U0084964

Chase dreams.
追求夢想。

Chase passions.
追求愛好。

Chase happiness.
追求幸福。

Embrace life.
擁抱生活。
Cherish life.
珍惜生命。
Celebrate life.
慶祝生命。

Keep hoping.
保持希望。
Look forward.
展望未來。
Expect good.
期待美好。

Embrace change.
擁抱改變。
Embrace progress.
擁抱進步。
Embrace innovation.
擁抱創新。

CONTENTS · 目 錄

📖BOOK ①

目
錄

▸ PART 3

📖 BOOK ❷

▸ PART 1

目錄

📖BOOK ❸

▸PART 1

▸ **PART 2**

▸ **PART 3**

目錄

📖BOOK ❹

▸ PART 1

📖 BOOK ❺

▶ PART 1

▶ PART 2

目錄

▸PART 3

Be good. 做好人。
Do good. 做好事。
Say good. 說好話。

這本書改變了我

　　教了 50 多年書，沒有一天停止，現在最快樂，進步使我快樂，今天比昨天好，今年比去年好。

　　自從編了「完美英語」以後，人生變得很有色彩。

　　編了那麼多書，沒有像「完美英語之心靈盛宴」讓我心中不停地澎湃，它改變了我，它給了我能量。你唸唸看，有沒有能量出現。

> ***Reach down.*** （彎下腰。）
> ***Lift people up.*** （拉人一把。）
> ***There is no better exercise.***
> 　　（沒有比這更好的運動。）

這三句話是雙關語，從此我更注意幫助他人，碰到乞丐，我會彎下腰，輕輕地把錢放到他的碗裡，最快樂的是我自己。

> ***Give happiness.*** （給人快樂。）
> ***Share happiness.*** （分享快樂。）
> ***That's the best gift.*** （那是最好的禮物。）

　　從此，無論到哪裡，無論見到誰，我的任務，就是讓別人有所得，給人快樂。你去見人，不要兩個肩膀、一個頭就去，不要空手去，讓人快樂是最好的禮物。

> ***Be kind.*** （存好心。）
> ***Be caring.*** （真關心。）
> ***You may change someone's life.***
> 　　（可能改變某人的一生。）

　　我們周圍有太多人需要關心了，講一些好聽的話，讓別人快樂，自己也快樂。

劉毅

PART 1

Unit 1
進 步

PART 1・Unit 1~9
英文錄音QR碼

Move forward.
向前進。

Make progress.
求進步。

Advance to be happy.
樂在進步。

Improve every day.
每天進步。

Advance every year.
每年進步。

**Feel accomplished
all the time.**
長存成就感。

Learn and grow.
學習讓你成長。

Never stop progressing.
永不停止進步。

Keep going forward.
持續進步。

BOOK 1 · PART 1

PART 1

Unit 1 背景説明

　　小孩最快樂的事情是「長大」，人生最快樂的事情，就是「進步」。只要今天比昨天好，今年比去年好，你就不會害怕變老。

Move forward.
Make progress.
Advance to be happy.

Move forward. ①向前進。②進步。(= *Go forward.* = *Make progress.* = *Advance.*)

move〔mʌv〕*v.* 移動　　forward〔ˈfɔrwəd〕*adv.* 向前

progress〔ˈprɑgrɛs〕*n.* 進步　　***make progress*** 進步

Advance to be happy. 樂在進步；進步才會快樂。

(= *Making progress will make you happy.*) 中文中沒有 /æ/ 的發音，所以唸 advance〔ədˈvæns〕的時候，嘴巴要裂開，否則會唸成〔ədˈvɛns〕(誤)。唸 happy〔ˈhæpɪ〕時，嘴巴不裂開，就唸成〔ˈhɛpɪ〕(誤)。所以，這句話要唸 100 遍以上才順口，**把中文的發音肌肉，改成適合英文的發音肌肉。**

advance〔ədˈvæns〕*v.* 前進；進步

　　你每天唸 Move forward.　Make progress. Advance to be happy. 唸熟以後，潛移默化，你就知道每天要進步，唸的時候已經讓你忘卻煩惱。

Improve every day.
Advance every year.
Feel accomplished all the time.

　　先是「每天」進步，再「每年」進步，「無時無刻」
都有成就感。　　improve〔ɪmˈpruv〕v. 改善；進步
Feel accomplished all the time. 要一直有成就感。
(= *Always have a sense of accomplishment.*)
一般字典上找不到 *feel accomplished*（覺得有成就感），
但美國人常用。**每分每秒都在進步，會讓你有成就感，**
這是人生最大的快樂。
accomplished〔əˈkɑmplɪʃt〕*adj.* 完成了的；達到了的；
　　已實現的
all the time 一直；總是 (= *always* = *at all times*)

Learn and grow.
Never stop progressing.
Keep going forward.

　　Learn and grow.（學習讓你成長。）也可說成：Learn
　　and get better.（學習才會變得更好。）不要停止進步，
　　要繼續向前進。　　progress〔prəˈgrɛs〕v. 進步
　　go forward 進步 (= *move forward* = *advance*
　　= *improve* = *progress* = *make progress*)

每天背誦「完美英語之心靈盛宴」，沒有煩惱，有成就感，
身心都會變得健康，會更受人尊敬。

BOOK 1・PART 1

PART 1

Unit 2
學 習

**Never stop
learning.**
學不停歇。

Stay young at heart.
永保赤子之心。

Be young forever.
永遠年輕。

BOOK 1 · PART 1

Stay curious.
保持好奇心。

Keep an open mind.
保持開放心。

**Learn something
new every day.**
每日學新知。

Be a lifelong student.

終生學習。

Never think you're too old.

絕不認老。

You're never too old to learn.

學不嫌老。

PART 1

Unit 2 背景説明

　　我今年 77 歲，我從未覺得自己老。我每天背「完美英語」，教「完美英語」，忙得不可開交，但我非常愉快。「董事長英語研習班」的同學，各個都活潑起來了，變得年輕。

Never stop learning.
Stay young at heart.
Be young forever.

Never stop learning.（學不停歇。）這是很好的句型。
　Never stop progressing.（永不停止進步。）叫別人「不要停止…」，都可以説：Never stop~.

never〔ˋnɛvɚ〕*adv.* 絕不　　***stop + V-ing*** 停止…

Stay young at heart.（永保赤子之心。）字面的意思是「心中保持年輕。」「Stay + 形容詞」是很好的句型，如：Stay hungry.（保持飢餓。）Stay foolish.（保持愚笨。）等。

stay〔ste〕*v.* 保持　　young〔jʌŋ〕*adj.* 年輕的
heart〔hɑrt〕*n.* 心　　***at heart*** 本質上；內心裡

Be young forever.（永遠年輕。）每天待在公園裡，閒話家常，不學習，沒有目標，老得很快，人的心態可以永遠年輕。　　forever〔fɚˋɛvɚ〕*adv.* 永遠

Stay curious.
Keep an open mind.
Learn something new every day.

Stay curious. (保持好奇心。) 會對新的事物有興趣。

也可說成：Always be curious. (要永遠有好奇

心。) 或 Be interested in new things. (對新事

物有興趣。)

curious 〔ˈkjʊrɪəs 〕*adj.* 好奇的

Keep an open mind. (保持開放心。) 表示「不抱任

何偏見；沒有成見。」人老了往往會頑固，堅持己見，

心態年輕就不會，開放接受新的想法。(= *Be open*

to new ideas.) open 〔ˈopən 〕*adj.* 開放的

mind 〔 maɪnd 〕*n.* 心；頭腦

Be a lifelong student.
Never think you're too old.
You're never too old to learn.

Be a lifelong student. (終生學習。) 我 58 歲時，有

人叫我退休，幸虧我堅持，這 20 年來，我過得很快樂。

這句話可說成：Be a student for life. 意思相同。

lifelong 〔ˈlaɪfˌlɔŋ 〕*adj.* 終身的；終生的

too…to V. 太…以致於不～

BOOK 1・PART 1

PART 1

Unit 3
努力工作

Work like crazy.
拼命工作。

Work like hell.
拼命工作。

Hard work pays off.
努力工作會有回報。

BOOK 1・PART 1

Do all you can.
盡你所能。

Do everything possible.
盡所有可能。

Do whatever it takes.
不惜一切代價。

Do what is needed.
做你必須做的事。

Do what is necessary.
做必要的事。

Complete it no matter what.
無論如何都要完成它。

PART 1

Unit 3 背景說明

　　我每天工作 12 小時以上，我不會累，我喜歡我的工作。如果只爲了錢工作，就像當奴隸一樣，身體會老得快。要做你喜歡做的事，見你喜歡見的人。我喜歡上「董事長英語研習班」，怎麼上課我都不會累。我喜歡看到王宣雯，和她聊天很愉快，學到很多東西。我喜歡看到 40 多年前的學生黃雯鈺，跟她開玩笑，她不會生氣。

Work like hell.　拼命工作。(= *Work like crazy.*
　= *Work very hard.*)
crazy〔'krezɪ〕*adj.* 瘋狂的　　*like crazy* 拼命地
hell〔hɛl〕*n.* 地獄　　*like hell* 拼命地

Hard work pays off.（努力工作會有回報。）也可說
　成：Hard work will pay off. 但前者較常用。也有美
　國人說：Hard work will be rewarded. 意思相同。
hard work 努力工作；努力
pay off 得到回報；有收穫

　　我從小功課就不好，但我很努力，自己也沒想到，到美國讀書，全班 50 多位同學，我第一名，因爲假日大家都出去玩了，我捨不得花錢，留在宿舍讀書。做什麼事，盡最大的力量，會有奇蹟出現。小 Amy 的媽媽許美完，每天早上 4 點鐘起來讀「完美英語」，可以看到她的未來，

一定讓人吃驚。沒有任何事情比努力重要。我努力教了
55 年的書，沒有一天缺席，沒有一天遲到，從沒想到退
休的一天。

Do all you can.
Do everything possible.
Do whatever it takes.
都表示「盡最大的力量。」

do all you can 盡力（= *do your best*）
possible〔'pɑsəbḷ〕*adj.* 可能的
whatever〔hwɑt'ɛvɚ〕*pron.* 任何⋯的事物
take〔tek〕*v.* 需要
do whatever it takes 盡一切可能；不惜一切代價（= *do*
  what is necessary = *do whatever you have to*）

　　人生最可悲的，就是什麼事都做一半，英文學一半，
沒交到好朋友。我有一位朋友，吃飯每次都吃一半，結果
她的小孩，沒辦法吞嚥，痛苦萬分。

need〔nid〕*v.* 需要
necessary〔'nɛsəˌsɛrɪ〕*adj.* 需要的；必須的
Complete it no matter what. 也可説成：Finish it
  whatever the circumstances.（無論在任何情況下
  都要完成它。）　　　complete〔kəm'plit〕*v.* 完成
no matter what 無論如何

PART 1

Unit 4
馬上做

Go for it.
去做就對了。

Just do it.
做就對了。

Make it happen.
實現它。

Don't hesitate.

不要猶豫。

Don't falter.

不要遲疑。

Start now.

現在開始。

BOOK 1 · PART 1

Do it today.
今天就做。

Don't put it off.
勿拖延。

Tomorrow never comes.
明日不復來。

PART 1

Unit 4 背景説明

　　我的朋友謝智芳在台大演講，説想要在菲律賓宿霧開語言學校。他問，有人同意嗎？我第一個站起來説：「同意！投資 100 萬。」當別人要募款時，你説「考慮考慮」或拖拖拉拉，都表示心不甘情不願。我喜歡 Bailey Aiken 説的三句話：

Give happily.（快樂地給。）
Accept gratefully.（感激地接受。）
Everyone benefits.（每個人都得到好處。）

　　很多人小時候跟媽媽要錢，往往是罵一頓再給。不給就不給，要給就要快，而且要高高興興地給，才是好媽媽。

　　當這本書開始預購時，「董事長英語研習班」的同學，反應好快，王宣雯 200 本、王李款 200 本、黄雯鈺 200 本、曾昭和 800 本、吳世勳 200 本、林玉坪 200 本、王敬紅 200 本、區路得 100 本，富翁的特性就是，反應很快、搶先、不拖拉，人人喜愛，才變成富翁。期待在我身旁所有的人：發大財→快樂→健康→慷慨。

Go for it. 大膽試一試（= *Try it.*）；冒一下險；去做就對了。（= *Do it.*）

Just do it.（去做就對了。）這句話原是國際知名運動品牌 Nike〔'naɪkɪ〕廣告行銷的標語，字面的意思是「只要做它。」引申為「去做就對了。」就是叫人「趕快做。」

Make it happen. 字面的意思是「使這件事發生。」也就是「去做就對了。」(= *Do it.*) 就是因為大家都不做，才有很多口號：*Go for it.* = *Just do it.* = *Make it happen.* = *Do it.* = *Try it.* 都表示「趕快做。」

make〔mek〕*v.* 使
happen〔'hæpən〕*v.* 發生

Don't falter. 字面的意思是「不要搖晃。」引申為「不要遲疑。」(= *Don't hesitate.* = *Don't be indecisive.*)

hesitate〔'hɛzə,tet〕*v.* 猶豫
falter〔'fɔltɚ〕*v.* 蹣跚；搖晃地走；猶豫；動搖；遲疑；畏縮

　　很多美國人和中國人一樣，喜歡說：I'll do it tomorrow.（我明天做。）所以，美國人常教小孩子：*Do it today.*（今天就做。）*Don't put it off.*（不要拖延。）*Tomorrow never comes.*（沒有明天。）溫和的說法是：Tomorrow may never come.（明天也許永遠不會來。）也可說成：Don't procrastinate.（不要拖延。）Don't put things off.（不要拖延事情。）Do what you need to do today.（做你今天必須做的事。）

PART 1

Unit 5
為今天而活

Yesterday is history.
昨日已成歷史。

Tomorrow is a mystery.
明日卻依然成謎。

Today is a present.
今日是禮物。

**Learn from
yesterday.**
向昨日學習。

Hope for tomorrow.
為明日充滿希望。

Live for today.
為今天而活。

Not yesterday.
非昨日。

Not tomorrow.
非明日。

Today is your day.
今日是你的好日子。

BOOK 1 · PART 1

PART 1

Unit 5 背景説明

Yesterday is history. Tomorrow is a mystery. Today is a present.

yesterday〔ˋjɛstɚˏde〕*n. adv.* 昨天　　history〔ˋhɪstrɪ〕*n.* 歷史　　tomorrow〔 təˋmoro 〕*n. adv.* 明天 mystery〔ˋmɪstrɪ〕*n.* 奧祕；謎　　today〔 təˋde 〕*n. adv.* 今天　　present〔ˋprɛznt〕*n.* 現在；禮物

這三句話是我在尼泊爾的牆上看到的。history 前面不能加 a，不能説成：*Yesterday is a history.*（誤）

Today is a present. = Today is a gift.

關鍵在 present 這個字，是雙關語，表示「現在」，也表示「禮物」，我們能有今天，就是上帝給我們的禮物。這三句話的意思是「昨天已經成歷史了，已經沒有了。明天是神祕的，還不知道有沒有。今天就是禮物，是最重要的。」這是美國人的文化，強調活在當下的急迫性。

Learn from yesterday. 也可説成：Learn from your past experience.（從過去的經驗中學習。）

Hope for tomorrow.（對明天充滿希望。）也可説成：Be hopeful about the future.（對未來抱持希望。）

hope〔 hop 〕*v.* 希望　　*hope for* 希望有

Live for today.（為今天而活。）也可説成：Live in the present.（要活在當下。）

Today is your day. 今天是你的好日子。(= *Today will be a good day for you.*)

one's day （某人）飛黃騰達的時候

PART 1

Unit 6
把握機會

Chances are everywhere.
機會無所不在。

Grab every chance.
把握每次機會。

Never miss a good chance.
絕不錯過好機會。

BOOK 1・PART 1

Seize the day.
把握時機。

Seize the moment.
抓住時機。

Carpe diem.
把握時機。

Seize the opportunity.
把握機會。

Seize the chance.
抓住機會。

Opportunity knocks only once.
機不可失。

PART 1

Unit 6 背景説明

　　我們每天都有很多機會，碰到好的人，也是機會，把握機會，就能成為贏家。

chance〔tʃæns〕*n.* 機會
everywhere〔'ɛvrɪˌhwɛr〕*adv.* 到處
grab〔græb〕*v.* 抓住　　miss〔mɪs〕*v.* 錯過

　　美國人喜歡説：***Seize the day. Seize the moment. Carpe diem.*** 除了叫你「把握時機」以外，還有「及時行樂」的意思。　　seize〔siz〕*v.* 抓住
moment〔'momənt〕*n.* 時刻　　carpe diem〔ˌkɑrpe 'diəm〕【拉丁語】把握時機；及時行樂 (= *seize the day*)

Seize the day. 把握時機。(= *Live for the day.* = *Grab the chance.* = *Take the chance.* = **Seize the chance.** = *Take the opportunity.* = **Seize the opportunity.** = *Carpe diem.*)

opportunity〔ˌɑpɚ'tjunətɪ〕*n.* 機會
Opportunity knocks only once. (機會只敲一次門；機不可失。) 也可説成：Opportunity seldom knocks twice. (機會很少敲兩次門。) You only get one chance. (你只有一次機會。) This chance is unlikely to come again. (這個機會不可能再來。)
knock〔nɑk〕*v.* 敲門　　once〔wʌns〕*adv.* 一次

PART 1

Unit 7
賺大錢

BOOK 1 · PART 1

Win!
要贏！

Be the winner!
成為贏家！

Come out on top!
出人頭地！

Make it big.
要飛黃騰達。

Hit it big.
一炮而紅。

Make big bucks.
賺大錢。

Make a move.
採取行動。

Make history.
創造歷史。

Make life amazing.
精彩人生。

PART 1

Unit 7 背景說明

難得活一次，要出人頭地，創造歷史，飛黃騰達，
精彩人生。

Win! 要贏！(= *Triumph! = Prevail! = Succeed!*
= *Dominate!*)   win〔wɪn〕*v.* 贏

Be the winner! 要成為贏家！(= *Be victorious!*)
winner〔'wɪnɚ〕*n.* 優勝者；贏家

Come out on top! 要得第一！(= *Come first! = Finish*
first! = Carry the day!)

come out 結果變成；(在考試中)獲得⋯成績

top〔tap〕*n.* 頂端   *on top* 在上邊；成功地；勝利地

come out on top 贏了；獲勝 (= *win*)；得第一
(= *come in first*)；出人頭地

Make it big.
Hit it big.
Make big bucks.
這三句話都有 big，很好背。

make it 成功；辦到

big〔bɪg〕*adj.* 大的；大受歡迎的；成功的

make it 是「成功」，*Make it big.* 是「大大成功；功成名就；飛黃騰達。」(= *Be very successful.*)

Hit it big. 成功；大紅大紫；一炮而紅。(= *Make it big.* = *Hit the big time.* = *Make your mark.* = *Be very successful.*)

hit〔hɪt〕*v.* 打擊；命中；成功；中獎

Make big bucks. 賺大錢。(= *Make a lot of money.* = *Earn a lot of money.*)

make〔mek〕*v.* 賺　　buck〔bʌk〕*n.* 一美元

big bucks 大筆的錢

Make a move. 採取行動。(= *Take action.*)

move〔muv〕*n.* 移動；行動

Make history 創造歷史。(= *Do something memorable.*)　history〔ˋhɪstrɪ〕*n.* 歷史

Make life amazing. 要使人生非常精彩。(= *Live an amazing life.*) 也可説成：Make your life amazing. 意思相同。

amazing〔əˋmezɪŋ〕*adj.* 驚人的；很棒的 (= *wonderful* = *fantastic* = *fabulous* = *great*)

PART 1

Unit 8
休 息

Rest.
好好休息。

Recover.
恢復精神。

Recharge your batteries.
恢復體力。

Inhale.

吸氣。

Exhale.

吐氣。

Don't forget to breathe.

不要忘記呼吸。

Hang easy.
放輕鬆。

Hang loose.
放輕鬆。

Let it all hang out.
放輕鬆。

PART 1

Unit 8 背景說明

累了要馬上休息，要放輕鬆，身體第一。

Rest. 休息。(= *Take a break.* = *Relax.*)

rest〔rɛst〕*v.* 休息

Recover. 恢復精神。(= *Regain your strength.*
  = *Bounce back.*)

recover〔rɪ'kʌvɚ〕*v.* 恢復（健康、精神等）(= *regain*
  = *restore*)

Recharge your batteries. 字面的意思是「把你的電
  池再充電。」引申為「恢復體力。」(= *Regain your*
  strength. = *Restore your energy.*)

recharge〔ri'tʃɑrdʒ〕*v.* 給（電池）再充電

battery〔'bætərɪ〕*n.* 電池

Inhale. 吸氣。(= *Breathe in.*)

inhale〔ɪn'hel〕*v.* 吸氣

Exhale. 呼氣。(= *Breathe out.*)

exhale〔ɪks'hel〕*v.* 呼氣；吐氣

Don't forget to breathe. (不要忘記呼吸。) 也可說
  成：Keep breathing. (要持續呼吸。)

forget〔fɚ'gɛt〕*v.* 忘記　　breathe〔brið〕*v.* 呼吸

Hang easy.（放輕鬆。）源自早年美國人出去玩的時
  候，都把帽子掛起來，這句話字面的意思是「輕鬆
  地掛起來。」也就是「放輕鬆。」（ = ***Hang loose.***
  = *Let it all hang out.* = *Relax.* = *Be relaxed.*
  = *Unwind.* = *Chill out.* = *Take it easy.*)

hang〔hæŋ〕*v.* 懸掛；閒蕩

easy〔ˈizɪ〕*adj.* 輕鬆的   *adv.* 輕鬆地

loose〔lus〕*adj.* 鬆的；不受束縛的；自由的

hang loose 放鬆（ = *relax* ）

hang out 掛出；伸出；閒蕩；出去玩

let it all hang out ①毫不保留地說出 ②輕鬆隨便；
  不拘禮節；自由隨意 ③盡情歡樂；做自己喜歡做的事
  【字面的意思是「讓頭髮披散」，也就是「毫無顧忌；放輕
  鬆」(= *let your hair down* = *relax*)】

PART 1

Unit 9
可休息，但不放棄

You can take a rest.
你可休息。

You can slow down.
你可慢活。

Fast or slow is okay.
安於步調快慢。

Never stop.
絕不停。

Never quit.
絕不退。

Never, ever give up.
永不放棄。

Carry on.

繼續。

Continue on.

繼續。

There's no finish line.

永無止線。

PART 1

Unit 9　背景説明

目標鎖定以後，可以休息、可以暫停，但絕不能放棄。

rest〔rɛst〕*n.* 休息
take a rest 休息一下（*= take a break*）
You can slow down.（你可以放慢腳步。）也可説成：
　You can take your time.（你可以慢慢來。）
slow〔slo〕*adj.* 慢的　*v.* 變慢　　***slow down*** 減慢速度
Fast or slow is okay.（快或慢都可以。）也可説成：It
　doesn't matter whether you do it quickly or not.
　（無論你做得快或慢，都沒關係。）
fast〔fæst〕*adj.* 快的
okay〔'o'ke〕*adj.* 好的；沒問題的（*= ok = OK = O.K.*）

never〔'nɛvɚ〕*adv.* 絕不　　stop〔stɑp〕*v.* 停止
Never quit. ①絕不停止。（*= Never stop.*）②絕不放棄。
　（*= Never give up.*）　　quit〔kwɪt〕*v.* 停止；放棄
Never, ever give up. 絕不放棄。（*= Never give up.*）
never, ever 絕不【never 的加強語氣】　　***give up*** 放棄

carry on 繼續堅持下去（*= continue on = keep going*
　= don't stop）　　continue〔kən'tɪnju〕*v.* 繼續
continue on 繼續下去（*= continue*）
There's no finish line.（沒有終點線。）是 1970 年代
　Nike 的廣告標語。也可説成：There is no end.（永
　無止境。）　　finish〔'fɪnɪʃ〕*n.* 終結；最後
line〔laɪn〕*n.* 線　　***finish line*** 終點線

PART 1　總整理

Unit 1

Move forward. 向前進。
Make progress. 求進步。
Advance to be happy.
樂在進步。

Improve every day.
每天進步。
Advance every year.
每年進步。
Feel accomplished all
　the time. 長存成就感。

Learn and grow.
學習讓你成長。
Never stop progressing.
永不停止進步。
Keep going forward.
持續進步。

Unit 2

Never stop learning.
學不停歇。
Stay young at heart.
永保赤子之心。
Be young forever.
永遠年輕。

Stay curious.
保持好奇心。
Keep an open mind.
保持開放心。
Learn something new
　every day. 每日學新知。

Be a lifelong student.
終生學習。
Never think you're too
　old. 絕不認老。
You're never too old to
　learn. 學不嫌老。

Unit 3

Work like crazy.
拼命工作。
Work like hell.
拼命工作。
Hard work pays off.
努力工作會有回報。

Do all you can. 盡你所能。
Do everything possible.
盡所有可能。
Do whatever it takes.
不惜一切代價。

BOOK 1・PART 1

Do what is needed.
做你必須做的事。
Do what is necessary.
做必要的事。
Complete it no matter what.
無論如何都要完成它。

Unit 4

Go for it. 去做就對了。
Just do it. 做就對了。
Make it happen. 實現它。

Don't hesitate. 不要猶豫。
Don't falter. 不要遲疑。
Start now. 現在開始。

Do it today. 今天就做。
Don't put it off. 勿拖延。
Tomorrow never comes.
明日不復來。

Unit 5

Yesterday is history.
昨日已成歷史。
Tomorrow is a mystery.
明日卻依然成謎。
Today is a present.
今日是禮物。

Learn from yesterday.
向昨日學習。
Hope for tomorrow.
爲明日充滿希望。
Live for today. 爲今天而活。

Not yesterday. 非昨日。
Not tomorrow. 非明日。
Today is your day.
今日是你的好日子。

Unit 6

Chances are everywhere.
機會無所不在。
Grab every chance.
把握每次機會。
Never miss a good
    chance. 絕不錯過好機會。

Seize the day. 把握時機。
Seize the moment.
抓住時機。
Carpe diem. 把握時機。

Seize the opportunity.
把握機會。
Seize the chance.
抓住機會。
Opportunity knocks only
    once. 機不可失。

Unit 7

Win!　要贏！
Be the winner!
成為贏家！
Come out on top!
出人頭地！

Make it big.
要飛黃騰達。
Hit it big.
一炮而紅。
Make big bucks.
賺大錢。

Make a move.
採取行動。
Make history.
創造歷史。
Make life amazing.
精彩人生。

Unit 8

Rest.　好好休息。
Recover.　恢復精神。
Recharge your batteries.
恢復體力。

Inhale.　吸氣。
Exhale.　吐氣。
Don't forget to breathe.
不要忘記呼吸。

Hang easy.　放輕鬆。
Hang loose.　放輕鬆。
Let it all hang out.
放輕鬆。

Unit 9

You can take a rest.
你可休息。
You can slow down.
你可慢活。
Fast or slow is okay.
安於步調快慢。

Never stop.　絕不停。
Never quit.　絕不退。
Never, ever give up.
永不放棄。

Carry on.　繼續。
Continue on.　繼續。
There's no finish line.
永無止線。

PART 2

Unit 1
做好人

PART 2・Unit 1~9
英文錄音QR碼

Be a good person.
做好人。

Do good things.
做好事。

Say good words.
說好話。

Be nice to people.

要對人好。

Win people over.

要贏得人心。

**You'll get what
you want.**

你就會得到你想要的。

Open your heart.
打開你的心門。

Show you care.
表現出你在乎。

Share your love.
愛要分享出去。

PART 2

Unit 1　背景說明

　　淨空法師說：「做好人。做好事。說好話。」剛好英文也可以找到。

Be a good person. 做好人。(= *Be good*.)
Do good things. 做好事。(= *Do good*.)
Say good words. 說好話。(= *Say good things*.)
words〔wɜdz〕*n. pl.* 言詞；話

nice〔naɪs〕*adj.* 好的；親切的 (= *kind*)
Win people over. 要贏得人心。(= *Persuade people*
　= *Gain others' support*.)
win** sb. **over 說服某人 (= *persuade sb*.)；把某人爭
　取過來 (= *get sb. to come over to your side*)

Open your heart. (敞開心扉。) 也可說成：
　Empathize. (要有同理心。) Sympathize. (要
　同情。)　　heart〔hɑrt〕*n.* 心
Show you care. (表現出你在乎。) 也可說
　成：Be compassionate. (要有同情心。)
show〔ʃo〕*v.* 展現　care〔kɛr〕*v.* 在乎
Share your love. 分享你的愛。(= *Share*
　your love with others.)　　share〔ʃɛr〕*v.* 分享

PART 2

Unit 2
要付出

Have a good heart.
要有好的心腸。

Create a beautiful inside.
創造內在美。

Beauty is as beauty does.
【諺】心美貌始美。

Give!
要付出！

Giving is a blessing.
能給是福。

You get what you give.
付出多少，得到多少。

Be grateful.
要心存感激。

Show gratitude every day.
每天都要表達感謝。

Gratitude is the key to success.
感恩是成功的關鍵。

PART 2

Unit 2 背景説明

　　美麗是沒辦法裝出來的，貌由心生。***Beauty is as beauty does.*** 漂亮的人做漂亮的事情；心美貌始美。能付出是福，不要想得到回報，就不會失望。

Have a good heart. (心地要好。) 也可説成：Be kind.
　(要仁慈。) Be a good person. (要做個好人。)
heart〔hɑrt〕*n.* (仁慈的) 心

Create a beautiful inside. (創造內在美。) 也可説
　成：Become a nice person. (要成爲一個好人。)
create〔krɪˈet〕*v.* 創造
inside〔ˈɪnˈsaɪd〕*n.* 人的內心；本性

Beauty is as beauty does. 是一句諺語，「行爲漂亮才
　是美；心美貌始美。」也可説成：Handsome is as
　handsome does. 意思相同。
beauty〔ˈbjutɪ〕*n.* 美

Give! (要付出！) 也可説成：Be generous! (要慷慨！)
give〔gɪv〕*v.* 給；給予；贈送；付出

Giving is a blessing. 能給是福。(= *Blessed are those who give.*) 也可説成：Giving is a good

BOOK 1・PART 2

thing to do. (付出是好事。) Giving helps both you and others. (付出對你和他人都有幫助。)

blessing〔'blɛsɪŋ〕 *n.* 幸福

You get what you give. (付出多少，得到多少。) 也可說成：The more you give, the more you will receive. (你給得越多，得到越多。)

Be grateful. 要心存感激。(= *Be thankful.*)

grateful〔'gretfəl〕 *adj.* 感激的

Show gratitude every day. 每天都要表示感激。
(= *Express your gratitude daily.*)

show〔ʃo〕 *v.* 表示；展現

gratitude〔'grætə,tjud〕 *n.* 感激

Gratitude is the key to success. (感恩是成功的關鍵。) 也可說成：Being grateful will help you to succeed in life. (心存感激能幫助你在人生中獲得成功。)

key〔ki〕 *n.* 關鍵 < *to* >

success〔sək'sɛs〕 *n.* 成功

PART 2

Unit 3
不能孤立

No man is an island.
【諺】沒有人是一座孤島。

Don't isolate yourself.
不要孤立自己。

Everyone relies on others.
每個人都要依賴別人。

Keep good company.
和好人在一起。

Avoid bad people.
避開壞人。

**A man is known
by the company
he keeps.**
【諺】觀其友，知其人。

Have good friends.
要有好的朋友。

Hang out with quality people.
要和優質的人在一起。

Successful people lift you up.
成功的人會提升你。

PART 2

Unit 3 背景説明

外國人常説：***No man is an island.*** (沒有人是一座孤島。) 也就是説，沒有人能夠孤立，單獨存在；人一定要有朋友。我自從上了「董事長班」以後，每天心情都很愉快，因爲不斷增加志同道合的朋友。經董事長們的介紹，買了很多好東西，向許奕買了十六萬多元的「韻律床」，和兩萬元的「天使能量帶」，有這些董事長背書，才敢買，的確是物超所値的好東西。

No man is an island. (【諺】沒有人是一座孤島。) 也可説
　　成：Everyone needs support. (每個人都需要支持。)
man 〔 mæn 〕 *n.* 男人；人　　island 〔ˈaɪlənd 〕 *n.* 島

Don't isolate yourself. 不要孤立自己。(= *Don't cut
　　yourself off from others.*)
isolate 〔ˈaɪsl̩ˌet 〕 *v.* 使孤立；使隔離

Everyone relies on others. (每個人都要依賴別人。)
　　也可説成：We all need others. (我們都需要別人。)
rely 〔 rɪˈlaɪ 〕 *v.* 依賴
rely on 依賴 (= *depend on* = *count on*)

Keep good company. 要結交益友。(= *Make good
　　friends.* = *Associate with good people.*)
company 〔ˈkʌmpənɪ 〕 *n.* 同伴；朋友

Avoid bad people. （要避開壞人。）也可說成：Don't
associate with bad people. （不要和壞人來往。）
avoid〔ə'vɔɪd〕*v.* 避免；避開

A man is known by the company he keeps. （觀其
友，知其人。）是一句諺語，也可說成：If you lie
down with dogs, you get up with fleas. 如果你
和狗躺在一起，你起來就會有跳蚤，引申為「近墨者
黑。」

Have good friends. 要有好的朋友。(= *Make friends
with good people.*)

Hang out with quality people, 要和優質的人在一起。
(= *Associate with good people.*)

hang out with 和⋯出去玩；和⋯在一起
(= *spend time with*)

quality〔'kwɑlətɪ〕*adj.* 優良的；優質的；高級的

Successful people lift you up. 成功的人會提升你。
(= *People who are successful can help you to
succeed, too.*)

successful〔sək'sɛsfəl〕*adj.* 成功的

lift〔lɪft〕*v.* 舉起；抬起；使向上；提高

lift up 提升

PART 2

Unit 4
要樂觀

Having a bad day?
你今天很倒楣嗎？

Take a deep breath.
做個深呼吸。

**It's just a day, not
a lifetime.**
只是倒楣一天，不是
倒楣一輩子。

You're still young!
你還年輕！

**You have many
opportunities.**
你有很多機會。

**The world is open
to you.**
整個世界都對你開放。

BOOK 1・PART 2

Life goes on.
生活還是得繼續。

Look to the future.
要展望未來。

Look on the bright side.
要看事物的光明面。

PART 2

Unit 4 背景說明

　　當你不舒服的時候，做個深呼吸，打開這本「完美英語之心靈盛宴」背一背，你就會忘卻煩惱。

Having a bad day? 源自 Are you having a bad day?
（你今天很倒楣嗎？）　　*have a bad day* 一整天都很倒楣
breath〔brɛθ〕*n.* 呼吸　　*take a deep breath* 深呼吸
It's just a day, not a lifetime.（只是倒楣一天，不是倒楣一輩子。）也可說成：It won't last forever.（它不會持續到永遠。）　　lifetime〔'laɪf,taɪm〕*n.* 一生；一輩子

still〔stɪl〕*adv.* 還；仍然
opportunity〔,ɑpə'tjunətɪ〕*n.* 機會
The world is open to you.（整個世界都對你開放。）
也可說成：You can do anything you want.（你可以做任何你想做的事。）Anything is possible.（什麼事都有可能。）　　open〔'opən〕*adj.* 開放的 < to >

Life goes on.（生活還是得繼續。）也可說成：You have to go on.（你必須繼續前進。）It's not the end of the world.（這不是世界末日。）　　*go on* 繼續
Look to the future. 要展望未來。(= *Think about the future.* = *Focus on the future.*)
look to 展望　　future〔'futʃə〕*n.* 未來
Look on the bright side. 也可說成：Look on the bright side of things.（要看事物的光明面。）也就是「要樂觀看待事物。」　　bright〔braɪt〕*adj.* 光明的

PART 2

Unit 5
要有志氣

You are able!
你很能幹！

You can do it!
你可以做到！

You got this!
你能搞定！

BOOK 1 · PART 2

Have ambition.
有志氣。

Have courage.
有勇氣。

Have a backbone.
有骨氣。

Have high hopes.
要有遠大的希望。

Have a winning attitude.
要有必勝的態度。

To succeed, be positive.
要成功，就得樂觀。

PART 2

Unit 5 背景説明

　　人貴有三氣：志氣、勇氣、骨氣。很多人陷入困境，就是因為沒有信心。像學英文，有人打死不學，就是不相信自己能夠學會。之前在「劉毅英文」當板哥的蔣萬安，現在已經當選台北市長了，只要有志氣，一步一步來，沒有達不到的事。

You are able! (你很能幹！) 也可說成：You are able to do it! (你能夠做到！)

able〔ˈebl〕*adj.* 能夠的；有能力的

You can do it! (你可以做到！) 也可說成：You have the ability! (你有能力！)

You got this! 你能搞定；你做得到！(= *You've got this!* = *You can do it!* = *You are able to do it!*)

Have ambition. 要有志氣。(= *Be ambitious.*)

ambition〔æmˈbɪʃən〕*n.* 野心；抱負

Have courage. (要有勇氣。) 也可說成：Be brave. (要勇敢。)

courage〔ˈkɝɪdʒ〕*n.* 勇氣

Have a backbone. (要有骨氣。) 也可説成：Show some spine. (要展現一些骨氣。) Don't be spineless. (不要沒有骨氣。)

backbone〔'bæk,bon〕*n.* 背脊骨；骨氣

Have high hopes. 要有遠大的希望。(= *Have big hopes.* = *Be hopeful.* = *Expect a lot.*)

high〔haɪ〕*adj.* 崇高的；遠大的

hope〔hop〕*n.* 希望　　***high hopes*** 遠大的希望

Have a winning attitude. (要有必勝的態度。) 也可説成：Believe in yourself. (要相信自己。) Be confident. (要有信心。)

winning〔'wɪnɪŋ〕*adj.* 得勝者的；獲勝的；(態度等) 吸引人的；迷人的　　attitude〔'ætə,tjud〕*n.* 態度

To succeed, be positive. (要成功，就得樂觀。) 也可説成：Be optimistic and you will succeed. (樂觀你就會成功。)

succeed〔sək'sid〕*v.* 成功

positive〔'pazətɪv〕*adj.* 正面的；樂觀的

PART 2

Unit 6
拒絕失敗

Refuse to lose.
拒絕失敗。

Refuse to give up.
拒絕放棄。

**Persistence wins
the day!**
堅持的人才會贏！

**Don't worry
about failures.**
不要擔心失敗。

**Worry about
missed chances.**
擔心錯過的機會。

Always try, try, try!
永遠嘗試再嘗試！

Turn the tables.
反敗為勝。

Turn the tide.
反敗為勝。

Reverse the situation.
反敗為勝。

PART 2

Unit 6 背景説明

　　所有成功的人，都經歷過無數次失敗，只要鎖定目標，做自己所喜歡的事，你會反敗爲勝。

refuse〔rɪˈfjuz〕v. 拒絶　　lose〔luz〕v. 輸掉；失敗
give up 放棄
Persistence wins the day!（堅持的人才會贏！）也可
　説成：If you persist, you will win!（如果你堅持，
　你就會贏！）If you don't give up, you will
　succeed!（如果你不放棄，你就會成功！）
persistence〔pɚˈsɪstəns〕n. 堅持　　win〔wɪn〕v. 贏
win the day 獲勝（＝ *be successful*）

worry about 擔心　　failure〔ˈfeljɚ〕n. 失敗
missed〔mɪst〕*adj.* 錯過的　　chance〔tʃæns〕n. 機會
Always try, try, try!（永遠嘗試再嘗試！）也可説成：
　Keep trying!（要持續嘗試！）Never give up!（絶
　對不要放棄！）　　try〔traɪ〕v. 嘗試；努力
這三句話的意思是：Not taking a chance would be
　the true failure.（沒有把握機會就是眞正的失敗。）

turn the tables 源自「西洋雙陸棋」（backgammon）
　的比賽者互換座位，引申爲「扭轉局勢；扭轉局面；反
　敗爲勝」（＝ ***turn the tide*** ＝ ***reverse the situation***）。
tide〔taɪd〕n. 潮汐；潮流；形勢　　reverse〔rɪˈvɝs〕v.
　逆轉；使倒轉　　situation〔ˌsɪtʃuˈeʃən〕n. 情況

PART 2

Unit 7
不要生氣

Forgive.

原諒。

Forget.

忘記。

Letting go will set
you free.

放下會讓你得到
心靈的自由。

Don't hate.
不要憎恨。

Don't get angry.
不要生氣。

Anger steals happiness.
生氣會偷走你的
幸福。

You can get angry.
你可以選擇生氣。

You can get even.
你可以選擇報仇。

Or you can get ahead.
或者，你可以選擇成功。

PART 2

Unit 7 背景説明

　　生氣很傷身體，生氣是用別人的錯誤來懲罰自己。
我們要訓練自己，不生氣、不懷恨。

Forgive.（原諒。）*Forget.*（忘記。）源自諺語：
　　Forgive and forget.（既往不咎。）Let bygones
　　be bygones.（讓過去的事成為過去。）
forgive〔fə'gɪv〕*v.* 原諒　　forget〔fə'gɛt〕*v.* 忘記

Letting go will set you free.（放下會讓你得到心靈的
　　自由。）也可説成：You will feel liberated when
　　you give up grudges.（當你放下怨恨，你就會感到
　　自由。）
let go　放開；鬆手；放下（不再想過去的某事或因之而
　　惱怒）　　set〔sɛt〕*v.* 使處於（某種狀態）
free〔fri〕*adj.* 自由的
set free　放…自由；釋放（= *liberate*）

Don't hate.　不要憎恨。（= *Don't be hateful.*）
hate〔het〕*v.* 憎恨

Don't get angry.　不要生氣。（= *Don't get mad.*）
angry〔'æŋgrɪ〕*adj.* 生氣的
get angry　生氣

BOOK 1・PART 2

Anger steals happiness. (生氣會偷走你的快樂。) 也
可說成 : If you are angry, you will not be happy.
(如果你生氣，你就不會快樂。) Anger will prevent
you from being happy. (生氣會讓你不快樂。)

anger〔'æŋgɚ〕*n.* 憤怒；生氣

steal〔stil〕*v.* 偷；偷偷取走

happiness〔'hæpɪnɪs〕*n.* 快樂；幸福

You can get angry. 你可以生氣。(= *You can get
mad.*)

You can get even. 你可以報仇。(= *You can get
revenge.*)

even〔'ivən〕*adj.* 平均的；不相上下的

get even 報仇 (= *get revenge*)

Or you can get ahead. ①或者，你可以選擇進步。
(= *Or you can progress.*) ②或者，你可以選擇成
功。(= *Or you can succeed.* = *Or you can win.*)
也可再繼續說 : You can use your energy on
them, or you can use your energy on yourself.
(你可以把精力用在生氣和報仇，或者你可以把精力用
在自己身上。)

ahead〔ə'hɛd〕*adv.* 在前面

get ahead 超前；進步；勝過；成功

PART 2

Unit 8
愛打敗憤怒

Love beats anger.
愛會打敗憤怒。

Be busy with love.
要忙著去愛。

Kill them with kindness.
要好得讓他們受不了。

Worry less.
少一點擔心。

Smile more.
多一點微笑。

**Don't regret, just
learn and grow.**
別後悔，
只要學習和成長。

BOOK 1 · PART 2

Let go of regrets.
不要後悔。

Let go of sadness.
不要悲傷。

Start a new life with love.
用愛開始新的生活。

PART 2

Unit 8 背景説明

　　小孩子剛出生，什麼也不懂，但他懂得愛。愛是求生存的最大武器，捨得付出愛，便得到愛。

Love beats anger. (愛會打敗憤怒。) 也可説成：
　Love is stronger than anger. (愛比憤怒更強大。)
　Love is better than anger. (愛比憤怒好。)
beat〔 bit 〕*v.* 打敗　　anger〔'æŋgɚ〕*n.* 憤怒；生氣

busy〔'bɪzɪ〕*adj.* 忙碌的
be busy with 忙著 (…事)；忙於
kill〔 kɪl 〕*v.* 殺死；使非常痛苦
kindness〔'kaɪndnɪs〕*n.* 仁慈；好意
kill sb. with kindness 以溺愛害人 (= *indulge sb.*)；好得讓人受不了【源自大猩猩會太用力抱小孩，使小孩被壓死】

worry〔'wɝɪ〕*v.* 擔心　　smile〔 smaɪl 〕*v.* 微笑
regret〔 rɪ'grɛt 〕*v. n.* 後悔　　just〔 dʒʌst 〕*adv.* 只要
grow〔 gro 〕*v.* 成長

Let go of regrets. (不要後悔。) 也可説成：Don't hold on to bad memories. (不要一直想著不好的回憶。)
let go of 字面的意思是「放開；鬆手」(= *release* = *stop holding on to*)，也可引申爲「放下；放棄」(= *stop thinking about* = *give up*)。
sadness〔'sædnɪs〕*n.* 悲傷　　start〔 stɑrt 〕*v.* 開始

PART 2

Unit 9
好好過日子

You only live once!
人只能活一次！

Don't waste any time.
不要浪費時間。

Make every day count.
每一天都要活得有意義。

Enjoy life!

享受人生！

Live it up!

盡情享受人生！

Use your time well!

好好地利用你的時間！

Live well!
好好地過日子！

Love life!
要愛你的生活！

Life is good!
生活很美好！

PART 2

Unit 9 背景説明

人只能活一次！（*You only live once!*）不要浪費
時間，每天都要活得有意義，每天都快樂，就是幸福。

once〔wʌns〕*adv.* 一次
waste〔west〕*v.* 浪費

Make every day count. 要讓每一天都重要。(= *Make
every day matter.*)；每一天都要活得有意義。(= *Make
every day meaningful.*) 也可説成：Make every
day valuable. (要讓每一天都很有價值。)
count〔kaʊnt〕*v.* 重要；有意義

Live it up! 盡情享受人生；過快樂好玩的日子！(= *Enjoy
life! = Have a good time! = Have fun*)
live〔lɪv〕*v.* 居住；生活；過 (生活)

Live well! 好好地過日子！(= *Live it up!*
= *Live a good life!*)

Love life! 要愛你的生活！(= *Enjoy life!*
= *Enjoy living!*)

PART 2 總整理

Unit 1

Be a good person.
做好人。
Do good things. 做好事。
Say good words. 說好話。

Be nice to people.
要對人好。
Win people over.
要贏得人心。
You'll get what you want.
你就會得到你想要的。

Open your heart.
打開你的心門。
Show you care.
表現出你在乎。
Share your love.
愛要分享出去。

Unit 2

Have a good heart.
要有好的心腸。
Create a beautiful inside.
創造內在美。
Beauty is as beauty does.
【諺】心美貌始美。

Give! 要付出！
Giving is a blessing.
能給是福。
You get what you give.
付出多少，得到多少。

Be grateful. 要心存感激。
Show gratitude every
  day. 每天都要表達感謝。
Gratitude is the key to
  success.
感恩是成功的關鍵。

Unit 3

No man is an island.
【諺】沒有人是一座孤島。
Don't isolate yourself.
不要孤立自己。
Everyone relies on others.
每個人都要依賴別人。

Keep good company.
和好人在一起。
Avoid bad people.
避開壞人。
A man is known by the
  company he keeps.
【諺】觀其友，知其人。

Have good friends.
要有好的朋友。
Hang out with quality
  people.
要和優質的人在一起。
Successful people lift you
  up. 成功的人會提升你。

Unit 4

Having a bad day?
你今天很倒楣嗎？
Take a deep breath.
做個深呼吸。
It's just a day, not a
  lifetime. 只是倒楣一天，
  不是倒楣一輩子。

You're still young!
你還年輕！
You have many
  opportunities.
你有很多機會。
The world is open to you.
整個世界都對你開放。

Life goes on.
生活還是得繼續。
Look to the future.
要展望未來。
Look on the bright side.
要看事物的光明面。

Unit 5

You are able! 你很能幹！
You can do it! 你可以做到！
You got this! 你能搞定！

Have ambition. 有志氣。
Have courage. 有勇氣。
Have a backbone. 有骨氣。

Have high hopes.
要有遠大的希望。
Have a winning attitude.
要有必勝的態度。
To succeed, be positive.
要成功，就得樂觀。

Unit 6

Refuse to lose. 拒絕失敗。
Refuse to give up.
拒絕放棄。
Persistence wins the day!
堅持的人才會贏！

Don't worry about
  failures. 不要擔心失敗。
Worry about missed
  chances.
擔心錯過的機會。
Always try, try, try!
永遠嘗試再嘗試！

Turn the tables.　反敗爲勝。
Turn the tide.　反敗爲勝。
Reverse the situation.
反敗爲勝。

Unit 7

Forgive.　原諒。
Forget.　忘記。
Letting go will set you
　　free.
放下會讓你得到心靈的自由。

Don't hate.　不要憎恨。
Don't get angry.　不要生氣。
Anger steals happiness.
生氣會偷走你的幸福。

You can get angry.
你可以選擇生氣。
You can get even.
你可以選擇報仇。
Or you can get ahead.
或者，你可以選擇成功。

Unit 8

Love beats anger.
愛會打敗憤怒。
Be busy with love.
要忙著去愛。
Kill them with kindness.
要好得讓他們受不了。

Worry less.　少一點擔心。
Smile more.　多一點微笑。
Don't regret, just learn
　　and grow.
別後悔，只要學習和成長。

Let go of regrets.
不要後悔。
Let go of sadness.
不要悲傷。
Start a new life with love.
用愛開始新的生活。

Unit 9

You only live once!
人只能活一次！
Don't waste any time.
不要浪費時間。
Make every day count.
每一天都要活得有意義。

Enjoy life!　享受人生！
Live it up!　盡情享受人生！
Use your time well!
好好地利用你的時間！

Live well!　好好地過日子！
Love life!　要愛你的生活！
Life is good!
生活很美好！

BOOK 1・PART 2

BOOK 1・PART 3

PART 3

Unit 1
有朋友真幸福

PART 3・Unit 1~9
英文錄音QR碼

Hard to find!
難尋！

Lucky to have!
幸有！

**Friends are truly
a joy.**
有朋真幸福。

Difficult to leave.

別離難。

Impossible to forget.

難忘懷。

Friends make life worthwhile.

有朋人生值。

Make new friends!
結新友！

Keep the old.
顧老友。

One is silver, the other is gold.
前者是銀，後者是金。

PART 3

Unit 1　背景說明

　　我們把長的句子簡化，才容易背，才容易說出來。如果你說：They're hard to find! 不如說 Hard to find!「他們很難找到！」不如說「難尋！」It's lucky to have them! 不如說 Lucky to have!「很幸運擁有他們！」不如說「幸有！」英文要短，中文也要短。「難尋！幸有！有朋真幸福。」中文和英文一起背。

Hard to find! 源自 They're hard to find!（他們很難找到！）

hard〔hɑrd〕*adj.* 困難的

Lucky to have! 源自 It's lucky to have them!（很幸運能擁有他們！）

lucky〔ˈlʌkɪ〕*adj.* 幸運的

Friends are truly a joy. 有朋友真是一件令人快樂的事。(*= It's joyful to have friends. = Friends bring joy to your life.*)

truly〔ˈtrulɪ〕*adv.* 真地

joy〔dʒɔɪ〕*n.* 快樂；快樂的事

Difficult to leave. 源自 It's difficult to leave them.（很難離開他們。）

Impossible to forget. 源自 It's impossible to forget them. (不可能忘記他們。) 也可說成：Good friends are never forgotten. (好朋友絕對不會被遺忘。)

Friends make life worthwhile. 朋友讓人生有價值。 (*= Friends give life meaning. = Without friendship, life is not worth living.*)

worthwhile〔ˈwɝθˈhwaɪl〕*adj.* 值得的

Make new friends! 結交新朋友！ (*= Meet new people!*)　***make friends*** 交朋友

Keep the old. (要留住老朋友。) 也可說成：Don't forget your old friends. (不要忘記你的老朋友。)

One is silver, the other is gold. (前者是銀，後者是 金。) 源自 One is silver and the other is gold. 也 可說成：New friends are attractive because they are shiny and new, but old friends have stood the test of time. (新朋友吸引人，因爲他們閃亮而且 新鮮，但老朋友則是經得起時間的考驗。)

silver〔ˈsɪlvɚ〕*adj.* 銀的
gold〔gold〕*adj.* 金的
one…the other (兩者) 一個…另一個～；前者…後者～

PART 3

Unit 2
好友至上

Friends are like gold.
朋友如金。

True friends are like diamonds.
真友如鑽。

Like-minded friends are a treasure.
志同道合的朋友是寶藏。

Value your friends.
重視你的朋友。

Have strong friendships.
有堅定友誼。

Friendship is a gift.
友誼是禮物。

Friendship is love.
友誼是愛。

Friends are like family.
友如家人。

Nothing beats a good friend.
好友至上。

PART 3

Unit 2 背景說明

　　有朋友就不簡單了，有真心的朋友更不容易，能找到志同道合的朋友，是人生最大的幸福。不要忘記，好朋友至上。

gold〔gold〕*n.* 黃金　　diamond〔'daɪəmənd〕*n.* 鑽石
Like-minded friends are a treasure.（志同道合的朋友是寶藏。）也可說成：Friends who think like you do are valuable.（和你想法相同的人很珍貴。）
like-minded〔'laɪk'maɪndɪd〕*adj.* 志趣相投的；看法相同的
treasure〔'trɛʒɚ〕*n.* 寶藏

Value your friends.（要重視你的朋友。）也可說成：Treasure your friends.（要珍惜你的朋友。）
value〔'vælju〕*v.* 重視

Have strong friendships.（要有堅定的友誼。）也可說成：Have deep friendships.（要有深厚的友誼。）
strong〔strɔŋ〕*adj.* 堅定的
friendship〔'frɛndʃɪp〕*n.* 友誼
gift〔gɪft〕*n.* 禮物

Nothing beats a good friend.（沒有什麼能勝過好朋友。）也可說成：There is nothing better than having a good friend.（沒有什麼比擁有好朋友還要好。）　　beat〔bit〕*v.* 打敗；勝過

PART 3

Unit 3
要有禮貌

Always say please.
一定要說「請」。

Always say thank you.
一定要說「謝謝你」。

Always be polite!
一定要有禮貌！

Have good manners.
要有禮貌。

It means a lot.
很重要。

It goes a long way.
很有用。

Respect others.
尊重別人。

Show kindness.
展現善意。

Show you really care.
表現真誠的關心。

PART 3

Unit 3 背景説明

　　美國人非常重視説 "please" 和 "thank you"，即使是很熟的朋友，也不能忘記。對任何人都要有禮貌。

Always be polite! 一定要有禮貌！(= *Always be courteous!*)
polite〔pəˈlaɪt〕*adj.* 有禮貌的

Have good manners. 要有禮貌。(= *Be courteous.*)
manners〔ˈmænɚz〕*n. pl.* 禮貌

It means a lot. (它意義重大。) 也可説成：It's meaningful. (它很有意義。) It's important. (它很重要。) 　　***mean a lot*** 意義重大

It goes a long way. (它很有用。) 也可説成：It means a lot. (它很重要。) (= *It counts for a lot.*) It can work wonders. (它能創造奇蹟。)
go a long way 很有用；很重要

Respect others. 尊重別人。(= *Show respect.*)
respect〔rɪˈspɛkt〕*v. n.* 尊敬；尊重
show〔ʃo〕*v.* 展現
kindness〔ˈkaɪndnɪs〕*n.* 善意
care〔kɛr〕*v.* 在乎；關心

PART 3

Unit 4
笑吧！

Smile!
笑吧！

It costs nothing!
不用花一毛錢！

It means everything.
其價值連城。

Smiling brings joy.
笑帶來歡樂。

Smiling gives confidence.
笑給你信心。

It makes you attractive.
使你魅力四射。

Brighten up a day.
照亮他人的一天。

Make someone happy.
讓他人快樂。

Make eye contact and smile.
做眼神交流，笑一笑。

PART 3

Unit 4 背景說明

　　笑太重要了，不花你一毛錢，卻帶來無比的歡樂，笑會讓你魅力四射。

smile〔smaɪl〕*v.* 微笑；笑
It costs nothing. 它不花一毛錢。(= *It's free.*)
cost〔kɔst〕*v.* 花費

It means everything. 它意義重大。(= *It means a lot.*)
mean everything 意義重大 (= *mean a lot*)

Smiling brings joy. 微笑帶來快樂。(= *A smile can make people happy.*)
bring〔brɪŋ〕*v.* 帶來　joy〔dʒɔɪ〕*n.* 快樂

Smiling gives confidence. 微笑給你信心。(= *A smile can make people more confident.*)
confidence〔'kɑnfədəns〕*n.* 信心　make〔mek〕*v.* 使
attractive〔ə'træktɪv〕*adj.* 吸引人的

Brighten up a day. 照亮他人的一天；讓某人高興起來。
　(= *Brighten up someone's day.* = *Cheer someone up.*)
brighten〔'braɪtn̩〕*v.* 使明亮；使歡樂 < *up* >

Make eye contact and smile. (要有目光接觸，並且微笑。) 也可說成：Look people in the eye and smile.
　(看著別人的眼睛並且微笑。)
contact〔'kɑntækt〕*n.* 接觸　*eye contact* 目光接觸

PART 3

Unit 5
失敗為前進之母

Fail fast.
快點失敗。

Fail often.
失敗連連。

Fail forward.
失敗為前進之母。

Be willing to fail.
甘於失敗。

Failure is learning.
失敗即是學習。

Failure is a badge of honor.
失敗是一枚榮譽勳章。

Failure can bring opportunities.

失敗可以帶來機會。

An ending can be a new beginning.

結束也可能是一個新開始。

One door closes, another opens.

上帝關一扇門，
會為你開另一扇門。

PART 3

Unit 5 背景説明

美國矽谷有個標語：Fail fast. Fail often. Fail forward. 意思是：快點失敗，常常失敗，失敗爲前進之母。怕失敗是不會成功的。

Fail fast. (快點失敗。) 也可説成：Don't hesitate to do something because you are afraid of failure. (不要因爲害怕失敗，就猶豫不決。) fail〔fel〕*v.* 失敗

Fail often. (常常失敗。) 也可説成：Be willing to fail again and again. (要心甘情願接連失敗。)

Fail forward. 一邊失敗，一邊前進，也就是「在失敗中前進。」也可説成：Fail in order to succeed. (失敗是爲了要成功。) Learn from your failures. (從失敗中學習。) Use your failures in order to advance. (利用失敗以求進步。) forward〔'fɔrwəd〕*adv.* 向前地

willing〔'wɪlɪŋ〕*adj.* 願意的 failure〔'feljə〕*n.* 失敗

Failure is a badge of honor. (失敗是一枚榮譽勳章。)

也可説成：There is honor in being willing to risk failure. (願意冒失敗的風險十分光榮。) There's nothing dishonorable about failure. (失敗並不可恥。)

badge〔bædʒ〕*n.* 徽章 honor〔'ɑnə〕*n.* 榮譽

opportunity〔ˌɑpə'tjunətɪ〕*n.* 機會

ending〔'ɛndɪŋ〕*n.* 結局；結束

beginning〔bɪ'gɪnɪŋ〕*n.* 開始

close〔kloz〕*v.* 關上 open〔'opən〕*v.* 打開

PART 3

Unit 6
人無完人

Nobody's perfect.
人無完人。

Everyone makes mistakes.
人皆可能犯錯。

Even Homer sometimes nods.
【諺】智者千慮，必有一失。

Don't blame others.

不要責備別人。

Don't accuse others.

不要指責別人。

Find the problem and solve it.

察覺問題，解決它。

Fix it.
解決它。

Correct it.
改正它。

Make it right.
修正它。

PART 3

Unit 6 背景説明

人無完人，每個人都可能犯錯。智者千慮，必有一失。

Nobody's perfect. (沒有人是完美的。) 也可説成：
　 Everyone makes mistakes. (每個人都會犯錯。)
perfect〔ˈpɝfɪkt〕 *adj.* 完美的
mistake〔məˈstek〕 *n.* 錯誤　 ***make a mistake*** 犯錯

Even Homer sometimes nods. 是一句諺語，就連希
　 臘著名的詩人荷馬都會不小心打瞌睡，更何況是一般
　 人，引申爲「人皆有錯；智者千慮，必有一失。」
even〔ˈivən〕 *adv.* 甚至；即使　 Homer〔ˈhomɚ〕 *n.*
荷馬【古希臘詩人】　 sometimes〔ˈsʌmˌtaɪmz〕 *adv.*
有時候　 nod〔nad〕 *v.* 打瞌睡

Don't blame others. 不要責備別人。(= *Don't hold
other people responsible.*)

Don't accuse others. 不要指控別人；不要譴責別人。
　 (= *Don't lay the blame on other people.*)
blame〔blem〕 *v.* 責備；責怪　 accuse〔əˈkjuz〕 *v.*
指控；譴責 (= *blame* = *fault*)　 solve〔salv〕 *v.* 解決

Fix it. 解決它。(= *Solve the problem.*)
fix〔fɪks〕 *v.* 修理；解決

Make it right. 使它正確；修正它。(= ***Correct it.***)
correct〔kəˈrɛkt〕 *v.* 改正

PART 3

Unit 7
現在就去做

Do it now.
現在就去做。

Now is best.
現在最好。

No time like the present.
現在最好。

Now is ideal.
現在正是時候。

It's the perfect time.
完美時刻。

The stars are aligned.
最佳時刻。

Behind you, all your memories.
回憶，拋諸腦後。

Before you, all your dreams.
夢想盡在前方。

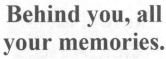

Be alive in the here and now!
要活在當下！

PART 3

Unit 7 背景説明

　　很多人喜歡拖延，中外皆然，所以美國人説：Do it now. Now is best. No time like the present. 意思是現在就做，現在最好，沒有比現在更好的時機了。有什麼夢想、計劃，要立刻付諸實踐，不要拖延。

Do it now.（現在就做。）也可説成：Take action right now.（現在就採取行動。）Don't delay.（不要拖延。）Don't hesitate.（不要猶豫。）

Now is best. 現在最好。(= *Now is the best time.*) 也可説成：It's best to do it now.（最好現在就做。）

No time like the present. 源自 There is no time like the present.（沒有像現在一樣的時機；現在最好。）　like〔laɪk〕*prep.* 像

present〔ˈprɛznt〕*n.* 現在

Now is ideal. 現在最理想；現在正是時候。(= *Now is the best time.*)

ideal〔aɪˈdiəl〕*adj.* 理想的

It's the perfect time. 現在是完美時刻。(= *It's the best time.*)

perfect〔ˈpɝfɪkt〕*adj.* 完美的

The stars are aligned. 占星家認為，星星
　連成一線，是上天的安排，表示「這是最
　佳時刻。」(= *It's the perfect moment.*)

align〔ə'laɪn〕*v.* 排成一直線

Behind you, ***all your memories***. 源自 Behind you
　are all your memories. (你所有的回憶都在你身
　後。) 也可說成：Your memories are in the past.
　(你的回憶已成過去。)

behind〔bɪ'haɪnd〕*prep.* 在…後面
memory〔'mɛmərɪ〕*n.* 回憶

Before you, ***all your dreams***. 源自 Before you are
　all your dreams. (你所有的夢想都在你的前方。) 也
　可說成：Your dreams are in the future. (你的夢
　想都在未來。) Your dreams are not real yet. (你
　的夢想尚未實現。)

Be alive in the here and now! 要活在當下！
　(= *Live in the present!*)

alive〔ə'laɪv〕*adj.* 活著的
here and now 此時此地

PART 3

Unit 8
要更努力

Try harder.
要更努力。

Work harder.
要更努力。

Give more effort.
要更加努力。

Devote yourself.
要全心投入。

Dedicate yourself.
要全心投入。

Commit yourself.
要全心投入。

Give your best effort.

盡己所能。

Do the best you can.

盡你所能。

Beat your brains out.

絞盡腦汁。

PART 3

Unit 8 背景說明

只要比別人更努力，全心投入，絞盡腦汁，沒有不成功的道理。

Try harder. ***Work harder***. ***Give more effort***. 意思相同，都等於 Try more.（多努力一點。）Do more.（多做一點。） try〔traɪ〕*v.* 嘗試；努力
hard〔hɑrd〕*adv.* 努力地 ***try harder*** 更努力（= *work harder*） effort〔ˈɛfət〕*n.* 努力

devote〔dɪˈvot〕*v.* 致力於；奉獻
dedicate〔ˈdɛdəˌket〕*v.* 奉獻
commit〔kəˈmɪt〕*v.* 專心致力
devote *oneself* 專心致力；全心投入（= ***dedicate*** *oneself*
= ***commit*** *oneself* = *be devoted* = *be dedicated*
= *be committed*）

Give your best effort. 要盡全力。（= *Do your best.*）
do the best *one can* 盡力（= *do one's best*）
Beat your brains out.（要絞盡腦汁。）也可說成：
Consider it carefully.（要仔細考慮。）Meditate on it.（要深思熟慮。）Contemplate it.（要仔細考慮。）Mull it over.（要仔細考慮。）Think very hard.（要非常認真地思考。） beat〔bit〕*v.* 打
brain〔bren〕*n.* 頭腦
beat *one's* ***brains out*** 絞盡腦汁

PART 3

Unit 9
不要半途而廢

Finish it.
事能結。

Complete it.
事能成。

Continue till it's done.
持續到底。

Go the distance.

堅持到底。

Go all the way.

走完全程。

Hang in till the end.

堅持到底。

Do it completely.
徹底完成。

**Never do things
halfway.**
絕不要半途而廢。

**Never do anything
by halves.**
【諺】絕不要半途而廢。

PART 3

Unit 9 背景説明

很多人學英文學一半,做事做一半,太浪費了。鎖定目標,徹底完成,不要半途而廢。

finish〔'fınıʃ〕*v.* 做完   complete〔kəm'plit〕*v.* 完成
Continue till it's done.(要持續到完成爲止。)也可説成:Don't stop until it is finished.(要直到完成才能停止。)   continue〔kən'tınju〕*v.* 繼續
till〔tıl〕*conj., prep.* 直到(= *until*)
done〔dʌn〕*adj.* 完成的

distance〔'dıstəns〕*n.* 距離
go the distance 堅持到底   *all the way* 一路
hang in 堅持   end〔ɛnd〕*n.* 結束

Do it completely.(徹底完成。)也可説成:Finish it.(把事情做完。)
completely〔kəm'plitlı〕*adv.* 完全地
Never do anything by halves.【諺】絕不要半途而廢。
(= *Never do things halfway.*)也可説成:Never leave anything undone.(不要有任何事沒完成。)
Don't quit before you finish something.(直到完成之前,都不要放棄。)Complete things.(要把事情做完。)
halfway〔'hæf'we〕*adv.* 到一半;不徹底地
half〔hæf〕*n.* 一半   *by halves* 不完全地

PART 3 總整理

Unit 1

Hard to find! 難尋！
Lucky to have! 幸有！
Friends are truly a joy.
有朋眞幸福。

Difficult to leave. 別離難。
Impossible to forget.
難忘懷。
Friends make life
　worthwhile. 有朋人生值。

Make new friends!
結新友！
Keep the old. 顧老友。
One is silver, the other is
　gold. 前者是銀，後者是金。

Unit 2

Friends are like gold.
朋友如金。
True friends are like
　diamonds. 眞友如鑽。
Like-minded friends are
　a treasure.
志同道合的朋友是寶藏。

Value your friends.
重視你的朋友。
Have strong friendships.
有堅定友誼。
Friendship is a gift.
友誼是禮物。

Friendship is love.
友誼是愛。
Friends are like family.
友如家人。
Nothing beats a good
　friend. 好友至上。

Unit 3

Always say please.
一定要說「請」。
Always say thank you.
一定要說「謝謝你」。
Always be polite!
一定要有禮貌！

Have good manners.
要有禮貌。
It means a lot. 很重要。
It goes a long way.
很有用。

Respect others. 尊重別人。
Show kindness. 展現善意。
Show you really care.
表現真誠的關心。

Unit 4

Smile! 笑吧！
It costs nothing!
不用花一毛錢！
It means everything.
其價值連城。

Smiling brings joy.
笑帶來歡樂。
Smiling gives confidence.
笑給你信心。
It makes you attractive.
使你魅力四射。

Brighten up a day.
照亮他人一天。
Make someone happy.
讓他人快樂。
Make eye contact and
smile. 做眼神交流，笑一笑。

Unit 5

Fail fast. 快點失敗。
Fail often. 失敗連連。
Fail forward.
失敗為前進之母。

Be willing to fail.
甘於失敗。
Failure is learning.
失敗即是學習。
Failure is a badge of honor.
失敗是一枚榮譽勳章。

Failure can bring
opportunities.
失敗可以帶來機會。
An ending can be a new
beginning.
結束也可能是一個新開始。
One door closes, another
opens. 上帝關一扇門，會
為你開另一扇門。

Unit 6

Nobody's perfect.
人無完人。
Everyone makes
mistakes. 人皆可能犯錯。
Even Homer sometimes
nods.
【諺】智者千慮，必有一失。

Don't blame others.
不要責備別人。
Don't accuse others.
不要指責別人。
Find the problem and
solve it. 察覺問題，解決它。

Fix it. 解決它。
Correct it. 改正它。
Make it right. 修正它。

Unit 7

Do it now. 現在就去做。
Now is best. 現在最好。
No time like the present.
現在最好。

Now is ideal.
現在正是時候。
It's the perfect time.
完美時刻。
The stars are aligned.
最佳時刻。

Behind you, all your
　memories.
回憶，拋諸腦後。
Before you, all your
　dreams. 夢想盡在前方。
Be alive in the here and
　now! 要活在當下！

Unit 8

Try harder. 要更努力。
Work harder. 要更努力。
Give more effort.
要更加努力。

Devote yourself.
要全心投入。
Dedicate yourself.
要全心投入。
Commit yourself.
要全心投入。

Give your best effort.
盡己所能。
Do the best you can.
盡你所能。
Beat your brains out.
絞盡腦汁。

Unit 9

Finish it. 事能結。
Complete it. 事能成。
Continue till it's done.
持續到底。

Go the distance.
堅持到底。
Go all the way. 走完全程。
Hang in till the end.
堅持到底。

Do it completely.
徹底完成。
Never do things halfway.
絕不要半途而廢。
Never do anything by
　halves.【諺】絕不要半途而廢。

【劉毅老師的話】

Appreciate blessings. 知福。
Cherish blessings. 惜福。
Create more blessings. 再造福。

劉毅老師給粉絲的話

學英文最好的方法，就是「使用」。我們要使用，就要使用最好的「中文」和「英文」。

背單字不如背句子，背一個句子，不如一次背三句，背三句，不如背「完美英語」，你會心想事成，與世界接軌，結交國際的朋友！

現在，我們可以在手機上，使用「完美英語之心靈盛宴」，寫出好的中文句子跟英文句子，會讓人產生共鳴，會交到更多志同道合的朋友，別人會因為你的完美中文和英文而佩服，進而喜歡跟你在一起！

當你心情不好的時候，你翻一翻這本書，你就會感到舒服；背一背這本書，你的煩惱全忘掉！照著做，你會交到好朋友，很多人喜歡你，財富自然跟著來！

無形中，你的英文會進步、你的心靈提升，你的中文程度，也跟著越來越好。

Move forward! 前進！
Go forward! 前進！
Run forward! 快速向前進！

每天進步，讓你有成就感，書中很多句子都出自經典，你說出來會振奮人心，讓別人驚喜。我在美國，曾經使用這些句子，美國人聽到以後，非常興奮，他們快樂，我自己也變得更快樂！很多人用書中的句子，和外國人交談，創造了奇蹟。

我們今年最大的成就，是建立「董事長團隊」，團結一心的力量，真的很大！董事長人脈更是金脈。《完美英語心靈饗宴①》6,000 本，尚未出版，已經銷售一空，就是最好的例子。

劉毅

PART 1

Unit 1
給人快樂

PART 1・Unit 1~9
英文錄音QR碼

Give happiness.
給人幸福。

Share happiness.
分享快樂。

That's the best gift.
是最棒的禮物。

Generosity pays off.
慷慨會得到回報。

Selflessness pays off.
無私會得到回報。

**Kindness is always
worth it.**
善良一定划得來。

Be kind.
存好心。

Be caring.
要關懷。

You may change someone's life.
也許你會改變別人的一生。

BOOK 2 · PART 1

PART 1

Unit 1 背景說明

　　有錢大家用，慷慨會得到回報。(Generosity pays off.) 給人快樂。(Give happiness.) 分享快樂。(Share happiness.) 自己最快樂。

　　以前我去買菜，還會還價，現在，我高高興興地買菜，賣菜的叫我再買其他的，我馬上說好；他又叫我再買其他的菜，我也會認真地去看一看。認真地聽別人講話，尊重別人，自己得到最大的快樂。

　　現在我一進菜市場，大家都跟我打招呼，把最好的給我。「心靈盛宴」改變了我，讓我每天都過好日子。

Give happiness. 給人幸福；給人快樂。(= *Give happiness to others.*) 也可說成：Make others happy. (讓別人快樂。)
give〔 gɪv 〕 *v.* 給與
happiness〔 ˋhæpɪnɪs 〕 *n.* 快樂；幸福

Share happiness. (分享快樂。) 也可說成：Share happiness with others. (和別人分享快樂。)
share〔 ʃɛr 〕 *v.* 分享
gift〔 gɪft 〕 *n.* 禮物

Generosity pays off. (慷慨會得到回報。) 也可說成：
It is worthwhile to be generous. (慷慨很值得。)
generosity 〔͵dʒɛnəˈrɑsətɪ 〕 *n.* 慷慨；大方
pay off 得到回報；有收穫

Selflessness pays off. (不自私會得到回報。) 也可
說成：It is worthwhile to be selfless. (不自私
很值得。)
selflessness 〔ˈsɛlflɪsnɪs 〕 *n.* 無私

Kindness is always worth it. 善良總是很值得；善良
一定划得來。(= *It is always worthwhile to be kind.*)
kindness 〔ˈkaɪndnɪs 〕 *n.* 仁慈；好心；善意
worth it 值得的

kind 〔 kaɪnd 〕 *adj.* 仁慈的；親切的
Be caring. (要關懷。) 也可說成：Be considerate.
(要體貼。) Be compassionate. (要有同情心。) Be
helpful. (要樂於助人。) Be loving. (要有愛心。)
caring 〔ˈkɛrɪŋ 〕 *adj.* 關愛的；有愛心的
change 〔 tʃendʒ 〕 *v.* 改變
life 〔 laɪf 〕 *n.* 生活；人生

PART 1

Unit 2
高興地給

Give happily.
高高興興地給。

Accept gratefully.
感激地接受。

Everyone benefits.
大家都受益。

Reach down.

彎下腰。

Lift people up.

拉人一把。

There is no better exercise.

沒有比這更好的運動。

Do nice things.
去做好事。

**Expect nothing
in return.**
不求回報。

**You'll never be
disappointed.**
永不失望。

PART 1

Unit 2 背景說明

　　有的母親給小孩零用錢，罵完才給，把自己的情緒發洩在小孩身上。不如 Give happily. (高高興興地給。) Accept gratefully. (感激地接受。) Everyone benefits. (大家都受益。) 以前我給乞丐錢，用扔的，現在是蹲下來，慢慢地把紙鈔放在他的碗裡。要做好事。(Do nice things.) 想要回報，是很痛苦的；不求回報，才不會失望。

Give happily. 高高興興地給。(= *Be happy to give.*)
happily〔ˈhæpɪlɪ〕*adv.* 愉快地；高興地

Accept gratefully. (感激地接受。) 也可說成：Be grateful for what others give you. (要對別人給你的東西心存感激。)
accept〔əkˈsɛpt〕*v.* 接受
gratefully〔ˈgretfəlɪ〕*adv.* 感激地；感謝地
benefit〔ˈbɛnəfɪt〕*v.* 獲益；獲利

Reach down.「向下伸手。」引申爲「彎下腰。」(= *Bend down.*) 也可說成：Reach out to those who need help. (對需要幫助的人伸出援手。)
reach〔ritʃ〕*v.* 伸手　　down〔daʊn〕*adv.* 向下

Lift people up. (拉人一把。) 也可說成：Help
others. (要幫助別人。) Improve the lives of
others. (要改善別人的生活。)

lift〔lɪft〕*v.* 抬高；使向上；提高；提升

lift sb. up 提升某人

There is no better exercise. (沒有比這更好的運動。)
也可說成：There is nothing better you can do.
(這是你能做的最好的事。)

exercise〔'ɛksə,saɪz〕*n.* 運動

Do nice things. 要做好事。(= *Do good things.* = *Do
kind things.* = *Do something nice.* = *Do something
kind.*)

nice〔naɪs〕*adj.* 好的

Expect nothing in return. (不求回報。) 也可說成：
Don't expect any reward. (不要期待任何的報酬。)

expect〔ɪk'spɛkt〕*v.* 期待　　***in return*** 作為回報

You'll never be disappointed. (你絕對不會失望。)
也可說成：You won't be disappointed if you are
not rewarded or thanked. (如果你沒有得到報酬或
被人感謝，也不會失望。)

never〔'nɛvə〕*adv.* 絕不

disappointed〔,dɪsə'pɔɪntɪd〕*adj.* 失望的

PART 1

Unit 3
全心投入

Clear eyes.
擦亮眼睛。

Full heart.
全心投入。

Can't lose.
不可能輸。

BOOK 2 · PART 1

Expect the unexpected.

期待意想不到的。

Believe in the unbelievablc.

相信不可置信的。

Achieve the unachievable.

達到無法達到的。

Notice the efforts of others.

注意到別人的努力。

Express appreciation.

要表達感謝。

Have an attitude of gratitude.

要有感恩的態度。

PART 1

Unit 3 背景說明

目標鎖定，全心投入，不可能輸。我一生發生過不少事情，都沒有影響研究發明和教學。非常感謝現在有「快手」和「抖音」，可以把我們研發的新作品放在上面，留給後人。

Clear eyes. (擦亮眼睛。) 源自 Have clear eyes. (要有明亮的雙眼。) 也可說成：See the world clearly. (看清楚這個世界。)

clear〔klɪr〕*adj.* 清楚的；明亮的

Full heart. (全心投入。) 源自 Have a full heart. (要全心投入。) 也可說成：Be committed. (要全心投入。) Be devoted. (要全心投入。)

full〔fʊl〕*adj.* 充實的；滿的；充分的

heart〔hɑrt〕*n.* 心

Can't lose. 源自 You can't lose. (你不可能輸。)

lose〔luz〕*v.* 輸；失敗

Expect the unexpected. (期待意想不到的。) 也可說成：Expect to be surprised. (期待感到驚訝。)

expect〔ɪk'spɛkt〕*v.* 期待

unexpected〔͵ʌnɪk'spɛktɪd〕*adj.* 意想不到的；意外的

Believe in the unbelievable.（相信不可置信的。）也
可說成：Believe that anything is possible.（要相
信任何事都有可能。）Be open-minded.（要心胸開
闊。）　***believe in*** 相信

unbelievable〔͵ʌnbə'livəḅl〕*adj.* 難以置信的；不可信的

Achieve the unachievable.（達到無法達到的。）也可
說成：Anything is achievable.（任何事情都可達成。）
Do great things.（要做大事。）

achieve〔ə'tʃiv〕*v.* 達成；實現；達到

unachievable〔͵ʌnə'tʃivəḅl〕*adj.* 無法達到的；不可
實現的

Notice the efforts of others.（要注意到別人的努力。）
也可說成：Recognize what others do.（要認可別人
所做的。）Appreciate what others do.（要重視別人
所做的。）

notice〔'notɪs〕*v.* 注意到

effort〔'ɛfət〕*n.* 努力

Have an attitude of gratitude.（要有感恩的態度。）
也可說成：Always be grateful.（一定要心存感激。）

attitude〔'ætə͵tjud〕*n.* 態度

gratitude〔'grætə͵tjud〕*n.* 感激

PART 1

Unit 4
不要假裝

Be true.
要真實。

Be you.
做自己。

Be yourself.
做你自己。

Don't pretend.
不要假裝。

Don't put on an act.
不要裝模作樣。

Show your true colors.
展現你真實的本色。

Be who you are.
做自己。

Be your own person.
自己做主。

Be the one and only you.
成為獨一無二的你。

PART 1

Unit 4 背景説明

　　有些人有職業病，尤其是做補習班的，打躬作揖，一天到晚感謝這個、感謝那個，天天講官話，好像生病了，大家反而不相信他。

***Be true*.** 要真實。(= *Be authentic.*)
true〔tru〕*adj.* 真實的

***Be you*.** 做你自己。(= *Just be yourself.*)

***Be yourself*.** 做你自己。(= *Be you.* = *Be true.*) 也可説成：Be true to yourself. (要忠於自己。) Don't try to be something you are not. (不要想變得不是你自己。)
yourself〔jʊr'sɛlf〕*pron.* 你自己

***Don't pretend*.** 不要假裝。(= *Don't fake it.*)
pretend〔prɪ'tɛnd〕*v.* 假裝

***Don't put on an act*.** 不要裝模作樣。(= *Don't put it on.*)
put on ①穿上 ②增加 ③演出（戲劇）
act〔ækt〕*n.* 行為；（戲的）一幕；裝腔作勢
put on an act 裝腔作勢；裝模作樣

Show your true colors. (展現你眞實的本色。) 也可
　説成 : Show who you really are. (表現出眞實的
　自己。) Don't pretend to be something you're
　not. (不要假裝成不是你自己。)

show〔 ʃo 〕*v.* 展現

color〔'kʌlɚ 〕*n.* 顏色；本質；本性；(*pl.*) 國旗；船旗

one's true colors 某人的眞面目【源自航海時，船旗代
　表船的身分，打仗時爲了獲勝，可能會偷掛敵人的船旗】

Be who you are. 做你自己。(*= Be yourself.*) 也可
　説成 : Don't pretend. (不要假裝。)

who you are ①你是誰 ②你是怎樣的人

Be your own person. 要獨立自主；要自己做主。
　(*= Be yourself. = Make your own decisions. = Be
　independent. = Don't be influenced by others.*)

own〔 on 〕*adj.* 自己的

Be the one and only you. 成爲獨一無二的你。(*= Be
　who you are.*) 也可説成 : Be true to yourself.
　(要忠於自己。) Don't pretend to be something
　you're not. (不要假裝不是你自己。) Don't put
　on an act. (不要裝模作樣。)

one and only 唯一的；僅有的

PART 1

Unit 5
超越巔峰

Be more.
人要變得更好。

Do more.
要做得更多。

Do better.
做得更好。

Go above.

超過。

Go beyond.

超越。

Go above and beyond.

超越巔峰。

Go the extra mile.
加倍努力。

Go beyond expectations.
超越預期。

You'll be sure to go far.
你一定會成功。

PART 1

Unit 5 背景説明

美國人喜歡説：Be more. Do more. Do better. 人要
變得更好，做得更多，做得更好。別人工作 8 小時。我工
作 12 小時；別人工作 30 年，我已經工作 55 年，當然我是
贏家。

Be more. 字面的意思是「要成爲更多。」引申爲：
① 人要變得更好。(= *Be better.*)
② 要更有成就。(= *Be more accomplished.*)
③ 要更成功。(= *Be more successful.*)

Do more. (要做得更多。) 也可説成：Do more than
you have done. (要做得比你已經做到的還要多。)
Accomplish more. (要完成更多事。)
do〔du〕*v.* 做；表現

Do better. ① 要做得更好。(= *Do a better job.*)
② 要表現得更好。(= *Behave better.*)

above〔ə'bʌv〕*adv.* 在上面
go above 超過；超越
beyond〔bɪ'jɑnd〕*adv.* 在更遠處
go beyond 超出；超過

Go above and beyond. 要出類拔萃；要超越巔峰。
(= *Go above.* = *Go beyond.*) 也可說成：Do
more. (要多做一些。) Do better. (要做得更好。)
Do more than is expected. (要做得比預期的多。)
Do more than you have to do. (要做得比你必須
做的多。)

go above and beyond 出類拔萃

Go the extra mile. 多走一英里，引申為「多付出一分
力；加倍努力。」(= *Do more.* = *Do more than is
expected.*)

extra〔'ɛkstrə〕*adj.* 額外的

mile〔maɪl〕*n.* 英里

Go beyond expectations. 要超越預期。(= *Exceed
expectations.*)

expectation〔͵ɛkspɛk'teʃən〕*n.* 期待

You'll be sure to go far. 你一定會成功。(= *You are
bound to succeed.* = *You'll definitely succeed.*)

sure〔ʃʊr〕*adj.* 確定的

go far 成功；有遠大的前程

BOOK 2 • PART 1

PART 1

Unit 6
自力更生

Rely on yourself.
靠自己。

Depend on yourself.
靠自己。

Self-reliance is best.
自力更生最好。

BOOK 2 · PART 1

Do things yourself.
事必躬親。

Don't count on others.
不要依賴別人。

Be the best you.
做最好的自己。

Be independent.
要獨立。

Be self-reliant.
要自主。

You'll be a great success.
你會非常成功。

PART 1

Unit 6 背景說明

要借錢，專門借你錢的地方是銀行，向人借錢，貶低了自己，一傳十，十傳百，人人對你敬而遠之。

rely〔rɪ'laɪ〕v. 依靠；信賴　　***rely on*** 依靠
yourself〔jʊr'sɛlf〕pron. 你自己

depend〔dɪ'pɛnd〕v. 依賴　　***depend on*** 依賴；依靠

Self-reliance is best.（自力更生最好。）也可說成：
　It is better to rely on yourself than on others.
（依靠自己比依靠別人好。）

self-reliance〔'sɛlfrɪ'laɪəns〕n. 依靠自己；自力更生

count〔kaʊnt〕v. 數；依賴　　***count on*** 依賴
others〔'ʌðəz〕pron. 別人

Be the best you. 成為最好的你，也就是展現出自己最好的一面，「做最好的自己。」（= ***Be the best person you can be.*** = ***Be the best version of yourself.***）

independent〔ˌɪndɪ'pɛndənt〕adj. 獨立的

self-reliant〔'sɛlfrɪ'laɪənt〕adj. 依靠自己的；自力更生的

You'll be a great success. 你會是一個偉大的成功的人，也就是「你會非常成功。」（= ***You'll be very successful.***）

great〔gret〕adj. 很棒的；偉大的

success〔sək'sɛs〕n. 成功；成功的人

PART 1

Unit 7
赤子之心

Be childlike.
要有童真。

Be like a child.
赤子之心。

Age doesn't matter.
年齡不重要。

Be playful.
要愛玩。

Be innocent.
要純潔。

Be loving.
要有愛。

Don't become old.
不要變老。

Don't age too quickly.
不要老得太快。

Never lose the child in you.
絕不要失去你的赤子之心。

PART 1

Unit 7 背景説明

　　不管你年齡多大，你想活得快樂、活得久，就要有童眞。（Be childlike.）要有赤子之心。（Be like a child.）天天喊我的兒子多大了、我的孫子多大了，你會老得很快。

childlike〔'tʃaɪld,laɪk〕*adj.* 孩子般的；單純的；純眞無邪的

Be like a child. 要像個孩子，引申爲「要有赤子之心。」

　（*= Be childlike.*）也可説成：Look at the world
　through a child's eyes.（要用孩子的眼光看世界。）
　Be as open to new ideas as a child.（要像孩子一
　樣樂於接受新的想法。）

like〔laɪk〕*prep.* 像　　child〔tʃaɪld〕*n.* 孩子

age〔edʒ〕*n.* 年紀　　matter〔'mætɚ〕*v.* 重要

playful〔'plefəl〕*adj.* 愛玩的；頑皮的（*= lively = spirited*）

innocent〔'ɪnəsṇt〕*adj.* 天眞的；單純的（*= uncorrupted*）

loving〔'lʌvɪŋ〕*adj.* 充滿著愛的（*= caring = affectionate*）

old〔old〕*adj.* 老的　　age〔edʒ〕*v.* 變老

quickly〔'kwɪklɪ〕*adv.* 快地

Never lose the child in you. 絶不要失去你心中的小孩，

　引申爲「絶不要失去你的赤子之心。」也可説成：Keep
　your inner child alive.（要保有赤子之心。）Be
　young at heart.（心態要年輕。）Don't be close-
　minded.（不要思想保守。）Don't become set in
　your ways.（不要固執己見。）

never〔'nɛvɚ〕*adv.* 絶不　　lose〔luz〕*v.* 失去

PART 1

Unit 8
穿著得體

Dress well.
穿著得體。

Dress like a winner.
著似勝者。

It determines success.
關乎成敗。

Have style.
要有品味。

Feel better.
會感覺更好。

Gain respect.
會贏得尊重。

**Clothes make
the man.**
【諺】人要衣裝。

**You are what
you wear.**
衣如其人。

**Dress your best
for success.**
為成功而裝。

PART 1

Unit 8 背景說明

穿衣服太重要了！你花了你萬分之一的財產，可以創造無限的可能。不管去哪裡，都要穿得好。你穿得破破爛爛，誰會理你？穿得好，自己會感覺更好，因爲受到尊重。

dress〔drɛs〕*v.* 穿衣服
dress well 衣服穿得好；穿得體面

Dress like a winner .（要穿得像個贏家。）也可說成：
   Dress for success.（要爲獲得成功而穿衣打扮。）
like〔laɪk〕*prep.* 像   winner〔'wɪnɚ〕*n.* 優勝者

It determines success. （它能決定成敗。）也可說成：
   People will judge you by the way you dress. （人們會根據你的穿著評斷你。）Dressing well can help you succeed. （穿得好能幫助你成功。）
determine〔dɪ'tɝmɪn〕*v.* 決定
success〔sək'sɛs〕*n.* 成功

Have style .（要有風格；要有型；要有品味。）也可說成：Be stylish. （要時髦。）Be fashionable. （要時髦。）   style〔staɪl〕*n.* 風格；時尚；風度

Feel better . 源自 You will feel better. （你會感覺更好。）也可說成：You will feel more comfortable.

（你會覺得更舒服。）You will feel more confident.
（你會覺得更有自信。）

Gain respect. 源自 You will gain respect. （你會獲
得尊重。）也可說成：You will win others' respect.
（你會贏得別人的尊重。）You will win others'
admiration. （你會贏得別人的讚賞。）

gain〔gen〕*v.* 獲得

respect〔rɪ'spɛkt〕*n.* 尊敬；尊重

Clothes make the man. 是一句諺語，「衣服造就一個
人。」也就是「人要衣裝，佛要金裝。」(= *The tailor
makes the man.*)【源自莎士比亞的悲劇 *Hamlet* （哈姆
雷特）】 clothes〔kloz〕*n. pl.* 衣服

make〔mek〕*v.* 造就 man〔mæn〕*n.* 男人；人

You are what you wear. （你穿什麼，就變成什麼樣的
人。）類似的說法有：You are what you eat. （你吃
什麼，就變成什麼樣了。） wear〔wɛr〕*v.* 穿著

Dress your best for success. 為了成功，要穿最好的衣
服；穿得好有助於成功。(= *If you dress well, you are
more likely to succeed.*)

*one's **best*** （某人的）最好的衣服

dress your best 穿上你最好的衣服 (= *wear your best
clothes = dress as well as you can*)

PART 1

Unit 9
不要爭吵

Don't argue.
別爭吵。

No one wins.
沒有人贏。

No one likes to admit their mistakes.
沒有人喜歡承認
自己的錯誤。

BOOK 2 · PART 1

Arguing wastes time.

爭吵浪費時間。

It wastes energy.

它浪費力氣。

It's just noise.

它只是噪音。

Avoid arguing.
避免爭吵。

Change the subject.
轉移話題。

Or just walk away.
或是走開。

PART 1

Unit 9 背景說明

　　爭吵沒有贏家，沒有人喜歡承認自己的錯誤。解決爭吵最好的方法，就是轉移話題，或走開，不要浪費時間在爭論上。

Don't argue. 不要爭吵。(= *Don't quarrel.*)
argue〔'ɑrgjʊ〕*v.* 爭論；爭吵

No one wins. 沒有人贏。(= *There are no winners.*)
win〔wɪn〕*v.* 贏

No one likes to admit their mistakes. (沒有人喜歡承認錯誤。) 現代英文中，多用代名詞 their 代替 his。
admit〔əd'mɪt〕*v.* 承認　mistake〔mə'stek〕*n.* 錯誤

waste〔west〕*v.* 浪費
energy〔'ɛnədʒɪ〕*n.* 精力；氣力；活力
It's just noise. (它只是噪音。) 也可說成：It means nothing. (它沒有意義。)
just〔dʒʌst〕*adv.* 只　noise〔nɔɪz〕*n.* 噪音；吵鬧

avoid〔ə'vɔɪd〕*v.* 避免　「***avoid* + *V-ing***」表「避免～」。
Change the subject. 轉移話題。(= *Drop the subject.*)
change〔tʃendʒ〕*v.* 改變
subject〔'sʌbdʒɪkt〕*n.* 主題；話題
walk away 走開 (= *leave*)

PART 1 總整理

Unit 1

Give happiness.
給人幸福。
Share happiness.
分享快樂。
That's the best gift.
是最棒的禮物。

Generosity pays off.
慷慨會得到回報。
Selflessness pays off.
無私會得到回報。
Kindness is always worth
　it. 善良一定划得來。

Be kind. 存好心。
Be caring. 要關懷。
You may change
　someone's life.
也許你會改變別人的一生。

Unit 2

Give happily.
高高興興地給。
Accept gratefully.
感激地接受。

Everyone benefits.
大家都受益。

Reach down. 彎下腰。
Lift people up. 拉人一把。
There is no better
　exercise.
沒有比這更好的運動。

Do nice things. 去做好事。
Expect nothing in return.
不求回報。
You'll never be
　disappointed. 永不失望。

Unit 3

Clear eyes. 擦亮眼睛。
Full heart. 全心投入。
Can't lose. 不可能輸。

Expect the unexpected.
期待意想不到的。
Believe in the
　unbelievable.
相信不可置信的。
Achieve the unachievable.
達到無法達到的。

BOOK 2・PART 1

Notice the efforts of
　others. 注意到別人的努力。
Express appreciation.
要表達感謝。
Have an attitude of
　gratitude.
要有感恩的態度。

Unit 4

Be true. 要真實。
Be you. 做自己。
Be yourself. 做你自己。

Don't pretend. 不要假裝。
Don't put on an act.
不要裝模作樣。
Show your true colors.
展現你真實的本色。

Be who you are. 做自己。
Be your own person.
自己做主。
Be the one and only you.
成為獨一無二的你。

Unit 5

Be more. 人要變得更好。
Do more. 要做得更多。
Do better. 做得更好。

Go above. 超過。
Go beyond. 超越。
Go above and beyond.
超越巔峰。

Go the extra mile.
加倍努力。
Go beyond expectations.
超越預期。
You'll be sure to go far.
你一定會成功。

Unit 6

Rely on yourself. 靠自己。
Depend on yourself.
靠自己。
Self-reliance is best.
自力更生最好。

Do things yourself.
事必躬親。
Don't count on others.
不要依賴別人。
Be the best you.
做最好的自己。

Be independent. 要獨立。
Be self-reliant. 要自主。
You'll be a great success.
你會非常成功。

Unit 7

Be childlike. 要有童真。
Be like a child. 赤子之心。
Age doesn't matter.
年齡不重要。

Be playful. 要愛玩。
Be innocent. 要純潔。
Be loving. 要有愛。

Don't become old.
不要變老。
Don't age too quickly.
不要老得太快。
Never lose the child in
　you.
絕不要失去你的赤子之心。

Unit 8

Dress well. 穿著得體。
Dress like a winner.
著似勝者。
It determines success.
關乎成敗。

Have style. 要有品味。
Feel better. 會感覺更好。
Gain respect. 會贏得尊重。

Clothes make the man.
【諺】人要衣裝。
You are what you wear.
衣如其人。
Dress your best for
　success. 爲成功而裝。

Unit 9

Don't argue. 別爭吵。
No one wins.
沒有人贏。
No one likes to admit
　their mistakes.
沒有人喜歡承認自己的錯誤。

Arguing wastes time.
爭吵浪費時間。
It wastes energy.
它浪費力氣。
It's just noise.
它只是噪音。

Avoid arguing.
避免爭吵。
Change the subject.
轉移話題。
Or just walk away.
或是走開。

BOOK 2・PART 1

PART 2

Unit 1
做你所愛

PART 2・Unit 1~9
英文錄音QR碼

Do what you love.
做你所愛。

Love what you do.
愛你所為。

**Big money will
follow you.**
財富跟隨你。

**Don't just work
for money.**
莫為錢工作。

**Money should come
from your passion.**
財富來自熱情。

**Passion, passion,
passion!**
熱情，熱情，熱情！

Have passion.
要有熱情。

Follow your passion.
跟隨熱情。

Make magic happen.
創造奇蹟。

PART 2

Unit 1 背景説明

Do what you love.
Love what you do.
Big money will follow you.

　　我最喜歡這三句話。我工作 50 多年，從不覺得累，因爲我喜歡我做的事。中國人説：「男怕入錯行，女怕嫁錯郎。」大家一定要選擇你喜歡的工作，你會快樂、身體好，錢就自然會來。不要只爲錢工作，錢應該來自你的愛好。

　　熱情最重要，平常你冷冷的，別人也對你冷冷的，人生太無趣了。所以，我們強調：Passion! Passion! Passion!（熱情！熱情！熱情！）注意 passion〔ˈpæʃən〕這個字，中國人會唸作〔ˈpeʃən〕（誤），因爲中文裡沒有 /æ/ 的音，我們唸的時候，把嘴巴裂開來即可。

> *Big money will follow you.*（大錢會跟隨你；大錢自然來。）也可説成：You will become rich.（你會變得有錢。）

big money 大筆的錢

follow〔ˈfalo〕*v.* 跟隨　　just〔dʒʌst〕*adv.* 只

Money should come from your passion.（錢應該來自你的熱情。）也可說成：You should make money by doing something you love.（你應該做你喜愛的事來賺錢。）

passion〔'pæʃən〕*n.* 熱情（= *enthusiasm*）；愛好

Have passion. 要有熱情。(= *Have enthusiasm.* = *Be enthusiastic.*)

Follow your passion.（跟隨你的熱情；跟著你的愛好走。）也可說成：Pursue what you really care about.（追求你真正在乎的。）

Make magic happen.（讓魔法發生；創造奇蹟。）也可說成：Make incredible things happen.（讓不可思議的事發生。）Do something amazing.（做令人驚奇的事。）Do great things.（做很棒的事。）

make〔mek〕*v.* 使

magic〔'mædʒɪk〕*n.* 魔法；魔術

happen〔'hæpən〕*v.* 發生

Passion, passion, passion!
也可以寫成三句話：Passion!
Passion! Passion!

BOOK 2・PART 2

PART 2

Unit 2
接受挑戰

Try it!
試試看！

Try to do it!
努力去做！

Take it on!
接受挑戰！

Have faith.
有信心。

Keep the faith.
保持信心。

**Don't give up
hope.**
不失希望。

Have no doubt.
不要懷疑。

Trust in yourself.
相信自己。

**Trust you can
do it.**
相信自己能做。

PART 2

Unit 2 背景説明

很多人不敢開口説英文，連試一試都不肯，因爲對自己沒有信心。所以我們要：Try it! (試試看！) Try to do it! (努力去做！) Take it on! (接受挑戰！)

每天背「完美英語之心靈盛宴」，背多了，你就會有信心。英文要使用，才不會忘記，可以在手機上使用。Have no doubt. (不要懷疑。) Trust in yourself. (相信自己。) Trust you can do it. (相信自己能做。)

Try it! 試試看！(= *Give it a try!*)

Take it on! 接受挑戰！(= *Accept the challenge!*)

take on 承擔 (工作、責任等) (= *undertake* = *accept* = *assume* = *shoulder*)

Have faith. 有信心。(= *Have confidence.*)

faith 〔 feθ 〕 *n.* 信念；信心

keep 〔 kip 〕 *v.* 保持；保有

give up 放棄　　hope 〔 hop 〕 *n.* 希望

Have no doubt. (不要懷疑。) 也可説成：Don't doubt it. (不要懷疑。)　　doubt 〔 daʊt 〕 *n. v.* 懷疑

Trust in yourself. 相信你自己的能力。(= *Believe in yourself.* = *Have confidence in yourself.*)

trust 〔 trʌst 〕 *v.* 信任；相信　　*trust in* 信任；信賴

Trust you can do it. 相信你可以做到。(= *Believe that you can do it.*)

PART 2

Unit 3
成為菁英

Think bigger.
敢想。

Look farther.
看遠。

Cast your net wider.
廣泛蒐羅機會。

Do it better.
做得更好。

Get an advantage.
取得優勢。

Try to get ahead.
努力領先。

Be the best.
要成為最好的。

Be the brightest.
要成為最耀眼的。

**Be the cream of
the crop.**
要成為菁英。

PART 2

Unit 3　背景説明

　　有位同學想要當廚師，結果他找了路邊攤的師父爲師。我介紹他去找大師父，現在已經成爲五星級飯店的主廚。所以，我們一定要有遠大的志向，要敢想 (Think bigger.)，要看得遠 (Look farther.)，要到處找機會 (Cast your net wider.)，要做就做最好的 (Be the best.)。

Think bigger.　要有較大的志向。(= *Be more ambitious*.)

think big　志向遠大；有雄心壯志

Look farther.　要看遠一點。(= *Look farther into the future*.) 也可説成：Consider more possibilities.（要考慮更多的可能性。）

look〔lʊk〕*v.* 看　　farther〔ˈfɑrðɚ〕*adv.* 更遠

Cast your net wider.　撒開人網，機會才多；要廣泛蒐羅機會。(= *Look for more opportunities*.)

cast〔kæst〕*v.* 投擲；撒（魚網）

net〔nɛt〕*n.* 網子

wide〔waɪd〕*adv.* 張大地；廣大地

cast one's *net wider*　撒開大網（機會才多）(= *spread* one's *net wider*)

Do it better.　要做得更好。(= *Do a better job*.)

Get an advantage.　要取得優勢。(= *Gain an edge*.)
advantage 〔 əd'væntɪdʒ 〕 *n.* 優勢

Try to get ahead. (努力領先。) 也可説成：Try to
get ahead of others. (努力領先別人。) (= *Put in
the effort to do better than others*.)
try to V. 努力…　　***get ahead***　領先

Be the best. 可加長爲：Be the best of the best.
(要成爲最好的。)

Be the brightest. (要成爲最耀眼的。) 可加長爲：
Be the brightest star. (要成爲最耀眼的星星。) 也
可説成：Be the best. (要成爲最好的。) Be the
smartest. (要成爲最聰明的。)
bright 〔 braɪt 〕 *adj.* 明亮的；聰明的

Be the cream of the crop.　要成爲菁英。
　(= *Be the best*. = *Be the best of the best*.
　= *Be the finest*. = *Be the best of the bunch*.
　= *Be the top of the line*. = *Be top-notch*.
　= *Be A-number-one*. = *Be above all the rest*.)
cream 〔 krim 〕 *n.* 奶油；精華
crop 〔 krɑp 〕 *n.* 農作物；一群；一組
the cream of the crop　最好的人或物；精選的東西；精粹

PART 2

Unit 4
稱讚要快

Compliment.
稱讚。

Compliment others.
稱讚他人。

**Be quick to
compliment.**
稱讚人要快。

Compliment often.

經常稱讚。

Compliment everywhere.

無處不稱讚。

Speak well of others.

說別人的好話。

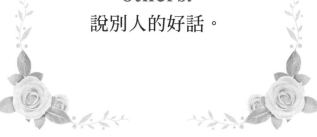

**Give sincere
compliments.**
真誠地稱讚。

Make someone smile.
讓別人笑。

**You'll be happier,
too.**
你也會更快樂。

PART 2

Unit 4　背景説明

　　稱讚（compliment）太重要了！不花你一毛錢，卻能給你帶來無窮的人脈和財富。稱讚別人要快，有機會就要稱讚，在背後也要稱讚。讓人快樂，自己也快樂。

Compliment.（稱讚。）也可說成：Give compliments.
（給人稱讚。）Be complimentary.（要稱讚。）Give
praise.（給人稱讚。）Praise others.（稱讚別人。）
compliment〔ˈkɑmpləˌmɛnt〕*v.* 稱讚（= *praise*）

Be quick to compliment.（要快速稱讚；稱讚人要快。）
也可說成：Don't hesitate to compliment.（要毫不
猶豫地稱讚。）　　quick〔kwɪk〕*adj.* 快的

often〔ˈɔfən〕*adv.* 常常
everywhere〔ˈɛvrɪˌhwɛr〕*adv.* 到處

Speak well of others. 說別人的好話。(= *Say nice
things about others.*) 也可說成：Speak highly of
others.（讚揚別人。）Applaud others.（稱讚別人。）
Pay tribute to others.（向別人致敬。）
speak well of 說…的好話

Give sincere compliments. 真誠地稱讚。(= *Give real
compliments.* = *Give honest compliments.* = *Give
genuine compliments.*)
sincere〔sɪnˈsɪr〕*adj.* 真誠的
compliment〔ˈkɑmpləmənt〕*n.* 稱讚
make〔mek〕*v.* 使　　smile〔smaɪl〕*v.* 微笑；笑

PART 2

Unit 5
徹底原諒

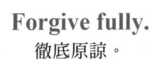

Forgive fully.
徹底原諒。

**It doesn't change
the past.**
無法改變過去。

**It brightens the
future.**
會照亮未來。

Forgive yourself.
原諒自己。

Forgive others.
原諒別人。

Forgiveness is healing.
寬容能治癒。

Forgiveness is a gift.

寬恕是恩賜。

You give it to yourself.

你給你自己的禮物。

It will set you free.

會使你獲得自由。

PART 2

Unit 5 背景説明

人無完人，要原諒別人，也要原諒自己，自己做錯了事，不去想它，給自己的心靈帶來自由。説起來容易，做起來難。天天背「完美英語之心靈盛宴」，會使你忘卻煩惱，寬恕別人。

Forgive fully. 徹底原諒。(= *Forgive others completely.*) 也可説成：Don't hang on to resentment. (不要一直憤恨。)
forgive〔fə'gɪv〕*v.* 原諒；寬恕
fully〔'fʊlɪ〕*adv.* 完全地

It doesn't change the past. (它無法改變過去。) 也可説成：Forgiveness doesn't change what happened. (原諒無法改變已經發生的事。)
change〔tʃendʒ〕*v.* 改變　　past〔pæst〕*n.* 過去

It brightens the future. (它會照亮未來。) 也可説成：Forgiveness makes the future better. (原諒會使未來更好。)　　brighten〔'braɪtn̩〕*v.* 使光明
future〔'fjutʃə〕*n.* 未來

Forgive yourself. (原諒自己。) 也可説成：Don't blame yourself. (不要責怪自己。)
others〔'ʌðəz〕*pron.* 別人

Forgiveness is healing. 寬恕有治療的效果。
(= *Forgiveness is therapeutic.*) 也可說成：
Forgiveness will make you feel better. (原諒
會使你感覺更好。)

forgiveness〔fə'ɡɪvnɪs〕*n.* 原諒

healing〔'hilɪŋ〕*adj.* 有治療功效的

Forgiveness is a gift. 寬恕是恩賜。(= *Forgiveness is a blessing.*)

gift〔ɡɪft〕*n.* 禮物；恩賜

You give it to yourself. 你把它給你自己，在此引申
為「你給你自己的禮物。」也可說成：Forgiveness
is a gift that you give to yourself. (寬恕是你給
你自己的禮物。) Forgiving others is beneficial
to you. (原諒別人對你有益。)

It will set you free. (它會使你自由。) 也可說成：
Forgiveness will liberate you. (寬恕會使你自由。)
Forgiving others will allow you to move on.
(原諒別人使你能繼續前進。)

set〔sɛt〕*v.* 使處於 (某種狀態)

free〔fri〕*adj.* 自由的

set free 放⋯自由；釋放

PART 2

Unit 6
團結一致

Let's stay united.
我們要團結。

Let's stick together.
我們團結一致。

Let's support
each other.
我們互相支持。

Let's work as a team.

我們要團隊合作。

Let's be like a family.

我們要像一個家庭。

Teamwork makes the dream work.

團隊合作使夢想成真。

Let's work side by side!

我們肩並肩工作！

Let's do it hand in hand!

我們手牽手合作！

Arm in arm, we are a team.

手挽手，我們同一隊。

PART 2

Unit 6　背景説明

Let's work *side by side*.（我們肩並肩工作。）
Let's do it *hand in hand*.（我們手牽手合作。）
Arm in arm, we are a team.
（手挽手，我們同一隊。）

你看看，這樣的三句話，有誰能夠説出這麼好的句子！
你去演講，你説出這樣的中文和英文，多麼讓人震撼！

你常常使用「完美英語之心靈盛宴」中的句子，你就成
為領袖，人人想和你在一起。背單字，利用文法造句，很容
易出錯，*side by side*（肩並肩）、*hand in hand*（手牽手）、
arm in arm（手挽手），表「對照」，都不加冠詞。*Arm
in arm, we are a team.* 就不能説成：*We are a team,
arm in arm.*（誤），而且 we are 也不會説成 we're，因為
加強語氣，所以，使用「完美英語」是學英文最好的方法。

stay〔ste〕*v.* 保持
united〔juˈnaɪtɪd〕*adj.* 聯合的；團結的
stick〔stɪk〕*v.* 黏貼
stick together 黏在一起；團結在一起（= *stay united*
　= *work together*）
support〔səˈport〕*v.* 支持　　*each other* 彼此；互相

Let's work as a team. 我們要團隊合作。(= *Let's cooperate*.) 也可說成 : Let's work together to reach the same goal. (我們要一起合作，達成同樣的目標。)　team〔tim〕*n.* 隊伍；團隊

Let's be like a family. (我們要像一個家庭。) 也可說成 : Let's support one another. (我們要互相支持。) Let's work closely together. (我們要密切合作。) like〔laɪk〕*prep.* 像

Teamwork makes the dream work. (團隊合作使夢想成眞；團隊力量大。) 這句話源自一本暢銷書的書名。也可說成 : If we work together as a team, we will achieve our dream. (如果我們團隊合作，就會達成我們的夢想。)

teamwork〔'tim,wɝk〕*n.* 團隊合作

make〔mek〕*v.* 使【是使役動詞，後面的 work 是原形動詞】

dream〔drim〕*n.* 夢想

work〔wɝk〕*v.* 運作；有效；行得通【在此指 be realized (被實現) 或 succeed (成功)】

side by side 並肩地；並排地；共同地 (= *hand in hand* = *shoulder to shoulder* = *together* = *jointly*)

hand in hand 手牽手；共同地

arm in arm 手臂挽著手臂

BOOK 2・PART 2

PART 2

Unit 7
時贏時輸

Win some, lose some.

時贏時輸。

That's life.

是人生。

C'est la vie.

人生如此。

Stand up after falling.

跌倒了再站起來。

Start again after failing.

失敗了再重新開始。

Get back on track.

重回正軌。

Bounce back.
捲土重來。

Make a comeback.
東山再起。

Get back on your feet.
重新站起來。

BOOK 2 · PART 2

PART 2

Unit 7　背景説明

　　失敗爲成功之母，有時失敗，有時成功，非常正常。跌倒了，再站起來。(Stand up after falling.) 失敗了，再重新開始。(Start again after failing.)「劉毅英文」從「升大學英文」轉向「完美英語」，經過 20 多年的折騰，終於又站起來了，轉虧爲盈的感覺非常美，好東西被人接受，是最愉快的事情。

Win some, lose some. 中文説「有輸有贏」，可是英文是 win 在前，lose 在後。這句話也可説成：You win some, you lose some. (你贏一些，你輸掉一些。) 意思就是 You can't win all the time in life. (在人生中，你不可能一直都贏。)

美語中往往摻雜了許多外來語，像 *C'est la vie.* 是法文，唸成〔ˌse lə ˈvi〕，翻譯成英文就是 *That's life.*「這就是人生；人生就是如此。」

stand up 站起來　　fall〔fɔl〕*v.* 跌倒　　start〔stɑrt〕*v.* 開始　　fail〔fel〕*v.* 失敗　　track〔træk〕*n.* 軌道
back on track 重回正軌；重新振作（= *back to normal*）

bounce〔bauns〕*v.* 彈回；反彈
bounce back 彈回；恢復；復原（= *recover* = *rebound*）
Make a comeback. 東山再起。（= *Return to success.*）
comeback〔ˈkʌmˌbæk〕*n.* 恢復；捲土重來；東山再起
　（= *return* = *revival*）
Get back on your feet. 重新站起來。（= *Regain your feet.* = *Stand up again.* = *Bounce back.* = *Recover.* = *Rebound.*）

PART 2

Unit 8
追求宏偉

Discard the bad.
丟棄不好的。

Keep the good.
保留好的。

Go for the great.
追求宏偉。

BOOK 2・PART 2

Try new things.
嘗試新事物。

Make mistakes!
勇於犯錯！

Change yourself.
改變自己。

Don't fear death.
不要害怕死亡。

Fear never really living.
要害怕沒真正活過。

Live your best life now.
活在最好的當下。

PART 2

Unit 8　背景説明

　　人生就是選擇，選擇對了，一生快樂，選擇錯了，一生痛苦。天天都在選擇，選擇吃什麼，選擇做什麼，小事情選錯沒有什麼關係，不好的餐廳，以後不要再去。要學會丟棄不好的（Discard the bad.）保留好的。（Keep the good.）要追求最好的。（Go for the great.）我們要嘗試新的事物。（Try new things.）勇於犯錯！（Make mistakes!）同樣的人做同樣的事，不可能有不同的結果。新人新事，就有新的結果。

Discard the bad.（丟棄不好的。）也可説成：Get rid of bad things.（擺脱不好的事物。）

discard〔 dɪsˈkɑrd 〕*v.* 拋棄【dis (*not*) + card（卡片）】

Keep the good.　保留好的。(= *Hold on to the good ones.*)

Go for the great.　追求最棒的。(= *Pursue the really good things.*)

go for　去拿；去追求；去爭取

great〔 gret 〕*adj.* 很棒的；偉大的

Try new things.　嘗試新事物。(= *Try something new.*)　　try〔 traɪ 〕*v.* 嘗試

Make mistakes!（勇於犯錯！）也可說成：Don't be afraid to make mistakes!（不要害怕犯錯！）

mistake〔mə'stek〕*n.* 錯誤

make a mistake 犯錯

Change yourself.（改變自己。）也可說成：Make a change.（要改變。）Change for the better.（要變得更好。）Become a better person.（要變成一個更好的人。）Turn over a new leaf.（翻開新的一頁；改過自新；重新開始。）　change〔tʃendʒ〕*v.* 改變

Don't fear death. 不要害怕死亡。（= *Don't be afraid of dying.*）　fear〔fɪr〕*v.* 害怕

death〔dɛθ〕*n.* 死亡

Fear never really living.（要害怕沒真正活過。）也可說成：Instead, be afraid of not living a full life.（而是要害怕沒有過充實的生活。）Be afraid of wasting your life instead.（而是要害怕浪費你的生命。）

never〔'nɛvɚ〕*adv.* 從未　　really〔'rɪəlɪ〕*adv.* 真地

Live your best life now.（現在要過得最好；活在最好的當下。）也可說成：Live life to the fullest now.（現在就過最充實的生活。）Live the best life you can.（儘可能過最好的生活。）

live〔lɪv〕*v.* 活；生活；過（…生活）

PART 2

Unit 9
中庸之道

Don't do too much.
不要做太多。

Don't do too little.
不要做太少。

Everything in moderation.
一切中庸。

Create balance.
創造平衡。

Balance your life.
平衡生活。

Life is all about balance.
人生全在於平衡。

Too far east is west.

【諺】物極必反。

Extreme right is extreme wrong.

【諺】過猶不及。

Find the middle ground.

尋求中庸之道。

PART 2

Unit 9　背景說明

　　中國的「中庸之道」太偉大了！不偏不倚，不要走極端。吃東西不要過度，也不要太少，身體才健康。什麼事都一樣，過猶不及。(Extreme right is extreme wrong.) 小偷來了，把他抓到就好，不要把他打死。股票暴跌了，買一點績優股，等他個 30 年，總是有機會。

Don't do too much. (不要做太多。) 也可說成：
　Don't overdo it. (別做得過火。)

Don't do too little. (不要做太少。) 也可說成：Make
　sure you do enough. (要確定你做得夠多。)

Everything in moderation. (一切中庸。) 這句話沒動
　詞，是慣用句，源自 Do everything in moderation.
　(做任何事都要適度。) Don't do anything to
　excess. (任何事都不要做得太超過。)
moderation〔͵mɑdə'reʃən〕*n.* 適度；適中；中庸

Create balance. (創造平衡。) 也可說成：Keep
　everything in balance. (凡事都要保持平衡。)
create〔krɪ'et〕*v.* 創造
balance〔'bæləns〕*n.* 平衡　*v.* 使平衡

Life is all about balance. (人生全在於平衡。) 也可
說成：Balance is important in life. (平衡在生活中
很重要。) A well-balanced life is a good life.
(均衡的生活才是好的生活。)

Too far east is west. 是一句諺語，地球是圓的，極東
就是西，引申為「物極必反。」(= *If you go too far,
you will end up back where you started*.)
east 〔 ist 〕 *n.* 東方　　west 〔 wɛst 〕 *n.* 西方

Extreme right is extreme wrong. 是一句諺語，「極端
正確，就是極端錯誤。」引申為「過猶不及；物極必反。」
也可說成：If you take things too far, you'll be in
thc wrong. (如果你做得過火，就會是錯的。)
extreme 〔 ɪk'strim 〕 *adj.* 極端的
right 〔 raɪt 〕 *n.* 正確；正當
wrong 〔 rɔŋ 〕 *n.* 錯誤；不當

Find the middle ground. (找到折衷辦法；尋求中庸之
道。) 也可說成：Find a compromise between two
extremes. (在兩個極端之間，找到一個折衷辦法。)
middle 〔 'mɪdḷ 〕 *adj.* 中間的
ground 〔 graʊnd 〕 *n.* (議論等的) 立場；意見
middle ground　中間立場；中間觀點；妥協；折衷辦法
　 (= *compromise*)

PART 2　總整理

Unit 1

Do what you love.
做你所愛。
Love what you do.
愛你所為。
Big money will follow
　you.　財富跟隨你。

Don't just work for
　money.　莫為錢工作。
Money should come
　from your passion.
財富來自熱情。
Passion, passion,
　passion!
熱情，熱情，熱情！

Have passion.　要有熱情。
Follow your passion.
跟隨熱情。
Make magic happen.
創造奇蹟。

Unit 2

Try it!　試試看！
Try to do it!　努力去做！
Take it on!　接受挑戰！

Have faith.　有信心。
Keep the faith.　保持信心。
Don't give up hope.
不失希望。

Have no doubt.　不要懷疑。
Trust in yourself.
相信自己。
Trust you can do it.
相信自己能做。

Unit 3

Think bigger.　敢想。
Look farther.　看遠。
Cast your net wider.
廣泛蒐羅機會。

Do it better.　做得更好。
Get an advantage.
取得優勢。
Try to get ahead.
努力領先。

Be the best.　要成為最好的。
Be the brightest.
要成為最耀眼的。
Be the cream of the crop.
要成為菁英。

Unit 4

Compliment. 稱讚。
Compliment others.
稱讚他人。
Be quick to compliment.
稱讚人要快。

Compliment often.
經常稱讚。
Compliment everywhere.
無處不稱讚。
Speak well of others.
說別人的好話。

Give sincere compliments.
真誠地稱讚。
Make someone smile.
讓別人笑。
You'll be happier, too.
你也會更快樂。

Unit 5

Forgive fully. 徹底原諒。
It doesn't change the past.
無法改變過去。
It brightens the future.
會照亮未來。

Forgive yourself.
原諒自己。
Forgive others. 原諒別人。

Forgiveness is healing.
寬容能治癒。

Forgiveness is a gift.
寬恕是恩賜。
You give it to yourself.
你給你自己的禮物。
It will set you free.
會使你獲得自由。

Unit 6

Let's stay united.
我們要團結。
Let's stick together.
我們團結一致。
Let's support each other.
我們互相支持。

Let's work as a team.
我們要團隊合作。
Let's be like a family.
我們要像一個家庭。
Teamwork makes the
    dream work.
團隊合作讓夢想成真。

Let's work side by side!
我們肩並肩工作！
Let's do it hand in hand!
我們手牽手合作！
Arm in arm, we are a team.
手挽手，我們同一隊。

Unit 7

Win some, lose some.
時贏時輸。
That's life.　是人生。
C'est la vie.　人生如此。

Stand up after falling.
跌倒了再站起來。
Start again after failing.
失敗了再重新開始。
Get back on track.
重回正軌。

Bounce back.　捲土重來。
Make a comeback.
東山再起。
Get back on your feet.
重新站起來。

Unit 8

Discard the bad.
丟棄不好的。
Keep the good.　保留好的。
Go for the great.
追求宏偉。

Try new things.
嘗試新事物。
Make mistakes!
勇於犯錯！

Change yourself.
改變自己。

Don't fear death.
不要害怕死亡。
Fear never really living.
要害怕沒真正活過。
Live your best life now.
活在最好的當下。

Unit 9

Don't do too much.
不要做太多。
Don't do too little.
不要做太少。
Everything in moderation.
一切中庸。

Create balance.　創造平衡。
Balance your life.
平衡生活。
Life is all about balance.
人生全在於平衡。

Too far east is west.
【諺】物極必反。
Extreme right is extreme
　　wrong.【諺】過猶不及。
Find the middle ground.
尋求中庸之道。

PART 3

Unit 1
率先開始

PART 3・Unit 1~9
英文錄音QR碼

Lead!

領導！

Launch!

行動！

Light the way!

點亮道路！

Take the lead.
要率先。

Take the first step.
跨出第一步。

Take the initiative.
率先開始。

BOOK 2・PART 3

Be the first to try.
第一個嘗試。

Be the first to change.
第一個改變。

Don't try to be the best, be the first.
試著不當最好，當第一。

PART 3

Unit 1 背景説明

當董事長，一定要會領導！（Lead!）要行動！
（Launch!）告訴別人怎麼走！（Light the way!）要成
爲世界上最好的，幾乎不可能，因爲最好的只有一個，奧運
金牌得主也只有一個人。企業成功的不二法門是創新、發
明。我們發明「完美英語」，獨一無二，我們就是第一了！

Lead!（領導！）也可説成：Take the lead!（要帶頭！；
　要領先！）Lead the way!（要帶路！；要領先！）
　Initiate things!（要帶頭做事！）
lead〔lid〕*v.* 引導；領先

Launch!（開始！）也可説成：Start!（開始！）
　Begin!（開始！）Get underway!（開始！）
launch〔lɔntʃ〕*v.* 發射；開始

Light the way! 字面的意思是「拿著燈帶路！」引申
　爲「當開路先鋒！」（= *Blaze a trail!*）也可説成：
　Innovate!（要創新！）Set an example!（要樹立
　典範！）Be the first!（一馬當先！）
light〔laɪt〕*v.* 給…點燈；照亮；點燈領（人）行路
way〔we〕*n.* 路
light the way 拿著燈帶路

Take the lead. 領先；率先。(= *Lead the way.*
  = *Be the leader.* = *Lead others.* = *Go first.*)
lead〔 lid 〕*n.* 領先

Take the first step. (跨出第一步。) 也可說成：
  Get started. (開始做。)
step〔 stɛp 〕*n.* 一步 *take a step* 走一步；邁出一步

Take the initiative. (採取主動；率先開始。) 也可說成：
  Take action. (採取行動。) Take responsibility.
  (負起責任。) Get started. (開始做。)
initiative〔 ɪˈnɪʃɪˏetɪv 〕*n.* 率先；主動權

try〔 traɪ 〕*v.* 嘗試；努力
change〔 tʃendʒ 〕*v.* 改變
Don't try to be the best, be the first. (試著不當最好，
  當第一。) 是慣用句。也可說成：It's more important
  to be the first one than to be the best one. (成為
  第一個，比成為最好的更重要。) Don't worry about
  how well you can do it; just do it. (不用擔心你能
  表現得多好；做就對了。)
try to V. 試圖…；努力…

PART 3

Unit 2
向前進

Step forward.
向前走。

Leap forward.
向前跳。

Run forward.
向前跑。

Press forward.
向前進。

Move ahead
向前進。

Take a step in the right direction.
朝正確的方向前進。

Never stand still.
千萬不要靜止不動。

**Always move
forward.**
一定要向前進。

**Run, jump, walk,
or crawl!**
不論是跑、跳、走，
或爬，都要向前進！

PART 3

Unit 2 背景説明

　　「進步」使人生變得更美。之前學過 Move forward. (向前進。) 我們再巧妙地編寫 Step forward. (向前走。) Leap forward. (向前跳。) Run forward. (向前跑。) 走、跳、跑,很好記。千萬不要靜止不動,一定要向前進,無論是跑、跳、走,或爬,都要向前進!

Step forward. 向前走。(= *Go forward.* = *Move forward.*) 也可説成: *Leap forward.* (向前跳。)
　　Run forward. (向前跑。)

step〔stɛp〕*v.* 跨出一步;走;步行
forward〔'fɔrwəd〕*adv.* 往前
leap〔lip〕*v.* 跳 (= *jump*)

leap forward 向前跳;躍進;快速發展

Press forward. 向前推進,引申爲「趕緊向前走;奮勇前進。」也可説成: Progress. (向前進。) Make progress. (要進步。) Advance. (要前進;要進步。)
press〔prɛs〕*v.* 壓;推擠而進

Move ahead. 向前移動,也就是「向前進。」(= *Move forward.*)
move〔muv〕*v.* 移動　　ahead〔ə'hɛd〕*adv.* 向前

BOOK 2 • PART 3

Take a step in the right direction. 朝正確的方向走一步，也就是「朝正確的方向前進。」

press〔prɛs〕*v.* 壓；推擠而進

step〔stɛp〕*n.* 一步   ***take a step*** 走一步；邁出一步

in〔ɪn〕*prep.* 朝（…方向）

direction〔dəˈrɛkʃən〕*n.* 方向

Never stand still.「絕不要站著不動。」引申為「絕不要靜止不動。」也可說成：Don't be complacent.（不要自滿。）Keep progressing.（要持續前進。）

stand〔stænd〕*v.* 站著；處於（某種狀態）

still〔stɪl〕*adj.* 靜止的；不動的

stand still 站著不動；靜止不動

Always move forward.（一定要向前進。）也可說成：Keep moving forward.（要一直向前進。）

Run, jump, walk, or crawl!（不論是跑、跳、走，或爬，都要向前進！）可加長為：Run, jump, walk, or crawl to do it!（不管是用跑的、跳的、走的，或是爬的，都要去做！）也可說成：Do it any way you can!（要設法做到！）

jump〔dʒʌmp〕*v.* 跳   crawl〔krɔl〕*v.* 爬

PART 3

Unit 3
敢做春秋大夢

Dream big.
敢做春秋大夢。

Have big dreams.
敢有春秋大夢。

**If you can dream it,
you can do it.**
你敢夢，就做得到。

Do your best.

盡己所能。

Become the best.

成為最好。

Be the best you can be.

盡自己最大可能。

Follow your goals.
追隨你的目標。

Focus on success.
專注於成功。

Keep your eyes on the prize.
專注於你的目標。

PART 3

Unit 3 背景說明

　　美國人常説：Dream big dreams.（做春秋大夢。）簡稱 Dream big. 有夢想、有希望，人生最美。

Dream big. 要有遠大的夢想。（= *Dream big dreams.* = *Have big dreams.* = *Don't limit yourself.*）
dream〔drim〕*n.* 夢想　*v.* 夢見；夢想

If you can dream it, you can do it.（如果你有夢想，你就能實現。）也可説成：You can do anything you imagine.（你可以做任何你想像得到的事。）If you want to do it, you can.（如果你想做，你就做得到。）Anything is possible.（任何事都有可能。）

do one's best 盡力

Be the best you can be. 要做最好的自己。（= *Be all you can be.* = *Be your best.* = *Strive to be as good as you can.*）也可引申爲「要發揮你所有的潛力。」（= *Realize your full potential.*）

Follow your goals.（追求你的目標。）也可説成：Pursue your goals.（追求你的目標。）Strive to achieve your goals.（努力達成你的目標。）　follow〔'falo〕*v.* 跟隨；追求　goal〔gol〕*n.* 目標　focus〔'fokəs〕*v.* 專注

focus on 專注於　success〔sək'sɛs〕*n.* 成功

Keep your eyes on the prize. 字面的意思是「你的眼睛要一直盯著獎品。」引申爲「要專注於你的目標。」（= *Remain focused on your goal.*）這句話源自美國民權運動時的一首歌曲。　prize〔praɪz〕*n.* 獎；獎品

PART 3

Unit 4
堅持不懈

Keep going.
堅持下去。

Keep trying.
持續努力。

**Keep working
at it.**
堅持不懈。

Hang on!
堅持下去！

Hang in there!
堅持下去！

Keep at it!
堅持下去！

Refuse to quit.
拒絕放棄。

**Keep trying to
the end.**
堅持到底。

Go down swinging!
永不放棄！

PART 3

Unit 4 背景說明

　　我教書和編書，持續了 50 多年，還要再持續下去，就像拳擊手被打倒在地，手還在揮拳！(Go down swinging!) 這九句話很有用，你可以在手機上使用，勸別人堅持下去。美國人常說：Keep at it! (堅持下去！) 加強語氣就是：Keep working at it! (堅持不懈！)

Keep going. 堅持下去。(= *Continue*. = *Don't stop.*
　= *Don't give up.*)　　try〔traɪ〕*v.* 嘗試；努力
keep + *V-ing* 持續~　　go〔go〕*v.* 進行
keep trying 持續努力
Keep working at it. 持續努力；堅持不懈。(= *Keep*
　working on it. = *Keep at it.*)
work at 致力於；在…上下功夫

hang〔hæŋ〕*v.* 懸掛　　*hang on* 持續；不放手；堅持下去
hang in there 堅忍不拔；堅持下去 (= *endure* = *persevere*)
Keep at it! 堅持下去！(= *Keep going!* = *Hang on!*
　= *Hang in there!* = *Don't give up!*)
keep at 努力不懈地做 (功課、工作等)；熱心地做

refuse〔rɪˈfjuz〕*v.* 拒絕　　quit〔kwɪt〕*v.* 放棄
end〔ɛnd〕*n.* 最後；結束　　*to the end* 到最後
Go down swinging! 奮戰到最後一刻！(= *Keep fighting*
　until the end!)；永不放棄！(= *Don't give up!*)【源自拳擊，拳擊手直到倒下去 (go down) 的那一刻，還在揮拳 (swing)，表示「奮戰到最後」】　　swing〔swɪŋ〕*v.* 揮動

PART 3

Unit 5
成功不是結束

Success is not final.

成功不是結束。

Failure is not fatal.

失敗並非劇終。

To achieve, persevere forever.

為達目的，堅持到底。

Lick your wounds.
自我療傷。

Regain your strength.
恢復精神。

Recover after defeat.
敗後重生。

Stand firm!
站穩！

Stay strong!
保持堅定！

Stay the course!
堅持到底！

PART 3

Unit 5 背景説明

　　成功不是永遠的。(Success is not final.) 一不小心就會失敗。失敗也不是永遠的，因爲可以反敗爲勝。管他失敗或成功，都要努力不懈。

Success is not final. 成功不是結束。(= *Success is not the end.*) 也可説成：Success is not permanent.
(成功不是永久的。)　　　success〔 sək'sɛs 〕 *n.* 成功
final〔'faınḷ 〕 *adj.* 最終的

Failure is not fatal. 失敗不會要人命。(= *Failure won't kill you.*) 也可説成：When you fail, you don't fail forever. (當你失敗時，你不會永遠失敗。)
You can always come back from failure. (失敗之後，你一定可以東山再起。)
failure〔'feljɚ 〕 *n.* 失敗　　fatal〔'fetḷ 〕 *adj.* 致命的

To achieve, persevere forever. 要成功，就要堅持到底。(= *If you want to win, you have to keep on trying.* = *If you want to succeed, you can never give up.*)
achieve〔 ə'tʃiv 〕 *v.* 達成；成功 (= *succeed* = *make it*)
persevere〔ˌpɝsə'vır 〕 *v.* 堅持；堅忍
forever〔 fɚ'ɛvɚ 〕 *adv.* 永遠

Lick your wounds. 「舔你的傷口。」引申為「(受到傷害或挫折後) 恢復元氣；休養生息。」(= *Get over it.* = *Recover.*)　　lick〔 lɪk 〕*v.* 舔

wound〔 wund 〕*n.* 傷口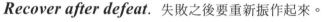

regain〔 rɪ'gen 〕*v.* 恢復

strength〔 strɛŋθ 〕*n.* 力氣；體力

Recover after defeat. 失敗之後要重新振作起來。(= *Get back on your feet.*)

recover〔 rɪ'kʌvɚ 〕*v.* 恢復健康；恢復正常，再獲得成功

defeat〔 dɪ'fit 〕*n.* 失敗；戰敗

Stand firm! (要堅定不移！；絕不讓步！) 也可說成：Persist! (要堅持！) Hold on! (要堅持！) Stand your ground! (要堅守立場！) Be determined! (要堅決！)　　stand〔 stænd 〕*v.* 處於 (某種狀態) (= *remain*)　　firm〔 fɝm 〕*adj.* 堅定的

Stay strong! (保持堅定！；一定要堅強！) 也可說成：Don't give up! (不要放棄！) Be determined! (要堅決！) Keep your chin up! (別灰心！)

stay〔 ste 〕*v.* 停留；保持

strong〔 strɔŋ 〕*adj.* 強壯的；堅定的

Stay the course! 堅持到底！(= *Stay on course!* = *Persevere to the end!*)　　course〔 kors 〕*n.* 前進路線；(船、飛機的) 航線；賽馬場【源自賽馬時，馬一直跑到最後，或船航行時不偏離航線】

PART 3

Unit 6
保持冷靜

Keep your cool.
保持冷靜。

Keep your composure.
保持冷靜。

Keep a stiff upper lip.
維持面部表情。

Remain calm.
保持冷靜。

Keep your shirt on.
稍安勿躁。

Keep your pants on.
沉住氣。

Calm yourself down.
自我冷靜。

Cool your jets.
平靜自身。

Take it down a notch.
莫過激動。

PART 3

Unit 6 背景説明

不管發生什麼事，冷靜最重要，不要讓小事影響你的心情。對我來説，編書、教書是我最大的興趣，也是最大的任務。期待這本書能夠拯救受苦受難的英文學習者。

cool〔kul〕*n.* 冷靜　composure〔kəmˋpoʒɚ〕*n.* 鎮靜
Keep a stiff upper lip. 要沈著冷靜。(= *Keep calm.*
= *Keep your emotions in check.*)

stiff〔stɪf〕*adj.* 僵硬的　upper〔ˋʌpɚ〕*adj.* 上面的
lip〔lɪp〕*n.* 嘴唇　***stiff upper lip*** 堅忍；剛毅；沈得住氣

remain〔rɪˋmen〕*v.* 保持 (= *stay*)

calm〔kɑm〕*adj.* 冷靜的

shirt〔ʃɝt〕*n.* 襯衫　on〔ɑn〕*adv.* 穿著
keep one's ***shirt on*** 不生氣；不發脾氣 (= *not get
annoyed*)；稍安勿躁 (= *hold your horses*)

pants〔pænts〕*n. pl.* 褲子
keep one's ***pants on*** 沉住氣；保持冷靜 (= *remain calm*)

Calm yourself down. 冷靜一點。(= *Calm down.*)

calm〔kɑm〕*v.* 使冷靜

cool〔kul〕*v.* 變涼；使冷卻　jet〔dʒɛt〕*n.* 噴射機
cool one's ***jets*** 冷靜一點 (= *calm down* = *settle down*
= *cool it* = *cool off* = *relax*)

Take it down a notch. 字面的意思是「調降一級。」也就
是「冷靜一點；不要太激動。」(= *Calm down a little.*
= *Relax a bit.* = *Be less excited.*)

notch〔nɑtʃ〕*n.* ①切口；刻痕 ②等級

BOOK 2．PART 3

PART 3

Unit 7
翻轉人生

Change.
要改變。

Change for the better.
變得更好。

Improve your situation.
優化情境。

Change to succeed.

為成功而改變。

Change to achieve.

為達成而改變。

**Change to better
your life.**

為美好人生而改變。

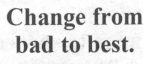

**Change from
bad to best.**
從劣變成優。

**Change from all
right to awesome.**
從普通變成傑出。

**Turn your life
around.**
翻轉你的人生。

PART 3

Unit 7 背景說明

　　台灣有一家有名的店，以前高朋滿座，現在我去，整間大餐廳只有我一個人，他們還堅持在那裡，沒有失去熱情。但是不改變、不進步，就落伍了。

　　即使你現在是第一，你不改變，你就會落到第二、第三。不管你現在好壞，都要求進步，保持不變，就會被淘汰。

Change!　Change!　Change!（改變！改變！改變！）
Change is the name of the game.（改變非常重要。）天下唯一不變的，就是「改變」。今天一定要跟昨天不一樣。

Change.（要改變。）也可說成：Evolve.（要進化。）
　Develop.（要發展。）
change〔tʃendʒ〕*v.* 改變

Change for the better.　要變得更好。(= *Improve yourself*.)

Improve your situation.（改善你的情況。）也可說成：Improve the conditions you live in.（要改善你的生狀況。）
improve〔ɪmˊpruv〕*v.* 改善；使進步
situation〔ˌsɪtʃʊˊeʃən〕*n.* 情況

Change to succeed. 爲成功而改變。(= *Make a change in order to thrive*.)　succeed ﹝ sək'sid ﹞ *v.* 成功

Change to achieve. 爲成功而改變。(= *You have to change if you want to succeed.* = *Make whatever changes you need to in order to succeed.*)

achieve ﹝ ə'tʃiv ﹞ *v.* 達成；成功；功成名就

Change to better your life. 爲改善你的生活而改變。(= *You have to change in order to have a better life.*)　better ﹝'bɛtɚ ﹞ *v.* 改善

Change from bad to best. 從不好變成最好。(= *Go from being the worst to being the best.* = *Go from the bottom to the top.*)

bad ﹝ bæd ﹞ *adj.* 壞的　*n.* 壞的事物；惡劣的狀態

best ﹝ bɛst ﹞ *adj.* 最好的　*n.* 最佳；最好

Change from all right to awesome. 要從還算可以變成很棒。(= *Go from mediocre to great.*)

all right 尚可的；還算可以的；馬馬虎虎

awesome ﹝'ɔsəm ﹞ *adj.* 很棒的

Turn your life around. 翻轉你的人生。(= *Make a big change.* = *Turn over a new leaf.*)

turn around 反轉；扭轉；翻轉；改變 (= *turn round*)

PART 3

Unit 8
做好事

Do good.
做好事。

Be helpful.
樂於助人。

You'll be blessed.
你會很有福氣。

Be kind to family.
對家人善。

Be generous to relatives.
對親友慨。

Charity begins at home.
【諺】仁愛先從家裡開始。

Do good deeds.
行善。

You'll be rewarded.
你會得到回報。

Good things happen to good people.
好心有好報。

PART 3

Unit 8 背景説明

　　「仁愛先從家裡開始。」(Charity begins at home.)
先愛周圍的人，越接近我的，我越愛他們。(The closer they
are to me, the more I love them.)

Do good. 要做好事。(= *Do good things*.)

helpful ('hɛlpfəl) *adj.* 願意幫忙的

You'll be blessed. (你會很有福氣。) 也可説成 : Good
　things will happen to you. (會有好事降臨在你身上。)
　You'll be rewarded. (你會得到回報。)

bless (blɛs) *v.* 祝福

kind (kaɪnd) *adj.* 仁慈的；友善的

generous ('dʒɛnərəs) *adj.* 慷慨的

relative ('rɛlətɪv) *n.* 親戚

Charity begins at home. 是一句諺語，「仁愛先從家裡開
　始；老吾老，以及人之老。」也可説成 : Take care of
　your family before caring for others. (先照顧家人，
　再照顧別人。)　　charity ('tʃærətɪ) *n.* 慈善；仁愛

Do good deeds. 要做好事。(= *Do good things*.)

reward (rɪ'wɔrd) *v.* 酬報；酬謝；獎賞

Good things happen to good people. (好心有好報。)
　也可説成 : If you do good things, then you will
　have good luck. (如果你做好事，那你就會有好運。) If
　you are a good person, then you will be rewarded.
　(如果你是個好人，那你就會得到回報。)

happen ('hæpən) *v.* 發生

PART 3

Unit 9
年齡只是數字

Stay healthy.
保持健康。

Stay happy.
保持快樂。

Stay kind.
保持善良。

Live without fear.
生之無懼。

Listen without judgment.
聽之無評。

Love without conditions.
愛無條件。

BOOK 2 • PART 3

**Count your age
by friends,
not years.**

以友情計算歲月，而非年齡。

**Count your life
by smiles,
not tears.**

以笑容衡量人生，而非淚水。

**Age is just a
number.**

年齡只是個數字。

PART 3

Unit 9 背景説明

美好的人生建議（Great Life Advice）：

1. 保持健康。(***Stay healthy.***)
2. 保持快樂。(***Stay happy.***)
3. 保持善良。(***Stay kind.***)
4. 永遠有錢。(Stay wealthy.)

stay〔ste〕v. 保持　　healthy〔'hɛlθɪ〕adj. 健康的
kind〔kaɪnd〕adj. 仁慈的；親切的；友善的

Live without fear.（毫無恐懼地生活。）也可説成：Don't
be fearful.（不要害怕。）Live courageously.（要勇
敢地生活。）　fear〔fɪr〕n. 恐懼

Listen without judgment. 毫不批評地傾聽。(= *Just
listen to others and do not judge them. = Don't
judge others.*)

listen〔'lɪsn̩〕v. 聽；傾聽
judgment〔'dʒʌdʒmənt〕n. 判斷；評判；批評

Love without conditions. 毫無條件地愛。(= *Love
unconditionally. = Don't put any restrictions on
your love.*)

condition〔kən'dɪʃən〕n. 狀況；條件

***Count your age by friends*, *not years*.** 字面的意思是
「你的年齡由朋友數來計算，不是歲數。」(= *It does not matter how old you are, only how many friends you have in your life.*) 引申爲「朋友越多越年輕。」

count〔kaʊnt〕*v.* 數；計算；評估 (= *evaluate*)

age〔edʒ〕*n.* 年齡；年紀

year〔jɪr〕*n.* 年；歲

***Count your life by smiles*, *not tears*.** 字面的意思是
「你的生命過得如何是靠微笑來衡量，不是眼淚。」
(= *Focus on the good times, not the bad.*) 引申爲
「笑容越多越幸福。」

smile〔smaɪl〕*n.* 微笑；笑

tear〔tɪr〕*n.* 眼淚

***Age is just a number*.** (年齡只是數字。) 意思是 Age
is not important. (年齡不重要。) Age is how you
feel. (年齡取決於你的感覺。)

just〔dʒʌst〕*adv.* 只

number〔'nʌmbɚ〕*n.* 數字

PART 3 總整理

Unit 1

Lead! 領導！
Launch! 行動！
Light the way!
點亮道路！

Take the lead.
要率先。
Take the first step.
跨出第一步。
Take the initiative.
率先開始。

Be the first to try.
第一個嘗試。
Be the first to change.
第一個改變。
Don't try to be the best,
  be the first.
試著不當最好，當第一。

Unit 2

Step forward. 向前走。
Leap forward.
向前跳。
Run forward. 向前跑。

Press forward. 向前進。
Move ahead. 向前進。
Take a step in the right
  dircction.
朝正確的方向前進。

Never stand still.
千萬不要靜止不動。
Always move forward.
一定要向前進。
Run, jump, walk, or
  crawl! 不論是跑、跳、
  走，或爬，都要向前進！

Unit 3

Dream big. 敢做春秋大夢。
Have big dreams.
敢有春秋大夢。
If you can dream it, you
  can do it.
你敢夢，就做得到。

Do your best. 盡己所能。
Become the best.
成為最好。
Be the best you can be.
盡自己最大可能。

Follow your goals.
追隨你的目標。
Focus on success.
專注於成功。
Keep your eyes on the
　　prize.　專注於你的目標。

Unit 4

Keep going.　堅持下去。
Keep trying.　持續努力。
Keep working at it.
堅持不懈。

Hang on!　堅持下去！
Hang in there!　堅持下去！
Keep at it!　堅持下去！

Refuse to quit.　拒絕放棄。
Keep trying to the end.
堅持到底。
Go down swinging!
永不放棄！

Unit 5

Success is not final.
成功不是結束。
Failure is not fatal.
失敗並非劇終。
To achieve, persevere
　　forever.
爲達目的，堅持到底。

Lick your wounds.
自我療傷。
Regain your strength.
恢復精神。
Recover after defeat.
敗後重生。

Stand firm!　站穩！
Stay strong!　保持堅定！
Stay the course!
堅持到底！

Unit 6

Keep your cool.
保持冷靜。
Keep your composure.
保持冷靜。
Keep a stiff upper lip.
維持面部表情。

Remain calm.　保持冷靜。
Keep your shirt on.
稍安勿躁。
Keep your pants on.
沈住氣。

Calm yourself down.
自我冷靜。
Cool your jets.
平靜自身。
Take it down a notch.
莫過激動。

Unit 7

Change.　要改變。
Change for the better.
變得更好。
Improve your situation.
優化情境。

Change to succeed.
為成功而改變。
Change to achieve.
為達成而改變。
Change to better your
　life.　為美好人生而改變。

Change from bad to best.
從劣變成優。
Change from all right to
　awesome.
從普通變成傑出。
Turn your life around.
翻轉你的人生。

Unit 8

Do good.　做好事。
Be helpful.　樂於助人。
You'll be blessed.
你會很有福氣。

Be kind to family.
對家人善。

Be generous to relatives.
對親友慨。
Charity begins at home.
【諺】仁愛先從家裡開始。

Do good deeds.　行善。
You'll be rewarded.
你會得到回報。
Good things happen to
　good people.
好心有好報。

Unit 9

Stay healthy.　保持健康。
Stay happy.　保持快樂。
Stay kind.　保持善良。

Live without fear.
生之無懼。
Listen without judgment.
聽之無評。
Love without conditions.
愛無條件。

Count your age by
　friends, not years.
以友情計算歲月，而非年齡。
Count your life by smiles,
　not tears.
以笑容衡量人生，而非淚水。
Age is just a number.
年齡只是個數字。

完美英語＋完美中文＋心靈盛宴

「完美英語之心靈盛宴」是「董事長英語研習班」的教材，我每天又在「快手」和「抖音」上教學，無形中，我的進步最大。

我變得更熱情，看到鄰居，我會主動上前打招呼，碰到喜歡的人，立刻獻上 1,000 元新台幣。過年，給管理員每人紅包 2,000 元。現在，回到家，從門口開始，所碰到的人，都是我的好朋友。

我家隔壁開了一間水果店，老闆叫我買這個，我就買這個；叫我買那個，我就買那個。我學會接受別人的意見，我買的水果都是價廉物美，他們一看到我，都很高興。

所有的書上都告訴你說，不要生氣，生氣有害。但你為什麼還會生氣呢？因為你忘了。

你每天背：Getting angry never benefits.（生氣無益。）It's never worth it.（全然不值。）You can only lose.（你只會輸。）背熟要花功夫，花了功夫，才能潛移默化，就自然不生氣了。

> *Your thoughts become your words.*
> （吾思成我語。）
> *Your words become your actions.*
> （吾語成我行。）
> *Your actions become your habits.*
> （吾行成我為。）

個性即是習慣，這本書能改變你的個性，邁向成功。

我教了 50 多年的書，發明無數的教材、教法，現在覺得「完美英語之心靈盛宴」的方法最棒，同時學會完美英語、完美中文，又提升了心靈。唸熟了這套書，真的會人人喜愛，心想事成，愉快無比，長命百歲！

劉毅

PART 1

Unit 1
自由思考

PART 1・Unit 1~9
中英文錄音QR碼
英文唸2遍，中文唸1遍

Think freely.
自由思考。

Think differently.
不同想法。

Think outside
the box.
奇思妙想。

BOOK 3 · PART 1

Have new ideas.
有新意。

Have no limits.
不受限。

Create new ways.
要創新。

Be original.
要原創。

Be creative.
有創意。

Break new ground.
要創新。

PART 1

Unit 1 背景説明

Think freely.（自由思考。）
Think differently.（不同想法。）
Think outside the box.（奇思妙想。）

用傳統方法、傳統思考，不會有驚人的結果。我新聘了一位
才女王宣雯老師，每月月薪 50 萬元，讓所有人跌破眼鏡，但
她創造歷史，使「劉毅英文」反敗爲勝。

Think freely.（要自由地思考。）也可説成：Don't
limit your imagination.（不要限制你的想像力。）
freely〔'frilɪ〕*adv.* 自由地；隨意地

Think differently.（要有不同的想法。）也可説成：
Think in a new way.（要用新的方法思考。）
differently〔'dɪfərəntlɪ〕*adv.* 不同地

Think outside the box. 字面的意思是「在框框外面思
考。」也就是「打破常規；跳脫舊思維；跳脫框架思考。」
也可説成：Be innovative.（要創新。）Be creative.
（要有創意。）Think unconventionally.（想法要不
落俗套。）Think creatively.（想法要有創意。）
outside〔aut'saɪd〕*prep.* 在…的外面
box〔baks〕*n.* 箱子；（報紙、雜誌上用線圍成的）框框

Have new ideas. 要有新的想法。(= *Think of
something novel.*)　　idea〔aɪ'diə〕*n.* 想法；點子

Have no limits. (不要有限制；不要受到限制。) 也可説
　成 : Have no boundaries. (不要有界限。) Don't
　limit yourself. (不要限制自己。) Don't be afraid
　of new ideas. (不要害怕新的想法。)
limit〔'lɪmɪt〕*n. v.* 限制

Create new ways. (要創造新的方法。) 也可説成 :
　Find new ways of doing things. (要找到新的做事
　的方法。)　　create〔krɪ'et〕*v.* 創造
way〔we〕*n.* 方法

Be original. (要有創意。) 也可説成 : Be unique.
　(要獨特。) Be imaginative. (要有想像力。)
original〔ə'rɪdʒənḷ〕*adj.* 獨創的

Be creative. 要有創意。(= *Be original.*) 也可説成 :
　Be innovative. (要創新。)
creative〔krɪ'etɪv〕*adj.* 有創造力的

Break new ground. 要開拓新天地；要創新。(= *Do
　or discover something new.*) 也可説成 : Lead the
　way. (要領先。) Blaze a trail. (要做開路先鋒。)
　Be the first. (要當第一。) Be in the vanguard.
　(要當先鋒。)
ground〔graʊnd〕*n.* 地面；土地

BOOK 3 · PART 1

PART 1

Unit 2
正向思考

Think positive.
正向思考。

Create a positive life.
創造積極人生。

**Your thoughts
are powerful.**
思想蘊含力量。

Your thoughts become your words.
吾思成我語。

Your words become your actions.
吾語成我為。

Your actions become your habits.
吾為成我行。

**Nurture your
mind.**

豐盛心智。

Have great thoughts.

豐偉思慮。

**You become what
you think.**

成為所願。

PART 1

Unit 2　背景説明

Think positive.（正向思考。）這句話不合文法，本來是錯誤的句子，講多了，就變成慣用句，變成正確了，可見 *Think positive.* 這句話多麼重要。也可説成：Think positively.（要正向思考。）Be positive.（要樂觀。）Be optimistic.（要樂觀。）

positive〔ˋpɑzətɪv〕*adj.* 正面的；積極的；樂觀的

Create a positive life.（創造積極的人生。）也可説成：Live a positive life.（要過積極的生活。）Always be positive.（一定要樂觀。）

create〔krɪˋet〕*v.* 創造

Your thoughts are powerful.（你的思想有強大的力量。）也可説成：Believing in yourself will give you strength.（相信自己的能力會給你力量。）

thought〔θɔt〕*n.* 想法；思想
powerful〔ˋpaʊəfəl〕*adj.* 強有力的

Your thoughts become your words.（你的思想成為你的話語。）也可説成：Express your ideas in words.（用言語表達你的想法。）

words〔wɝdz〕*n. pl.* 言詞；話

Your words become your actions. (你的言語成爲你
的行爲。) 也可説成 : Do what you say. (躬行己
說。)　　action〔'ækʃən〕*n.* 行動;行爲

Your actions become your habits. (你的行爲成爲你
的習慣。) 也可説成 : Do those things regularly.
(要定期做那些事。)

habit〔'hæbɪt〕*n.* 習慣

Nurture your mind. (孕育你的思想。) 也可説成 :
Feed your mind. (充實你的思想。) Seek out new
information. (搜尋新資訊。)

nurture〔'nɝtʃɚ〕*v.* 滋養;孕育 (計劃、想法等)
mind〔maɪnd〕*n.* 心;精神;想法

Have great thoughts. (要有很棒的想法。) 也可説成 :
Have good ideas. (要有好的想法。) Think of
good ideas. (要想到好的點子。)

great〔gret〕*adj.* 很棒的;偉大的

You become what you think. (你的心智反映你整個
人。) 也可説成 : What you think influences the
kind of person you become. (你的想法會影響你成
爲什麼樣的人。)

BOOK 3 • PART 1

PART 1

Unit 3
要想清楚

Think clearly.
要想清楚。

Make good decisions.
做好決定。

**Have your wits
about you.**
隨機應變。

See the big picture.
大局為重。

Have an overall view.
綜觀全局。

Know what's important.
分清緩急。

Know the facts.
了解事實。

Know the score.
知道事實的真相。

Know what's what.
搞清楚狀況。

PART 1

Unit 3 背景說明

　　做任何決定以前，要知道真相，以大局為重，分清
輕重緩急，千萬不要急著下決定。如結婚、買賣房屋，
都是重大決定，一失足成千古恨。小事情不必考慮，如
買菜，就不那麼重要了。

Think clearly. (要想清楚。) 也可說成：Be
　coolheaded. (頭腦要冷靜。)
clearly〔'klɪrlɪ〕*adv.* 清楚地；清晰地

Make good decisions. (要做好的決定。) 也可說成：
　Decide wisely. (要明智地決定。)
decision〔dɪ'sɪʒən〕*n.* 決定
make a decision 做決定

Have your wits about you. 保持頭腦清醒；隨機應變。
(= *Keep your head*. = *Keep a cool head*.) 也可說
成：Stay calm. (保持冷靜。) Be aware of what's
going on. (要知道發生了什麼事。) Stay alert. (保持
警覺。) Think and react quickly. (要很快地思考和
反應。)
wit〔wɪt〕*n.* 機智
have one's wits about one 保持警覺；隨機應變

See the big picture.（以大局爲重。）也可說成：
　Consider the whole situation.（要考慮整個情況。）
picture〔'pɪktʃɚ〕 *n.* 情況；局面（= *situation*）
the big picture 大局；全局（= *the situation as a whole*）

Have an overall view.（要綜觀全局。）也可說成：
　Consider all the circumstances.（要考慮所有的情況。）　overall〔'ovɚ,ɔl〕 *adj.* 全面的；整體的
view〔vju〕 *n.* 視野；概觀

Know what's important. 要知道什麼是重要的。
　（= *Understand what matters.*）
important〔ɪm'pɔrtn̩t〕 *adj.* 重要的

Know the facts. 了解事實。（= *Know what's true.*）
fact〔fækt〕 *n.* 事實

Know the score.（知道事實的眞相。）也可說成：
　Know what's going on.（要知道發生了什麼事。）
　Know the situation.（要了解情況。）
score〔skor〕 *n.* 分數；成績；情況；眞相

Know what's what.（要知道是怎麼回事。）也可說成：Know what to do.（要知道該做什麼。）
　Know the ropes.（要熟悉內情；要懂得訣竅。）

PART 1

Unit 4
種瓜得瓜

Pay less, get less.
付少得少。

Pay more, get more.
付多得多。

You get what you pay for.
一分錢，一分貨。

You get what you deserve.
得所應當。

You reap what you sow.
【諺】種瓜得瓜。

What goes around comes around.
【諺】種什麼因，得什麼果。

Getting less is OK.
少點可以。

**Getting something
beats nothing.**
有比沒有好。

**Half a loaf is better
than no bread.**
【諺】聊勝於無。

BOOK 3・PART 1

PART 1

Unit 4 背景説明

　　不怕付出，才會有所得，越怕吃虧，越吃虧。把上班當作苦差事，自己身心受到傷害。回家後還在專心研發的人，必成大器。

　　這一回全部是 A-A-B 的排列方式，前兩句開頭相同，容易背。

$$\left.\begin{array}{l} \underline{Pay} \ less, \ get \ less. \\ \underline{Pay} \ more, \ get \ more. \\ \underline{You} \ get \ what \ you \ pay \ for. \end{array}\right\} \begin{array}{l} A \\ | \\ A \\ | \\ B \end{array}$$

pay〔pe〕v. 支付

You get what you pay for. 你得到你付錢買的，也就是「一分錢，一分貨。」也可説成：You pay what the item is worth.（你付的是和物品等值的錢。）You can't get more than you pay for.（你無法得到超過你支付的；你付多少，就得到多少。）

pay for 付⋯的錢

You get what you deserve. 你得到你該得到的。
(= *You will get what is just.*)

deserve〔dɪ'zɜv〕v. 應得

You reap what you sow. 是一句諺語，你收割你所播
種的，也就是「種瓜得瓜，種豆得豆。」

reap〔rip〕*v.* 收割　　sow〔so〕*v.* 播種

What goes around comes around. 是一句諺語，怎麼
去就怎麼來，引申為「種什麼因，得什麼果。」(= *What
you do or say will come back to you in the future.*)

what goes around 你做的事 (= *things that you do*)

what comes around 發生在你身上的事 (= *things that
happen to you*)

Getting less is OK. 得到少一點沒關係。(= *It's fine to
get less than you want.*)

less〔lɛs〕*adj., adv., n.* 較少

OK〔'o'ke〕*adj.* 好的；沒問題的

Getting something beats nothing. (有得到東西，勝
過沒得到東西；有比沒有好。) 源自 Getting something
beats getting nothing. (得到一些比什麼都沒得到好。)

beat〔bit〕*v.* 打敗；勝過 (= *be better than*)

Half a loaf is better than no bread. 【諺】半條麵包
勝過沒有麵包；聊勝於無。(= *Half a loaf is better
than none.*) 也可說成：Something is better than
nothing. (有總比沒有好。)

half〔hæf〕*n.* 一半　*adj.* …的一半的

loaf〔lof〕*n.* 一條 (麵包)　　bread〔brɛd〕*n.* 麵包

PART 1

Unit 5
天下無不散的筵席

Nothing lasts forever.

沒所謂永恆。

Nothing is set in stone.

沒所謂不可改。

All good things must end.

天下無不散的筵席。

**Nothing is
permanent.**
沒永垂不朽。

**Nothing stays
the same.**
沒世事不變。

**Change always
happens.**
萬事皆改變。

Nothing is certain.
沒有什麼是確定的。

Nothing is for sure.
沒有什麼是一定的。

**Even the best plans
can go wrong.**
神仙打鼓有時錯。

PART 1

Unit 5 背景說明

在水中悠游的小魚，一下子就被大魚吃掉了。人生無常，不必想太多，遇到挫折，沒什麼了不起。這一回九句，每一組的前兩句都是 Nothing 開頭，「A-A-B」形式很好背。

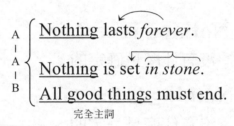

$$
\begin{matrix}
A \\
| \\
A \\
| \\
B
\end{matrix}
\left\{
\begin{matrix}
\underline{\text{Nothing}} \text{ lasts } \textit{forever.} \\
\underline{\text{Nothing}} \text{ is set } \textit{in stone.} \\
\underline{\text{All good things}} \text{ must end.}
\end{matrix}
\right.
$$

完全主詞

Nothing lasts forever. 沒有什麼能永遠持續存在，也就是「沒有什麼是永恆的。」

last〔 læst 〕*v.* 持續；持續存在
forever〔 fə'ɛvə 〕*adv.* 永遠

Nothing is set in stone. 沒有什麼是鑲在石頭上的，引申為「沒有什麼是不可改變的。」也可說成：Nothing is eternal.（沒有什麼是永恆的。）Nothing is constant.（沒有什麼是不變的。）

set〔 sɛt 〕*v.* 嵌入；鑲入   stone〔 ston 〕*n.* 石頭
set in stone 永久的；不可改變的（*= permanent = not able to be changed*）

BOOK 3・PART 1

All good things must end. 「所有美好的事物都必須結束。」引申為「天下無不散的筵席；好景不常。」源自諺語：All good things come to an end. 意思相同。

end〔ɛnd〕*v.* 結束（= *come to an end*）

Nothing is permanent. 沒有什麼是永恆的。(= *Nothing is eternal*.)   permanent〔'pɜmənənt〕*adj.* 永久的

Nothing stays the same. 「沒有什麼能保持同樣。」也就是「沒有什麼是不變的。」也可說成：Nothing lasts forever. (沒有什麼能持續到永久。)

stay〔ste〕*v.* 保持   same〔sem〕*adj.* 相同的

Change always happens. 改變隨時都在發生。(= *There will always be change*.) 也可說成：Change is constant. (改變是一定的。)

change〔tʃendʒ〕*n.* 改變   happen〔'hæpən〕*v.* 發生

Nothing is certain. 沒有什麼是確定的。(= *Nothing is definite*.)   certain〔'sɜtn̩〕*adj.* 確定的

Nothing is for sure. 沒有什麼是一定的。(= *Nothing is certain*.)   ***for sure*** 確實的；當然的；一定

Even the best plans can go wrong. (即使是最好的計劃也可能出錯。) 也可說成：There are no perfect plans. (沒有完美的計劃。)

even〔'ivən〕*adv.* 甚至；連   plan〔plæn〕*n.* 計劃

go wrong 出錯

PART 1

Unit 6
越老越有智慧

Age is an asset.
年齡是一項資產。

**Aging brings
wisdom.**
越老越有智慧。

Age like a fine wine.
變老要像酒一樣，
越陳越香。

BOOK 3・PART 1

I get wiser.
我越來越聰明。

I gain more friends.
我朋友越來越多。

Getting older is great.
越老越棒。

**I work to get better
every day.**
我與日俱進。

**I'm happier and
smarter.**
我更快樂、更聰明。

**That's my
secret to life.**
這是我人生的祕訣。

PART 1

Unit 6 背景說明

　　通常，年輕人喜歡展望未來，老人喜歡回想過去。但是我過去的記憶很模糊，我老是想到未來，不斷進步，越來越聰明，朋友越來越多，反倒覺得越老越棒。（Getting older is great.）

Age is an asset.（年齡是一項資產。）也可說成：Age is an advantage.（年紀大是個優點。）

age〔edʒ〕*n.* 年齡；年老；高齡
asset〔'æsɛt〕*n.* 資產

Aging brings wisdom.「變老會帶來智慧。」也就是「越老越有智慧。」也可說成：Insight comes with age.（年紀越大越有洞察力。）

age〔edʒ〕*v.* 老化；變老
bring〔brɪŋ〕*v.* 帶來
wisdom〔'wɪzdəm〕*n.* 智慧

Age like a fine wine.（變老要像美酒一樣，越陳越香。）
　age 在此是動詞，作「變老」解。也可說成：Old age is mellow and better than youth.（年老很成熟，比年輕更好。）

fine〔faɪn〕*adj.* 好的　　wine〔waɪn〕*n.* 葡萄酒
fine wine 美酒；上等葡萄酒

I get wiser. (我變得更聰明。) 也可説成：I gain wisdom. (我增長智慧。) I gain insight. (我更有洞察力。) wise〔waɪz〕*adj.* 聰明的；有智慧的

I gain more friends. (我獲得更多朋友。) 也可説成：I widen my circle of friends. (我拓展了朋友圈。) gain〔gen〕*v.* 獲得

Getting older is great. 變老很棒。(*= Aging is fantastic*.) *get old* 變老 (*= grow old*)
great〔gret〕*adj.* 很棒的

I work to get better every day. (我非常努力，每天進步。) 也可説成：I always try to improve. (我總是努力求進步。) work〔wɜk〕*v.* 努力

I'm happier and smarter. 我更快樂而且更聰明。(*= I'm more cheerful and more intelligent*.)

That's my secret to life. (這是我人生的祕訣。) 也可説成：That's how I live a good life. (那就是我擁有美好人生的方法。) That's how I live a long life. (那就是我長壽的方法。)
secret〔'sikrɪt〕*n.* 祕密；祕訣 < *to* >

PART 1

Unit 7
常 樂

Be glad.

常樂。

Give thanks.

感恩。

Count your blessings.

知足。

Be thankful.
心懷感激。

Appreciate everything.
感謝一切。

Appreciate what you have.
感激所有。

Be happy.
知足常樂。

Be satisfied.
知足滿意。

**Look on the
sunny side.**
樂觀看待。

PART 1

Unit 7 背景說明

做到兩個字，你就快樂、幸福了，那就是「知足」，再加上「感恩」，交到志同道合的朋友，人生就太美了。

Be glad. 要高興。(= *Be happy*. = *Be cheerful*. = *Be pleased*.)
glad〔glæd〕*adj.* 高興的

Give thanks. 要感謝；要感恩；要感激。(= *Be thankful*.) 也可說成：Say thank you. (要說謝謝。) Show appreciation. (要表示感激。)(= *Show gratitude*.)
give thanks 致謝

Count your blessings. 數數你幸運的事，引申爲「要往好處想；要知足。」也可說成：Be happy. (要快樂。) Be pleased. (要高興。) Be grateful. (要心存感激。)
count〔kaʊnt〕*v.* 數
blessing〔'blɛsɪŋ〕*n.* 幸福；幸運之事

Be thankful. (要感謝。) 也可說成：Always be thankful. (要一直心存感激。)
thankful〔'θæŋkfəl〕*adj.* 感謝的 (= *grateful*)

Appreciate everything. 有兩個意思：①要感激一切。
(= *Be thankful for everything you have.*) ②要重
視一切。(= *Recognize the importance of*
everything.)
appreciate〔əˋpriʃɪ͵et〕*v.* 欣賞；重視；感激

Appreciate what you have. 有兩個意思：①要對你
所擁有的心存感激。(= *Be thankful for everything*
you have.) ②要重視你所擁有的一切。(= *Recognize*
the importance of what you have.)
what you have 你所擁有的

Be happy. 要快樂。(= *Be glad.* = *Be cheerful.*)
也可說成：Have fun. (要過得愉快。) (= *Have*
a good time. = *Enjoy yourself.*)

Be satisfied. 要知足。(= *Be content.*)
satisfied〔ˋsætɪs͵faɪd〕*adj.* 滿意的；滿足的

Look on the sunny side. 要看事物的光明面；要樂觀。
(= *Look on the bright side.* = *Look on the bright*
side of things. = *Be positive.* = *Be optimistic.*)
look on 看
sunny〔ˋsʌnɪ〕*adj.* 晴朗的；開朗樂觀的
side〔saɪd〕*n.* 邊；面

PART 1

Unit 8
熱情好客

Be welcoming.
熱情好客。

Be open to strangers.
敞開心扉。

Be friendly and polite.
友善有禮。

**Be quick to
greet people.**
快打招呼。

Be glad to meet others.
樂結新友。

**Enjoy making
friends.**
喜交朋友。

Receive openly.
公開接受。

Accept readily.
欣然接受。

**Always have an
open heart.**
打開心房。

PART 1

Unit 8 背景說明

　　要學會看到陌生人，主動打招呼，不要害怕被拒絕。要成為一個熱情的人。

Be welcoming.　要熱情好客。(= *Be hospitable.*)
welcoming〔ˈwɛlkʌmɪŋ〕*adj.* 熱情友好的；好客的

Be open to strangers.（要用開懷的心胸面對陌生人。）
　也可說成：Welcome strangers.（要歡迎陌生人。）
　Don't discriminate against strangers.（不要歧視
　陌生人。）
open〔ˈopən〕*adj.* 開放的 < *to* >
stranger〔ˈstrendʒɚ〕*n.* 陌生人

Be friendly and polite.　要友善而且有禮貌。(= *Be
　courteous.*)
friendly〔ˈfrɛndlɪ〕*adj.* 友善的
polite〔pəˈlaɪt〕*adj.* 有禮貌的

Be quick to greet people.（和人打招呼要快。）也可說
　成：Be quick to greet others.（和別人打招呼要快。）
　Don't hesitate to say hello.（要毫不猶豫地打招呼。）
quick〔kwɪk〕*adj.* 快的
greet〔grit〕*v.* 打招呼；迎接

Be glad to meet others. ①要樂於認識新朋友。(= *Be happy to get acquainted with new people.*) ②要樂於見到別人。(= *Be happy to see others.*)

glad 〔 glæd 〕 *adj.* 高興的　　meet 〔 mit 〕 *v.* 遇見；認識

Enjoy making friends. (要喜歡交朋友。) 也可說成：Enjoy making new friends. (要喜歡結交新朋友。) (= *Take pleasure in making new friends.*)

enjoy 〔 ɪnˈdʒɔɪ 〕 *v.* 享受；喜歡

make friends 交朋友

Receive openly. (要公然接受；要大大方方接受。) 也可說成：Receive others openly. (要公然接受別人。) Accept others. (要接受別人。)

receive 〔 rɪˈsiv 〕 *v.* 接受；接待；歡迎

openly 〔ˈopənlɪ 〕 *adj.* 公開地；公然地；坦率地

Accept readily. (要欣然接受；要高高興興接受。) 也可說成：Accept others readily. (要欣然接受別人。)

accept 〔 əkˈsɛpt 〕 *v.* 接受

readily 〔ˈrɛdɪlɪ 〕 *adv.* 欣然地 (= *willingly*)；迅速地 (= *quickly*)

Always have an open heart. (一定要有開闊的心胸。) 也可說成：Be willing to accept others. (要願意接受別人。)　　heart 〔 hɑrt 〕 *n.* 心

BOOK 3・PART 1

PART 1

Unit 9
找到天職

Find your calling.
找到天職。

Follow your bliss.
追求最愛。

Fulfill your destiny.
實踐命運。

BOOK 3．PART 1

Serve others.
服務他人。

Be a shining star.
成為明星。

**Make your life
remarkable.**
非凡人生。

Change the world.

改變世界。

Make a difference.

產生影響。

Make it a better place.

讓世界更好。

BOOK 3・PART 1

PART 1

Unit 9 背景説明

　　我很幸福，從小就找到自己喜歡做的事，連續做了50多年，上班也研究，下班也研究。現在可以在「快手」和「抖音」上教學，能夠把好的學英文的方法，留給後人，是最大的幸福。

Find your calling. (找到你的天職。) 也可説成：Find out what you are meant to do. (要知道你註定該做什麼。)　　calling〔ˋkɔlɪŋ〕*n.* 天職；職業

Follow your bliss. 追求你最喜愛的事。(= *Follow your passion*.) 也可説成：Pursue your dream. (追求你的夢想。) Do what you love to do. (做你喜歡做的事。) Do what makes you happy. (做會讓你快樂的事。)　　follow〔ˋfɑlo〕*v.* 追隨；追求 (= *go after*)　　bliss〔blɪs〕*n.* 極大的幸福

Fulfill your destiny.「實現你的命運。」引申為「做你註定要做的事。」(= *Do what you are meant to do*.) fulfill〔fʊlˋfɪl〕*v.* 實現　　destiny〔ˋdɛstənɪ〕*n.* 命運

Serve others. (要服務別人。) 也可説成：Help others. (要幫助別人。) Be helpful to others. (要對別人有幫助。)　　serve〔sɝv〕*v.* 服務 others〔ˋʌðəz〕*pron.* 別人

Be a shining star. (要做一顆閃亮的星星。) 也可説
成：Light up the world. (要照亮全世界。) Be a
guiding light. (要成爲指引人的明燈。)

shining〔ˈʃaɪnɪŋ〕*adj.* 閃閃發光的；閃耀的

star〔star〕*n.* 星星

Make your life remarkable. (讓你的人生精彩非凡。)
也可説成：Make your life worth living. (讓你的人
生很有價值。) Live a meaningful life. (要讓人生很
有意義。) Live an amazing life. (要過著很棒的生
活。)　　make〔mek〕*v.* 使；使成爲

remarkable〔rɪˈmarkəbḷ〕*adj.* 引人注目的；傑出的

Change the world. (改變世界。) 也可説成：Make
the world a better place. (讓世界成爲一個更好的
地方。)　　change〔tʃendʒ〕*v.* 改變

world〔wɝld〕*n.* 世界

Make a difference. 要產生影響。(= *Have an impact*.)
也可説成：Have a positive impact on the world.
(要對世界有正面的影響。)

difference〔ˈdɪfərəns〕*n.* 不同

Make it a better place. (使它成爲一個更好的地方。)
也可説成：Improve the world. (改善這個世界。)

PART 1 總整理

Unit 1

Think freely. 自由思考。
Think differently.
不同想法。
Think outside the box.
奇思妙想。

Have new ideas. 有新意。
Have no limits. 不受限。
Create new ways.
要創新。

Be original. 要原創。
Be creative. 有創意。
Break new ground.
要創新。

Unit 2

Think positive. 正向思考。
Create a positive life.
創造積極人生。
Your thoughts are
powerful. 思想蘊含力量。

Your thoughts become
your words. 吾思成我語。
Your words become your
actions. 吾語成我為。

Your actions become
your habits. 吾為成我行。
Nurture your mind.
豐盛心智。
Have great thoughts.
豐偉思慮。
You become what you
think. 成為所願。

Unit 3

Think clearly. 要想清楚
Make good decisions.
做好決定。
Have your wits about
you. 隨機應變。

See the big picture.
大局為重。
Have an overall view.
綜觀全局。
Know what's important.
分清緩急。

Know the facts. 了解事實。
Know the score.
知道事實的真相。
Know what's what.
搞清楚狀況。

Unit 4

Pay less, get less.
付少得少。
Pay more, get more.
付多得多。
You get what you pay for.
一分錢，一分貨。

You get what you deserve.
得所應當。
You reap what you sow.
【諺】種瓜得瓜。
What goes around comes around.
【諺】種什麼因，得什麼果。

Getting less is OK.
少點可以。
Getting something beats nothing. 有比沒有好。
Half a loaf is better than no bread. 【諺】聊勝於無。

Unit 5

Nothing lasts forever.
沒所謂永恆。
Nothing is set in stone.
沒所謂不可改。
All good things must end.
天下無不散的筵席。

Nothing is permanent.
沒永垂不朽。
Nothing stays the same.
沒世事不變。
Change always happens.
萬事皆改變。

Nothing is certain.
沒有什麼是確定的。
Nothing is for sure.
沒有什麼是一定的。
Even the best plans can go wrong.
神仙打鼓有時錯。

Unit 6

Age is an asset.
年齡是一項資產。
Aging brings wisdom.
越老越有智慧。
Age like a fine wine.
變老要像酒一樣，越陳越香。

I get wiser.
我越來越聰明。
I gain more friends.
我朋友越來越多。
Getting older is great.
越老越棒。

I work to get better every
day. 我與日俱進。
I'm happier and smarter.
我更快樂、更聰明。
That's my secret to life.
這是我人生的祕訣。

Unit 7

Be glad. 常樂。
Give thanks. 感恩。
Count your blessings.
知足。

Be thankful. 心懷感激。
Appreciate everything.
感謝一切。
Appreciate what you
have. 感激所有。

Be happy. 知足常樂。
Be satisfied. 知足滿意。
Look on the sunny side.
樂觀看待。

Unit 8

Be welcoming. 熱情好客。
Be open to strangers.
敞開心扉。
Be friendly and polite.
友善有禮。

Be quick to greet people.
快打招呼。
Be glad to meet others.
樂結新友。
Enjoy making friends.
喜交朋友。

Receive openly. 公開接受。
Accept readily. 欣然接受。
Always have an open
heart. 打開心房。

Unit 9

Find your calling.
找到天職。
Follow your bliss.
追求最愛。
Fulfill your destiny.
實踐命運。

Serve others. 服務他人。
Be a shining star. 成為明星。
Make your life remarkable.
非凡人生。

Change the world.
改變世界。
Make a difference.
產生影響。
Make it a better place.
讓世界更好。

PART 2

Unit 1
與人為善

PART 2・Unit 1~9
中英文錄音QR碼
英文唸2遍，中文唸1遍

**Be good
to everyone.**
與人為善。

**Be good
at your job.**
善盡職責。

**Be good
with money.**
善於理財。

Do the right thing.
行之正確。

Take the high road.
光明磊落。

**Don't take the
low road.**
勿走歪路。

Do good, and good will find you.

善有善報。

Do bad, and bad will happen.

惡有惡報。

Actions have consequences.

凡有因必有果。

PART 2

Unit 1 背景説明

　　要有美好人生，非常簡單，只要：①與人爲善，做個好人。②精通你的工作，善盡職責。③善於理財。

Be good to everyone. 要對每一個人好。(= *Treat everyone well.*)　***be good to*** 對…好

Be good at your job. 要精通你的工作。(= *Be good at what you do.* = *Excel at your work.* = *Excel at your profession.*)　***be good at*** 精通；擅長

Be good with money. 要善於理財。(= *Manage your money well.*)

be good with 善於應付；對…有辦法

money (錢) 是抽象名詞。

Do the right thing. 要做對的事。(= *Do the proper thing.* = *Do the honorable thing.* = *Do the decent thing.*)

Take the high road. 要光明磊落。(= *Do the right thing.* = *Do what is right.*)

take the high road 選擇正當、道德的方法 (= *choose the course of action which is the most moral or acceptable*)

BOOK 3・PART 2

Don't take the low road. (不要用卑劣的手段。) 也可說成 : Don't be unscrupulous. (不要不道德。)

low road 低劣卑鄙的方法 (= *behavior or practice that is deceitful or immoral*)

Do good, and good will find you. 如果你做好事，好事就會找上你。(= *Do good, and good will come to you.* = *If you do good things, then good things will happen to you.*)

good 〔 gʊd 〕 *n.* 好事

do good 行善；做好事 (= *do good things*)

Do bad, and bad will happen. 如果你做壞事，壞事就會發生。(= *If you do bad things, bad things will happen to you.*)

bad 〔 bæd 〕 *n.* 壞事

do bad 做壞事 (= *do bad things*)

Actions have consequences. 行動會有後果，也就是「有因必有果。」也可說成 : Every action produces a reaction. (每個行動都會造成某種反應。)

action 〔ˈækʃən 〕 *n.* 行動；行為

consequence 〔ˈkɑnsəˌkwɛns 〕 *n.* 後果

PART 2

Unit 2
走完全程

Go the whole way.
走完全程。

Go the whole distance.
堅持到底。

Go till you finish.
直到完成。

Make every effort.
竭盡全力。

Make every attempt.
嘗試一切。

**Jump through
hoops.**
赴湯蹈火，在所不辭。

Finish great.
好好地結束。

End strong.
強而有力地結束。

**Go out with
a bang.**
轟轟烈烈地結束。

PART 2

Unit 2 背景説明

任何事情做一半最浪費，一定要走完全程，並且轟轟烈烈地結束。

Go the whole way. 走完全程；一直這樣做下去。
(*= Go all the way. = Persevere. = Continue until you're finished.*)

go〔go〕*v.* 進行工作 (*= do sth.*)；努力 (*= make an effort*)；嘗試 (*= try*)

whole〔hol〕*adj.* 全部的　　way〔we〕*n.* 路

Go the whole distance. 堅持到最後。(*= Go the distance. = Complete it. = Finish it. = Continue until the end.*)【源自拳擊，指撐完排定的場次，在棒球方面，則是指投球投完整場比賽】

distance〔'dɪstəns〕*n.* 距離；路程

Go till you finish. 要持續到你做完為止。(*= Don't stop until you complete it.*) 也可説成：Don't stop until you achieve your goal. (直到你達成目標才能停止。)

till〔tɪl〕*conj.* 直到

finish〔'fɪnɪʃ〕*v.* 做完；完成；結束

Make every effort. 盡一切努力。(= *Do everything you can.*)　　effort〔'ɛfət〕 *n.* 努力
make an effort 努力

Make every attempt. 千方百計；費盡心機；想盡一切辦法。(= *Try everything possible.*)
attempt〔ə'tɛmpt〕 *n.* 嘗試　　***make an attempt*** 嘗試

Jump through hoops. 克服種種障礙；赴湯蹈火，在所不辭。【源自馬戲團動物跳躍穿過鐵環】也可說成：Exert yourself. (要盡力。) Give it your best shot. (要全力以赴。) Move heaven and earth. (要竭盡全力。)
jump〔dʒʌmp〕 *v.* 跳
through〔θru〕 *prep.* 穿過
hoop〔hup〕 *n.* 環；圈

Finish great. 好好地結束。(= *Finish successfully.*)
great〔gret〕 *adv.* 很好地

End strong. 強而有力地結束。(= *End impressively.*)
end〔ɛnd〕 *v.* 結束
strong〔strɔŋ〕 *adv.* 強而有力地；強大地

Go out with a bang. 轟轟烈烈地結束。(= *Finish in a dramatic fashion.* = *Finish in an exciting way.*)
go out 結束；終止
bang〔bæŋ〕 *n.* 砰砰的聲音；巨大影響；轟動

PART 2

Unit 3
要做好人

Try to be kind.
要做好人。

Strive to be caring.
努力關懷。

**Seek to be happy
and helpful.**
幫人得樂。

Make a special effort.
特別努力。

**Give more than
expected.**
予人出乎預料。

**Go out of your way
to be nice.**
盡你所能，成為好人。

Be glad to help others.

樂於助人。

Happiness comes from giving.

助人為快樂之本。

The more you give, the happier you are.

付出越多，快樂越多。

PART 2

Unit 3 背景說明

樂於助人，做好人，自己受益最大。付出越多，越快樂。

Try to be kind. 要努力做個好人。(= *Make an effort to be nice.*)　***try to V.*** 努力…

kind〔kaɪnd〕*adj.* 親切的；善意的；體貼的

Strive to be caring. 努力關懷。(= *Try to be considerate.*)　strive〔straɪv〕*v.* 努力

caring〔ˈkɛrɪŋ〕*adj.* 有愛心的；關心他人的

Seek to be happy and helpful. 努力成爲樂於助人的人。(= *Try to be cheerful and supportive.*)

seek〔sik〕*v.* 尋求　***seek to V.*** 嘗試…；試圖…

helpful〔ˈhɛlpfəl〕*adj.* 願意幫忙的；有幫助的

Make a special effort. 要特別努力。(= *Go out of your way.*)　special〔ˈspɛʃəl〕*adj.* 特別的

effort〔ˈɛfɚt〕*n.* 努力　***make an effort*** 努力

Give more than expected. 付出比預期的多。(= *Give more than asked.* = *Go above and beyond.* = *Do more than you have to.*)

give〔gɪv〕*v.* 給與；付出

expect〔ɪkˈspɛkt〕*v.* 預期；期待

Go out of your way to be nice. 要特別努力去善待
他人。(= *Make an effort to be nice.* = *Be kind even
when it causes you some inconvenience.*)

go out of one's ***way*** 做出特別的努力

nice〔naɪs〕*adj.* 好的；親切的

Be glad to help others. 要樂於助人。(= *Be happy
to give others a hand.*)

glad〔glæd〕*adj.* 高興的

others〔ˈʌðɚz〕*pron.* 別人

Happiness comes from giving. 快樂來自於付出。
(= *Giving to others will make you happy.*) 也可說
成：Helping others is the root of all happiness.
（助人為快樂之本。）

happiness〔ˈhæpɪnɪs〕*n.* 快樂；幸福

The more you give, the happier you are. （付出越
多，快樂越多。）也可說成：The more you help
others, the happier you will be.（你幫助別人越
多，就會越快樂。）Helping others will make
you happy.（幫助別人會使你快樂。）

「the＋比較級，the＋比較級」表「越…越～」。

PART 2

Unit 4
放輕鬆

Let it go.
放下吧。

Don't sweat it.
冷靜點。

Don't get worked up.
不要生氣。

Relax.

放輕鬆。

Chill out.

要冷靜。

Chillax.

冷靜，放輕鬆。

**It's not life
or death.**
這並非生死攸關。

**It's not the end
of the world.**
這並非世界末日。

**Get a hold of
yourself.**
要控制自己。

PART 2

Unit 4　背景説明

　　碰到不如意的事情，要學會放下。要冷靜、輕鬆，控制自己。

Let it go. (隨它吧；放手別管；順其自然；不讓某事或某人困擾你。) 也可説成：Forget about it. (算了吧。) ***Don't sweat it.*** ①不要擔心。(= *Don't worry.*) ②冷靜點。也可説成：Relax. (放輕鬆。) It's fine. (沒關係。)

sweat〔swɛt〕*v.* 流汗；擔心

Don't get worked up.　不要生氣。(= *Don't get angry.*)；不要激動。(= *Don't get too excited.*)；不要擔心。

work up　激發；使激動　　***get worked up***　激動；生氣

Relax.　放輕鬆。(= *Take it easy.*)　　relax〔rɪ'læks〕*v.* 放鬆
Chill out.　要冷靜。(= *Calm down.*)
chill〔tʃɪl〕*v.* 變冷；冷靜

Chillax.　冷靜，放輕鬆。(= *Chill out.* = *Relax.*)
chillax〔tʃɪ'læks〕*v.* 冷靜和放鬆【源自 chill 和 relax】

It's not life or death. (這並非生死攸關。) 也可説成：
　It's not important. (這並不重要。)
life or death　生死攸關的
It's not the end of the world. (這並非世界末日。) 也可説成：It's not that important. (這沒那麼重要。)
the end of the world　世界末日
Get a hold of yourself. (要控制自己。) 也可説成：
　Get control of yourself. (要控制自己。)
hold〔hold〕*n.* 掌握；支配力；影響力
get a hold of oneself　控制自己；冷靜下來；放輕鬆

PART 2

Unit 5
事過境遷

It will pass.
事過境遷。

It will blow over.
終將平息。

**It will come to
an end.**
將會結束。

All will be OK.
全將變好。

All will end well.
終獲好果。

All will be fine in the end.
水到渠成。

It'll ease up.
它會緩和。

It will die down.
它將平息。

Things will calm down again.
萬事終將平靜。

PART 2

Unit 5　背景說明

　　在成功的過程中，碰到挫折，是正常的事情，不要影響到自己的心情，一切都將會平息。

It will pass. 事情會過去的。(= *It will go away.*) 也可說成：Everything will be fine. (一切都會沒事的。)

pass〔pæs〕*v.* 過去　　***It will blow over.*** (風暴會平息。) 也可說成：It will die down. (它會平息。)

blow〔blo〕*v.* 吹　　***blow over*** 平息；停止

It will come to an end. 它會結束。(= *It will end.* = *It won't last forever.*)

come to an end 結束 (= *end* = *finish*)

All will be OK. 全都會沒事的。(= *Everything will be all right.*)　　OK〔'o'ke〕*adj.* 好的；沒問題的

All will end well. 全都會有好的結局。(= *Everything will be OK.*)　　end〔ɛnd〕*v.* 結束；終了 *n.* 結束；末尾

All will be fine in the end. 最後一切都會沒事的。(= *It will turn out fine.*)　　fine〔faɪn〕*adj.* 好的

in the end 最後

It'll ease up. 它會平息。(= *It'll let up.*)　　ease〔iz〕*v.* 緩和；減輕 *n.* 容易；輕鬆　　***ease up*** 緩和；減輕 (= *subside* = *diminish*)　　***It will die down.*** 它會平息。(= *It will calm down.*)　　die〔daɪ〕*v.* 死亡；熄滅；消失；變微弱　　***die down*** 靜下來；平息 (= *blow over*)　　***Things will calm down again.*** 一切都會平息；很快就會沒事。(= *Things will be fine soon.*)

calm down 平靜下來

PART 2

Unit 6
絕不生氣

Never get angry.
絕不生氣。

**Anger brings
you down.**
生氣會拉低氣場。

**Anger only
hurts you.**
憤怒只會傷害你自己。

**Don't hold on
to anger.**
不要一肚子怨氣。

**It consumes
your energy.**
精力將消耗殆盡。

**It replaces
your love.**
此將替代你的愛。

**Getting angry
never benefits.**
生氣無益。

It's never worth it.
全然不值。

You can only lose.
你只會輸。

PART 2

Unit 6　背景説明

　　我背了這一回以後，開始不生氣了，別人怎麼説，我都不會生氣。世界變成有彩色，美麗無比。

Never get angry. 絕對不要生氣。(= *Don't ever get upset.*)　　never〔'nɛvə〕*adv.* 絕不
angry〔'æŋgrɪ〕*adj.* 生氣的　　***get angry*** 生氣

Anger brings you down. 生氣會使你沮喪。(= *Anger will depress you.* = *Being angry will make you unhappy.*)
anger〔'æŋgə〕*n.* 憤怒；生氣
bring down 打倒；使垮台；使沮喪
bring you down 使你沮喪 (= *depress you* = *bring your mood down*)

Anger only hurts you. (生氣只會傷害你自己。) 也可説成：Anger does you no good. (生氣對你沒好處。)　　hurt〔hɝt〕*v.* 傷害

Don't hold on to anger. 不要一直生氣。(= *Let go of your anger.* = *Don't stay angry.*)
hold on to 堅持；緊緊抓住；抓住不放

It consumes your energy. (它會消耗你的精力。) 也
可說成：It takes a lot of energy. (它需要很多的精
力。) It will exhaust you. (它會使你筋疲力盡。)

consume〔kən'sum〕*v.* 消耗
energy〔'ɛnɚdʒɪ〕*n.* 精力；活力

It replaces your love. (它會取代你的愛。) 也可說成：
If you are angry, you cannot love. (如果你生氣，
你就無法愛。) You cannot feel love and anger
at the same time. (你無法同時感受到憤怒和愛。)

replace〔rɪ'ples〕*v.* 取代 (= *take the place of*)

Getting angry never benefits. 生氣一點好處都沒有。
(= *There is no profit in anger*.) 也可說成：Getting
angry doesn't help anyone. (生氣對任何人都沒有
幫助。)   benefit〔'bɛnəfɪt〕*v.* 獲利；獲益

It's never worth it. (一點都不值得。) 也可說成：It's
not worth it to get angry. (生氣不值得。) It's a
waste of time. (那是在浪費時間。)

worth〔wɝθ〕*adj.* 值得…的   ***worth it*** 值得的

You can only lose. (你只會輸。) 也可說成：It can
only hurt you. (它只會傷害你。) It's of no benefit
to you. (它對你沒好處。)

lose〔luz〕*v.* 輸；損失

PART 2

Unit 7
笑有傳染力

A smile is contagious.
笑有傳染力。

It spreads happiness.
笑能散播幸福。

Let your smile change the world.
笑容力量大。

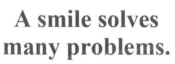

**A smile solves
many problems.**
一笑解恩仇。

**Silence avoids
many problems.**
沉默避衝突。

**Both are powerful
tools.**
皆為有力工具。

Stress gives you pimples.
壓力帶來痘子。

Crying gives you wrinkles.
哭能帶來皺紋。

Smiling brings you dimples.
笑能帶來酒窩。

PART 2

Unit 7 背景説明

Smile, and the whole world smiles with you.
笑有傳染力，能散播幸福，笑容力量最大。

A smile is contagious. (笑是有傳染力的。) 也可説
成：When you smile, others will smile, too.
(當你笑的時候，別人也會笑。)
smile〔smaɪl〕*n. v.* 微笑；笑
contagious〔kən'tedʒəs〕*adj.* 傳染的

It spreads happiness. (它能散播快樂。) 也可説成：
A smile makes other people happy. (笑能使其他
人快樂。)　　spread〔sprɛd〕*v.* 散播
happiness〔'hæpɪnɪs〕*n.* 快樂；幸福

Let your smile change the world. (讓你的笑容改變
世界。) 也可説成：Your smile will make a
difference. (你的笑容具有影響力。) Your smile
will make the world a better place. (你的笑容能
讓世界成爲更美好的地方。)
change〔tʃendʒ〕*v.* 改變　　world〔wɜld〕*n.* 世界

A smile solves many problems. (微笑能解決很多問
題。) 也可説成：Smiling can make many things
better. (微笑能讓很多事情變得更好。)
solve〔sɑlv〕*v.* 解決　　problem〔'prɑbləm〕*n.* 問題

BOOK 3・PART 2

Silence avoids many problems. (沉默能避免很多問題。) 也可説成：If you say nothing, you will avoid causing trouble. (如果你什麼話都不說，就能避免造成麻煩。)

silence〔'saɪləns〕*n.* 沉默　　avoid〔ə'bɪcd〕*v.* 避免

Both are powerful tools. (兩者都是強而有力的工具。) 也可説成：They are both very effective. (它們兩個都很有效。)

powerful〔'pauəfəl〕*adj.* 強有力的

tool〔tul〕*n.* 工具

Stress gives you pimples. 壓力會使你長青春痘。

(= *Stress will make you break out.*)

stress〔strɛs〕*n.* 壓力　　pimple〔'pɪmpḷ〕*n.* 青春痘

Crying gives you wrinkles. (哭會使你長皺紋。) 也可説成：If you often cry, you will develop wrinkles. (如果你常哭，你就會產生皺紋。) Crying ages you. (哭會讓你變老。)

wrinkle〔'rɪŋkḷ〕*n.* 皺紋

Smiling brings you dimples. 微笑能帶給你酒窩。

(= *When you smile, you have dimples.*)

dimple〔'dɪmpḷ〕*n.* 酒窩

---

pimple *n.* 青春痘 (p 是爆裂音)
dimple *n.* 酒窩 (d 是 dent，凹痕)

PART 2

Unit 8
人生苦短

Life is short.
人生苦短。

Make the most of it.
善加利用。

Work hard, study hard, play hard.
工作、讀書、玩樂，
盡情揮灑。

Treasure time.
珍愛光陰。

Time is a treasure.
時間即寶藏。

**Time beats
diamonds or gold.**
時間勝過鑽或金。

Use time wisely.
有智慧利用時間。

**Use every hour
and minute.**
時刻善用。

**Live life to the
fullest.**
充實人生。

PART 2

Unit 8 背景説明

　　我的座右銘是：Work hard, study hard, play hard. (拼命工作、努力學習、盡情玩樂。) 時間非常寶貴，無聊、沒事做、不快樂，就是在浪費時間。

Life is short. (人生很短暫。) 也可説成：Time passes quickly. (時間過得很快。)

Make the most of it. 要充分利用它。(= *Take full advantage of it.*)

make the most of 充分利用 (= *make the best use of* = *take full advantage of*)

Work hard, *study hard*, *play hard*. 努力工作，用功讀書，盡情玩樂。(= *Work, study and play enthusiastically.*) 句中沒有連接詞 and，是慣用句。也可説成：Be devoted to your work, but never turn down a chance to have a good time. (全心投入你的工作，但絕不要拒絕可以玩樂的機會。)

work hard, study hard 和 play hard 的順序可以隨意調換。

hard〔hɑrd〕*adv.* 拼命地；努力地；認眞地；充分地

Treasure time. 珍惜時間。(= *Cherish time.*)
treasure〔ˈtrɛʒɚ〕*v.* 珍惜　*n.* 寶藏

BOOK 3・PART 2

Time is a treasure. 時間很寶貴。(= *Time is valuable.* = *Time is invaluable.* = *Time is priceless.*)

Time beats diamonds or gold. (時間勝過鑽石或黃金。) 也可說成：Time is more valuable than diamonds or gold. (時間比鑽石或黃金更珍貴。)
beat〔bit〕*v.* 打敗；戰勝；比⋯好
diamond〔'daɪmənd〕*n.* 鑽石
gold〔gold〕*n.* 黃金

Use time wisely. (要聰明地使用時間。) 也可說成：Use your time well. (要好好地運用你的時間。)
wisely〔'waɪzlɪ〕*adv.* 聰明地

Use every hour and minute. (運用每個小時和每一分鐘。) 也可說成：Use every second of every day. (運用每一天的每一秒。)
hour〔aʊr〕*n.* 小時　　minute〔'mɪnɪt〕*n.* 分鐘

Live life to the fullest. (過最充實的生活。) 也可說成：Have a fulfilling life. (要有充實的生活。) Enjoy yourself. (要玩得愉快。) Make the most of it. (要充分利用它。)　　***live life*** 過生活
full〔fʊl〕*adj.* 滿的；充滿的；充實的
to the fullest 充分地；盡情地

PART 2

Unit 9
簡化事情

Simplify things.
簡化事情。

Don't complicate things.
勿複雜化。

The simple way is the best way.
簡單為上。

Value simplicity.
珍視純樸。

Simplicity is superior.
純樸是優勢。

Simplicity is the key.
純樸是重要的。

Simple is best.
簡單最好。

Keep it simple.
保持簡單。

**A simple life is
a happy life.**
簡單生活最快樂。

PART 2

Unit 9　背景説明

　　要把複雜的事情簡單化，簡單的事情要制度化。簡單爲上，簡單是成功之道。

***Simplify things*.**　要簡化事情。(= *Make things simpler.*)　　simplify〔'sɪmplə,faɪ〕*v.* 簡化

***Don't complicate things*.**　不要把事情複雜化。
(= *Don't make things more difficult.*)
complicate〔'kɑmplə,ket〕*v.* 使複雜

***The simple way is the best way*.** 簡單的方式，就是
最好的方式，即「簡單是最好的。」(= *The best way is the least complicated way.*) 也可説成：It's
best to do it the easy way. (用簡單的方式做最好。)
The best approach is the straightforward one.
(最好的方法就是簡單的方法。)
simple〔'sɪmp!〕*adj.* 簡單的
way〔we〕*n.* 方式；方法

***Value simplicity*.** (重視簡單。) 也可説成：
Appreciate simplicity. (重視簡單。)
Appreciate the simple things. (重視簡單的事物。)
value〔'væljʊ〕*v.* 重視
simplicity〔sɪm'plɪsətɪ〕*n.* 簡單；簡樸

***Simplicity is superior*.** 簡單比較好。(= *Simplicity is better*.)

superior〔 sə'pɪrɪə 〕 *adj.* 較好的；優秀的

***Simplicity is the key*.** (簡單是關鍵。) 也可説成：
Simplicity is important. (簡單很重要。)

key〔 ki 〕 *n.* 關鍵；解答；祕訣

***Simple is best*.** (簡單最好。) 也可説成：The simple way is the best. (簡單的方式最好。) The simple things are the most important. (簡單的事物最重要。)

***Keep it simple*.** (保持簡單。) 也可説成：Don't complicate it. (不要弄得太複雜。)

keep〔 kip 〕 *v.* 使保持

***A simple life is a happy life*.** (簡單的生活就是快樂的生活。) 也可説成：If your life is uncomplicated, you will be happier. (如果你的生活不複雜，你就會比較快樂。)

PART 2　總整理

Unit 1

Be good to everyone.
與人為善。
Be good at your job.
善盡職責。
Be good with money.
善於理財。

Do the right thing.
行之正確。
Take the high road.
光明磊落。
Don't take the low road.
勿走歪路。

Do good, and good will
　find you.　善有善報。
Do bad, and bad will
　happen.　惡有惡報。
Actions have
　consequences.
凡有因必有果。

Unit 2

Go the whole way.
走完全程。
Go the whole distance.
堅持到底。

Go till you finish.
直到完成。

Make every effort.
竭盡全力。
Make every attempt.
嘗試一切。
Jump through hoops.
赴湯蹈火，在所不辭。

Finish great.　好好地結束。
End strong.
強而有力地結束。
Go out with a bang.
轟轟烈烈地結束。

Unit 3

Try to be kind.　要做好人。
Strive to be caring.
努力關懷。
Seek to be happy and
　helpful.　幫人得樂。

Make a special effort.
特別努力。
Give more than expected.
予人出乎預料。
Go out of your way to be
　nice.　盡你所能，成為好人。

BOOK 3・PART 2

Be glad to help others.
樂於助人。
Happiness comes from
　giving.　助人為快樂之本。
The more you give, the
　happier you are.
付出越多，快樂越多。

Unit 4

Let it go.　放下吧。
Don't sweat it.　冷靜點。
Don't get worked up.
不要生氣。

Relax.　放輕鬆。
Chill out.　要冷靜。
Chillax.　冷靜，放輕鬆。

It's not life or death.
這並非生死攸關。
It's not the end of the
　world.　這並非世界末日。
Get a hold of yourself.
要控制自己。

Unit 5

It will pass.　事過境遷。
It will blow over.
終將平息。
It will come to an end.
將會結束。

All will be OK.　全將變好。
All will end well.
終獲好果。
All will be fine in the end.
水到渠成。

It'll ease up.　它會緩和。
It will die down.　它將平息。
Things will calm down
　again.　萬事終將平靜。

Unit 6

Never get angry.　絕不生氣。
Anger brings you down.
生氣會拉低氣場。
Anger only hurts you.
憤怒只會傷害你自己。

Don't hold on to anger.
不要一肚子怨氣。
It consumes your energy.
精力將消耗殆盡。
It replaces your love.
此將替代你的愛。

Getting angry never
　benefits.　生氣無益。
It's never worth it.
全然不值。
You can only lose.
你只會輸。

Unit 7

A smile is contagious.
笑有傳染力。
It spreads happiness.
笑能散播幸福。
Let your smile change the
world.　笑容力量大。

A smile solves many
problems.　一笑解恩仇。
Silence avoids many
problems.　沉默避衝突。
Both are powerful tools.
皆爲有力工具。

Stress gives you pimples.
壓力帶來痘子。
Crying gives you
wrinkles.　哭能帶來皺紋。
Smiling brings you
dimples.　笑能帶來酒窩。

Unit 8

Life is short.　人生苦短。
Make the most of it.
善加利用。
Work hard, study hard,
play hard.　工作、讀書、
玩樂，盡情揮灑。

Treasure time.　珍愛光陰。
Time is a treasure.
時間即寶藏。
Time beats diamonds or
gold.　時間勝過鑽或金。

Use time wisely.
有智慧利用時間。
Use every hour and
minute.　時刻善用。
Live life to the fullest.
充實人生。

Unit 9

Simplify things.　簡化事情。
Don't complicate things.
勿複雜化。
The simple way is the
best way.　簡單爲上。

Value simplicity.　珍視純樸。
Simplicity is superior.
純樸是優勢。
Simplicity is the key.
純樸是重要的。

Simple is best.　簡單最好。
Keep it simple.　保持簡單。
A simple life is a happy
life.　簡單生活最快樂。

PART 3

Unit 1
善用生命

PART 3 · Unit 1~9
中英文錄音QR碼
英文唸2遍，中文唸1遍

**Our life is not
our own.**
吾命不由己。

We can't control it.
沒有控制權。

We can only use it.
只有使用權。

**Make the most
of life.**
善用生命。

Take full advantage.
充分利用。

Put it to good use.
善加運用。

Live fully every day.
時刻充實。

Don't waste a second.
勿失分秒。

Make it count.
使其有價。

PART 3

Unit 1 背景說明

　　我們的生命，就是我們的時間，往往由不得自己，被外界控制，身不由己，想做的事不能做到。所以，我們一定要善用生命，做自己想做的事。

Our life is not our own.（我們的生命不是我們自己的。）也可說成：Our life does not belong to us.（我們的生命不屬於我們。）

life〔laɪf〕*n.* 生命；生活；人生

own〔on〕*adj.* 自己的

We can't control it.（我們無法控制它。）也可說成：We can't rule it.（我們無法支配它。）

control〔kən'trol〕*v.* 控制

We can only use it. 我們只能使用它。(= *We can only make use of it.* = *We can only take advantage of it.*)

Make the most of life.（要善用生命。）也可說成：Take full advantage of your time on earth.（要充分利用你在這世上的時間。）

make the most of 善加利用

Take full advantage. (要充分利用。) 也可說成：
Take full advantage of your life. (要充分利用你的
生命。)　　　full〔fʊl〕*adj.* 充分的

advantage〔əd'væntɪdʒ〕*n.* 優點；利益；好處

take advantage 利用

Put it to good use. (要好好利用它。) 也可說成：Use
your time well. (要善用你的時間。)

put〔pʊt〕*v.* 使　　use〔jus〕*n.* 使用；利用

put…to use 利用 (= *make use of* = *take advantage of*)

put…to good use 善加利用 (= *take full advantage of*
= *make the most of*)

Live fully every day. 要充實地過每一天。(= *Live
every day to the fullest*.)　　live〔lɪv〕*v.* 過

fully〔'fʊlɪ〕*adv.* 充分地

Don't waste a second. (不要浪費任何一秒。) 也可說
成：Don't waste any time. (不要浪費任何時間。)
Don't waste your time. (不要浪費你的時間。)

waste〔west〕*v.* 浪費　　second〔'sɛkənd〕*n.* 秒

Make it count. (要使它很有價值。) 也可說成：Make
it worthwhile. (要使它有價值。) Make it matter.
(要使它很重要。)　　　make〔mek〕*v.* 使

count〔kaʊnt〕*v.* 有價值；有重要性

PART 3

Unit 2
流芳百世

Make life worthwhile.
生命有價。

Leave your mark.
淵遠流長。

Leave something behind.
流芳百世。

Leave no stone unturned.
不遺餘力。

Leave no path unwalked.
竭盡全力。

Leave no problem unsolved.
克服困難。

Strike while the iron is hot.

【諺】打鐵趁熱。

Make hay while the sun shines.

【諺】把握時機。

Take a chance while you have it.

機不可失。

PART 3

Unit 2 背景說明

要盡全力，把握機會，讓所花費的時間有價值。讓好的東西流芳百世，是最高的境界。

Make life worthwhile. 讓生命有價值。(= *Make life worth it.* = *Make life worth living.*) 也可說成：Do something worthwhile with your life. (用你的生命做有價值的事。)

worthwhile〔'wɝθ'hwaɪl〕*adj.* 值得的；有價值的

Leave your mark. 要留下深遠的影響。(= *Have a lasting effect.*) 也可說成：Make an impact. (要產生影響。)　　mark〔mɑrk〕*n.* 標誌；記號；名聲

leave one's mark 留下不可磨滅的痕跡；留下深遠的影響

Leave something behind. (要留下些什麼。) 也可說成：Do something with lasting impact. (要做一些具有持久影響力的事。) Leave a legacy. (要留下遺產。)　　*leave behind* 遺留；留下

Leave no stone unturned. 要讓沒有石頭沒被翻過，引申為「要不遺餘力。」(= *Spare no effort.*)

leave〔liv〕*v.* 使處於 (某種狀態)

unturned〔ʌn'tɝnd〕*adj.* 未翻轉的

leave no stone unturned 竭盡全力；千方百計

Leave no path unwalked. 要讓沒有一條路沒被走過，
引申為「要竭盡全力。」也可說成：Try everything.
（什麼都嘗試。）Take every opportunity.（要把握
每一個機會。） path〔pæθ〕*n.* 小路
unwalked〔ʌn'wɔkt〕*adj.* 未被走過的

Leave no problem unsolved. 要解決每一個問題。
（= *Solve all the problems.*）也可說成：Deal with
all the challenges.（要應付所有的挑戰。）
unsolved〔ʌn'sɑlvd〕*adj.* 未被解決的

Strike while the iron is hot. 是一句諺語，鐵燒得火熱
時，容易打出形狀，也就是「打鐵趁熱；把握時機。」
strike〔straɪk〕*v.* 打擊　iron〔'aɪən〕*n.* 鐵

Make hay while the sun shines. 是一句諺語，「曬草
要趁陽光好。」也就是「把握時機。」（= *Strike while
the iron is hot.*）
hay〔he〕*n.* 乾草　***make hay*** 曬乾草
sun〔sʌn〕*n.* 太陽　shine〔ʃaɪn〕*v.* 照耀

Take a chance while you have it. 一有機會就要好好把
握。（= *Take the opportunity while you can.*）
take〔tek〕*v.* 使用（機會）；利用
chance〔tʃæns〕*n.* 機會

PART 3

Unit 3
追求所想

Have the nerve.
有魄力。

Have the courage.
有勇氣。

Have the guts.
有膽量。

Be self-assured.
要自信。

Have self-esteem.
要自尊。

Have self-respect.
要自重。

**Go after what
you want.**
追求所想。

Target your goal.
瞄準目標。

Pull out all the stops.
全力以赴。

PART 3

Unit 3 背景説明

只要有勇氣、有膽量，瞄準目標，全力以赴，人生非常精彩。

Have the nerve. 要有魄力。(= *Be brave.*)
nerve〔nɝv〕*n.* 神經；勇氣；膽量；魄力
Have the courage. 要有勇氣。(= *Be courageous.*)
courage〔'kɝɪdʒ〕*n.* 勇氣　　***Have the guts.*** 要有膽量。
(= *Be bold.*)　　guts〔gʌts〕*n. pl.* 勇氣；膽量

Be self-assured. 要有自信。(= *Be confident.*)
self-assured〔,sɛlfə'ʃʊrd〕*adj.* 有自信的
Have self-esteem. (要有自尊。) 也可説成：Have
confidence. (要有自信。)
self-esteem〔,sɛlfə'stim〕*n.* 自尊 (= *self-respect*)
Have self-respect. (要自重。) 也可説成：Believe in
your own worth. (要相信你自己的價值。)
self-respect〔'sɛlfrɪ'spɛkt〕*n.* 自尊心；自重

Go after what you want. 追求你想要的。(= *Pursue
what you want.*)　　***go after*** 追求 (= *pursue*)
Target your goal. (瞄準你的目標。) 也可説成：Stay
focused on your goal. (專注於你的目標。)
target〔'tɑrgɪt〕*v.* 把…作爲目標；瞄準 (= *aim at*)
goal〔gol〕*n.* 目標
Pull out all the stops. 竭盡全力；全力以赴。(= *Do
everything you can.*)　　pull〔pul〕*v.* 拉；拔；拉開
pull out 拔掉；拔出　　stop〔stɑp〕*n.* 塞住；阻礙

PART 3

Unit 4
精彩人生

Life is a blessing.
活著真幸福。

Health is a blessing.
健康是幸福。

Love is a blessing.
愛即是幸福。

Enjoy yourself.
享受人生。

Savor life.
品味人生。

Relish life.
欣賞人生。

Live your best life.
精彩人生。

You only get one.
生不重來。

**Get all you can
out of it.**
盡情揮灑。

PART 3

Unit 4 背景說明

　　能活著、能吃、能睡，就是一大幸福。要好好享受人生、品味人生，欣賞人生。人只活一次，***You only get one***. (= *You only get one life.* = *You only live once.*) 這句話不能把 You 改成 We，因爲美國人用的次數太多，已經成爲慣用句。

Life is a blessing. (活著眞幸福。) 也可説成：You're
　　lucky to be alive. (活著很幸運。) Life is a
　　miracle. (生命是個奇蹟。)
life〔laɪf〕*n.* 生命；生活；人生
blessing〔'blɛsɪŋ〕*n.* 賜福；祝福；幸福；幸運的事

Health is a blessing. (健康是幸福。) 也可説成：
　　Health is a good thing. (健康是一件好事。)
　　Good health is a wonderful thing to have. (擁有
　　良好的健康是很棒的事。)　　health〔hɛlθ〕*n.* 健康

Love is a blessing. (愛是幸福。) 也可説成：You
　　are lucky to have love. (你很幸運能擁有愛。)
love〔lʌv〕*n.* 愛

Enjoy yourself. 要過得愉快。(= *Have a good time.*
　　= *Have a ball.* = *Live it up.*)
enjoy oneself 玩得愉快；過得愉快

Savor life.（品味人生。）也可說成：Revel in life.
（盡情享受人生。）

savor〔ˈsevɚ〕v. 品嚐；欣賞；喜好；享受

Relish life.　①欣賞人生。(＝*Appreciate life.*) ②享受人
生。(＝*Enjoy life.*＝*Take great pleasure in living.*)

relish〔ˈrɛlɪʃ〕v. 喜愛；欣賞；品味；享受

Live your best life.　要活出精彩的人生。(＝*Have the
best life you can.*) 也可說成：Make the most of
your life.（要善用你的生命。）

live~life　過~生活

You only get one.　你只能活一次。(＝*You only get
one life.*＝*You only live once.*)

get〔gɛt〕v. 得到

Get all you can out of it.　要儘量利用它。(＝*Get
everything you can from it.*＝*Get the most out
of it.*＝*Make the most of it.*＝*Take full advantage
of it.*)

all one can　力所能及；竭盡全力

out of　從…當中 (＝*from*)

PART 3

Unit 5
健康無價

Appreciate your health.
重視健康。

Take care of it.
照顧自己。

Don't throw it away.
不要忽視。

Good health is priceless.
健康無價。

With it, you have no limits.
有則不限。

Without it, your world is smaller.
無則命苦。

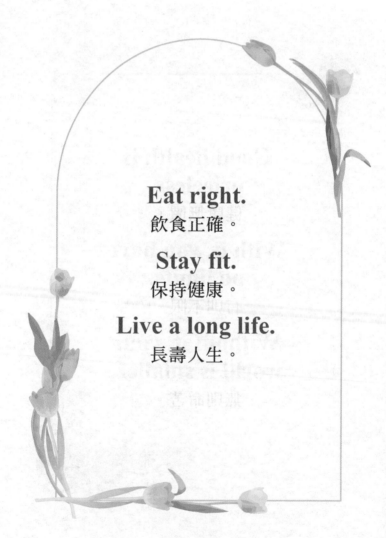

Eat right.
飲食正確。

Stay fit.
保持健康。

Live a long life.
長壽人生。

BOOK 3・PART 3

PART 3

Unit 5 背景説明

要重視你的健康，感冒是萬病之源，快要出現時，要危機
處理。我的方法是：

　　1. 喝杯熱咖啡，再喝幾杯溫開水，上小號排毒。

　　2. 做半身浴，不停流汗，排毒。

Appreciate your health. 要重視你的健康。(= *Value
your health.*)
appreciate〔əˋpriʃ1‚et〕v. 欣賞；重視；珍視
health〔hɛlθ〕n. 健康

Take care of it.（要照顧它。）也可説成：Protect it.
（要保護它。）
take care of 照顧

Don't throw it away.（不要拋棄它。）也可説成：
Don't neglect it.（不要忽視它。）Don't waste it.
（不要浪費它。）
throw away 拋棄；扔掉；浪費

Good health is priceless. 良好的健康是無價的。
(= *Good health is invaluable.*) 也可説成：Health
is irreplaceable.（健康是無可取代的。）
priceless〔ˋpraɪslɪs〕adj. 無價的

With it, you have no limits. (有了它，你就沒有限制。)
也可說成：If you have good health, you can do
anything. (如果你有良好的健康，你就可以做任何事。)
with〔 wɪθ 〕*prep.* 有…
limit〔'lɪmɪt 〕*n.* 限制
have no limits 沒有限制；無止境

Without it, your world is smaller. (沒有它，你的世界
會變小。) 也可說成：If you don't have good
health, your options will be limited. (如果你沒有
良好的健康，你的選擇會受限。)

Eat right. (要吃得正確；要注意飲食。) 也可說成：
Eat a healthy diet. (飲食要健康。)
right〔 raɪt 〕*adv.* 正確地

Stay fit. 要保持健康。(= *Stay in good shape.*)
stay〔 ste 〕*v.* 保持　　fit〔 fɪt 〕*adj.* 健康的

Live a long life. 要長壽。(= *Live a long time.*)
live a ~ life 過~生活

BOOK 3．PART 3

PART 3

Unit 6
珍惜真愛

Appreciate love.
珍惜真愛。

Not everyone has it.
非人皆有。

Know how lucky you are.
知所幸運。

Cherish those who love you.

珍惜所愛。

Love them back.

回饋所愛。

Let them know how you feel.

知你所受。

Love others.
多愛他人。

**Love people
around you.**
愛你身邊。

**Love
unconditionally.**
愛無條件。

PART 3

Unit 6 背景説明

　　不是每個人都能擁有愛。有人可以愛，是幸福；你被愛，也是幸福，一定要珍惜美好的時光。

Appreciate love. （要珍惜愛。）也可説成：Value love.（要重視愛。）

appreciate〔ə'priʃɪˏet〕*v.* 欣賞；重視；珍視

Not everyone has it. （不是每個人都能擁有愛。）也可説成：Some people don't have love. （有些人沒有愛。）

not everyone 並非每個人【部份否定】

how〔haʊ〕*adv.* 多麼地　　　lucky〔'lʌkɪ〕*adj.* 幸運的

cherish〔'tʃɛrɪʃ〕*v.* 珍惜

Love them back. 要用愛回報他們。（ = *Give them love in return.* ）　　back〔bæk〕*adv.* 返回；回報

Let them know how you feel. （讓他們知道你的感受。）也可説成：Tell them how much you love them. （告訴他們你有多愛他們。）　　***how you feel*** 你的感受

Love others. （要愛別人。）也可説成：Share your love.（分享你的愛。）Express your love. （表達你的愛。）（ = *Show your love.* ）

around〔ə'raʊnd〕*prep.* 在⋯周圍

Love unconditionally. （要無條件地愛。）也可説成：Place no conditions on your love. （你的愛不要有條件。）

unconditionally〔ˏʌnkən'dɪʃənlɪ〕*adv.* 無條件地

PART 3

Unit 7
培育愛心

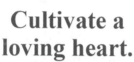

**Cultivate a
loving heart.**
培育愛心。

Fill it with kindness.
滿懷善意。

**Leave no room
for negativity.**
沒有負面。

**Fill your heart
with joy.**

滿懷歡喜心。

**Fill your mind with
good thoughts.**

腦中皆好意。

**Fill your life with
happiness.**

生活滿幸福。

Encourage others.
鼓勵別人。

Support others.
支持別人。

You won't be disappointed.
你不失落。

PART 3

Unit 7 背景說明

　　要培養愛心，滿腦子充滿著善意，負面的思想就沒有空間了。常常鼓勵別人、支持別人，自己最受益。

Cultivate a loving heart.（要培養充滿愛的心。）也可說成：Develop a kind heart.（要培養善良的心。）Develop empathy.（要培養同理心。）

cultivate〔ˈkʌltəˌvet〕v. 培養　　loving〔ˈlʌvɪŋ〕adj. 充滿愛的；深情的　　heart〔hɑrt〕n. 心

Fill it with kindness.（使它充滿善意。）也可說成：Have a kind heart.（要有善良的心。）

fill〔fɪl〕v. 裝滿；使充滿

fill A with B 用 B 裝滿 A；使 A 充滿 B

kindness〔ˈkaɪndnɪs〕n. 仁慈；善意

Leave no room for negativity. 不要有負面的想法。（= *Don't let negativity into your life.* = *Don't be negative.*）　　leave〔liv〕v. 留下

room〔rum〕n. 空間　　***leave no room for*** 不要留下任何…的餘地；不要留下…的機會

negativity〔ˌnɛgəˈtɪvətɪ〕n. 否定性；負面性；消極的態度；負面的想法

Fill your heart with joy. (讓你的心充滿喜悅。) 也可
說成：Be joyful. (要快樂。)　　joy〔dʒɔɪ〕*n.* 喜悅

Fill your mind with good thoughts. (讓你的頭腦充
滿好的想法。) 也可說成：Think only positive
thoughts. (要只有正面的想法。)

mind〔maɪnd〕*n.* 頭腦；心
thought〔θɔt〕*n.* 想法

Fill your life with happiness. (讓你的生活充滿快
樂。) 也可說成：Be happy. (要快樂。) Pursue
happiness. (要追求快樂。)

happiness〔'hæpɪnɪs〕*n.* 快樂；幸福

Encourage others. (鼓勵別人。) 也可說成：
Motivate other people. (激勵別人。)

encourage〔ɪn'kɝɪdʒ〕*v.* 鼓勵
others〔'ʌðɚz〕*pron.* 別人 (= *other people*)

Support others. (支持別人。) 也可說成：Help other
people. (幫助別人。)

support〔sə'port〕*v.* 支持

You won't be disappointed. (你不會失望。) 也可說
成：It will be worth it. (這會很值得。)

disappointed〔,dɪsə'pɔɪntɪd〕*adj.* 失望的

PART 3

Unit 8
絕不卑鄙

Never be mean.
絕不卑鄙。

Never be harsh.
絕不嚴厲。

Never be cruel.
絕不殘酷。

Don't tear others down.

勿拆人台階。

Don't embarrass them.

勿羞辱他人。

Don't take the wind out of their sails.

勿盛氣凌人。

**Kindness costs
you nothing.**
仁慈免費。

**It brings you
riches in return.**
帶進錢財。

**A kind heart is a
rich heart.**
善心富足。

PART 3

Unit 8 背景説明

 A kind heart is a rich heart. (善良的心，就是富足的心；善良致富。) 太多例子了，善良的窮人會變成有錢人。

Never be mean. (絕不要卑鄙。) 也可説成：Don't
 be unkind. (不要刻薄。)
never〔'nɛvɚ〕*adv.* 絕不
mean〔min〕*adj.* 卑鄙的；刻薄的；吝嗇的；小氣的

Never be harsh. 絕不要嚴厲。(= ***Don't be severe***.)
harsh〔harʃ〕*adj.* 嚴厲的

Never be cruel. 絕不要殘忍。(= ***Don't be brutal***.)
cruel〔'kruəl〕*adj.* 殘忍的

Don't tear others down. 不要輕視別人。(= ***Don't
 disparage others***. = ***Don't belittle other people***.)
tear〔tɛr〕*v.* 撕掉
tear down ①拆掉 ②撕掉 ③詆毀；駁斥 ④輕視

Don't embarrass them. (不要使人尷尬。) 也可説成：
 Don't humiliate other people. (不要羞辱別人。)
embarrass〔ɪm'bærəs〕*v.* 使尷尬

***Don't take the wind out of their sails*.** 不要使人洩氣。
  (= *Don't discourage other people.*)
wind〔wɪnd〕*n.* 風 ***out of*** 離開 (= *from*)
sail〔sel〕*n.* 帆

take the wind out of one's *sails* 源自航海，船帆沒有
  風吹動，就無法航行，拿走某人船帆上的風，引申爲
  「使人洩氣；使人不堅定」。

***Kindness costs you nothing*.** (仁慈不花你半毛錢。)
  也可說成：It is easy to be kind. (要仁慈很容易。)
kindness〔'kaɪndnɪs〕*n.* 仁慈；善良
cost〔kɔst〕*v.* 使花費

***It brings you riches in return*.** (它能帶給你財富作爲
  回報。) 也可說成：Being kind is worthwhile. (仁
  慈很值得。) Be kind and you will be rewarded.
  (善良會有回報。)
bring〔brɪŋ〕*v.* 帶給 (某人) (某物)
riches〔'rɪtʃɪz〕*n. pl.* 財富 ***in return*** 作爲回報

***A kind heart is a rich heart*.** (善良的心是富足的心。)
  也可說成：If you are kind, you will be blessed.
  (如果你善良，你會很有福氣。)
kind〔kaɪnd〕*adj.* 仁慈的；善良的
heart〔hɑrt〕*n.* 心 rich〔rɪtʃ〕*adj.* 有錢的；富有的

PART 3

Unit 9
勿低估自己

Never underestimate yourself.
勿低估自己。

Never belittle yourself.
勿小看自己。

Don't sell yourself short.
勿輕視自己。

Set your sights high.
訂標要高。

Your potential is limitless.
潛力無窮。

There is nothing you can't do.
無所不能。

Set your own course.

規劃人生。

Find your own way.

尋求出路。

Expand your horizons.

擴張視野。

PART 3

Unit 9 背景說明

　　只要有信心，設定好的目標，潛力無窮。不要低估自己，不要小看自己，你一定做得到。

Never underestimate yourself. 絕不要低估自己。
(= *Don't undervalue yourself.*)
never〔ˋnɛvɚ〕*adv.* 絕不
underestimate〔ˋʌndɚˋɛstəˌmet〕*v.* 低估

Never belittle yourself. 絕不要小看自己。(= *Don't underestimate yourself.* = *Don't think little of yourself.*)　　belittle〔bɪˋlɪt!〕*v.* 輕視；貶低

Don't sell yourself short. 絕不要輕視自己。(= *Don't underestimate yourself.* = *Don't disparage yourself.*)　　short〔ʃɔrt〕*adv.* 以賣空的方式
sell sb. short 小看某人；低估某人

Set your sights high. 要把目標訂得很高。(= *Set high goals.*) 也可說成：Have high ambitions. (要有崇高的志向。)
set〔sɛt〕*v.* 設定；使處於 (特定位置)
sights〔saɪts〕*n. pl.* (槍砲等的) 瞄準器；準星；目標 (= *goals*)；志向 (= *aspirations*)

high〔 haɪ 〕*adv.* 高地

set one's sights high 把目標訂很高；立志高遠；把眼光放遠

Your potential is limitless. 你的潛力無限。(＝ *Your potential is unlimited.*) 也可說成：You can do anything. (你可以做任何事。)

potential〔 pəˈtɛnʃəl 〕*n.* 潛力

limitless〔 ˈlɪmɪtlɪs 〕*adj.* 無限的

There is nothing you can't do. 沒有什麼是你做不到的。(＝ *You can do anything.*)

Set your own course. (設定你自己的路線。) 也可說成：Go your own way. (走你自己的路。)

course〔 kors 〕*n.* 前進路線

Find your own way. 找到你自己的路。(＝ *Find your own road.*) 也可說成：Decide your own life. (決定你自己的人生。)　　way〔 wc 〕*n.* 路

Expand your horizons. 要擴展你的眼界。(＝ *Broaden your horizons.*) 也可說成：Seek out new experiences. (要尋求新的經驗。)

expand〔 ɪkˈspænd 〕*v.* 擴大

horizon〔 həˈraɪzn̩ 〕*n.* 地平線；*(pl.)* 知識範圍；眼界

PART 3 總整理

Unit 1

Our life is not our own.
吾命不由己。
We can't control it.
沒有控制權。
We can only use it.
只有使用權。

Make the most of life.
善用生命。
Take full advantage.
充分利用。
Put it to good use.
善加運用。

Live fully every day.
時刻充實。
Don't waste a second.
勿失分秒。
Make it count. 使其有價。

Unit 2

Make life worthwhile.
生命有價。
Leave your mark.
淵遠流長。
Leave something behind.
流芳百世。

Leave no stone unturned.
不遺餘力。
Leave no path unwalked.
竭盡全力。
Leave no problem
　unsolved. 克服困難。

Strike while the iron is
　hot. 【諺】打鐵趁熱。
Make hay while the sun
　shines. 【諺】把握時機。
Take a chance while you
　have it. 機不可失。

Unit 3

Have the nerve. 有魄力。
Have the courage. 有勇氣。
Have the guts. 有膽量。

Be self-assured. 要自信。
Have self-esteem. 要自尊。
Have self-respect. 要自重。

Go after what you want.
追求所想。
Target your goal.
瞄準目標。
Pull out all the stops.
全力以赴。

Unit 4

Life is a blessing.
活著真幸福。
Health is a blessing.
健康是幸福。
Love is a blessing.
愛即是幸福。

Enjoy yourself.　享受人生。
Savor life.　品味人生。
Relish life.　欣賞人生。

Live your best life.
精彩人生。
You only get one.
生不重來。
Get all you can out of it.
盡情揮灑。

Unit 5

Appreciate your health.
重視健康。
Take care of it.
照顧自己。
Don't throw it away.
不要忽視。

Good health is priceless.
健康無價。

With it, you have no
　limits.　有則不限。
Without it, your world is
　smaller.　無則命苦。

Eat right.　飲食正確。
Stay fit.　保持健康。
Live a long life.　長壽人生。

Unit 6

Appreciate love.
珍惜真愛。
Not everyone has it.
非人皆有。
Know how lucky you are.
知所幸運。

Cherish those who love
　you.　珍惜所愛。
Love them back.
回饋所愛。
Let them know how you
　feel.　知你所受。

Love others.　多愛他人。
Love people around you.
愛你身邊。
Love unconditionally.
愛無條件。

Unit 7

Cultivate a loving heart.
培育愛心。
Fill it with kindness.
滿懷善意。
Leave no room for
  negativity. 沒有負面。

Fill your heart with joy.
滿懷歡喜心。
Fill your mind with good
  thoughts. 腦中皆好意。
Fill your life with
  happiness. 生活滿幸福。

Encourage others.
鼓勵別人。
Support others. 支持別人。
You won't be
  disappointed. 你不失落。

Unit 8

Never be mean. 絕不卑鄙。
Never be harsh. 絕不嚴厲。
Never be cruel. 絕不殘酷。

Don't tear others down.
勿拆人台階。
Don't embarrass them.
勿羞辱他人。

Don't take the wind out of
  their sails. 勿盛氣凌人。

Kindness costs you
  nothing. 仁慈免費。
It brings you riches in
  return. 帶進錢財。
A kind heart is a rich
  heart. 善心富足。

Unit 9

Never underestimate
  yourself. 勿低估自己。
Never belittle yourself.
勿小看自己。
Don't sell yourself short.
勿輕視自己。

Set your sights high.
訂標要高。
Your potential is limitless.
潛力無窮。
There is nothing you can't
  do. 無所不能。

Set your own course.
規劃人生。
Find your own way.
尋求出路。
Expand your horizons.
擴張視野。

賠本求利爲上策

我爲「完美英語之心靈盛宴」瘋狂！它改變了我，我不再斤斤計較。

> *Don't be cheap.*（不要小氣。）
> *Don't be stingy.*（不要吝嗇。）
> *Try to treat others first.*（搶先請客。）

有幾位友人，和一位女性朋友，一起去餐廳吃飯，女生付了錢，其他人默不作聲，以致於她很生氣。按照中國文化，要搶著付錢才對，至少，也應該要道謝，説下次要付。

> *Give back.*（要回饋。）
> *Return favors.*（要報答。）
> *Give more, gain more.*（付出多，得到多。）

我每天背，準備教材，上課又教，潛移默化，不但自己改變，而且帶來太多好處。「董事長班」同學愈來愈多，愈來愈熱情，補習班已由虧轉盈了！

> *Enjoy giving.*（樂於付出。）
> *Enjoy sharing.*（樂於分享。）
> *You'll always win.*（定會獲益。）

吃虧就是佔便宜。（The best gain is to lose.）我請外國老師寫：I enjoy being taken advantage of.（我喜歡被佔便宜。）她不肯，因爲她不相信！

將本求利，賺不到錢，因爲競爭太多，有許多促銷費。應該是賠本求利，物超所值，無人可比。

世界上，有多少好東西，未被人發現，就是因爲發明者怕吃虧，以致於好東西見不到光。

劉毅

PART 1

Unit 1
知 福

PART 1・Unit 1~9
中英文錄音QR碼
英文唸2遍，中文唸1遍

Appreciate blessings.
知福。

Cherish blessings.
惜福。

Create more blessings.
再造福。

BOOK 4 · PART 1

Don't feel inferior.
勿感自卑。

Don't feel insecure.
勿感不安。

**You're better
than you think.**
比想像好。

Wise men are broad-minded.
君子量大。

Foolish men are narrow-minded.
小人氣大。

Be more open-minded.
偉人寬大。

BOOK 4・PART 1

PART 1

Unit 1 背景說明

看到證嚴法師的標語：「知福，惜福，再造福。」最簡潔的英文是：Appreciate blessings. Cherish blessings. Create more blessings.

Appreciate blessings. ①重視幸福。(= *Value blessings.*) ②對幸福心存感激。(= *Be thankful for blessings.* = *Be grateful for all of the good things.*)
appreciate〔ə'priʃɪˌet〕*v.* 欣賞；重視；珍視；感激
blessing〔'blɛsɪŋ〕*n.* 幸福；幸運的事

Cherish blessings. 珍惜幸福。(= *Treasure blessings.*) cherish〔'tʃɛrɪʃ〕*v.* 珍惜

Create more blessings. (要創造更多的幸福。) 也可說成：Share your good fortune. (要分享你的幸運。) Create more good in the world. (要為世界創造更多美好的事物。) create〔krɪ'et〕*v.* 創造

Don't feel inferior. 不要覺得比別人差，也就是「不要自卑。」【相反的說法是：Don't feel superior. (不要覺得比別人好；不要驕傲。)】也可說成：Don't think you're second-rate. (不要認為自己很平庸。)
inferior〔ɪn'fɪrɪɚ〕*adj.* 較差的

Don't feel insecure. (不要感到不安。) 也可說成：

Don't doubt yourself. (不要懷疑自己。)

insecure〔͵ɪnsɪˈkjʊr〕*adj.* (人) 感到不安的；沒有自信的

You're better than you think. (你比你所想的更好。)

也可說成：You're more capable than you realize.

(你比你所想的更有能力。)

以下三句話改編自「靜思語」。

Wise men are broad-minded. 聰明的人心胸寬大。

(= *Intelligent people are tolerant.*)

broad-minded〔ˈbrɔdˈmaɪndɪd〕*adj.* 心胸開闊的；

度量大的

Foolish men are narrow-minded. 愚蠢的人心胸狹

窄。(= *The silly are intolerant.*)

foolish〔ˈfulɪʃ〕*adj.* 愚蠢的

narrow-minded〔ˈnæroˈmaɪndɪd〕*adj.* 心胸狹窄的

Be more open-minded. 心胸要更寬大。(= *You should be liberal.* = *You should be tolerant.* = *You should be accepting.*)

open-minded〔ˈopənˈmaɪndɪd〕*adj.* 心胸寬大的

PART 1

Unit 2
遵守金科玉律

Follow the golden rule.

遵守金科玉律。

Do as you would be done by.

【諺】己所欲，施於人。

Treat others as you want to be treated.

己所不欲，勿施於人。

BOOK 4 · PART 1

Give all you can.
盡所能付出。

Give to live well.
付出過得好。

Give to receive.
有捨才有得。

Have sympathy.
要有同情心。

Have empathy.
要有同理心。

Put yourself in others' shoes.
設身處地想。

BOOK 4・PART 1

PART 1

Unit 2 背景説明

美國人所說的 golden rule（金科玉律），即是

Do *as you would be done by*.（己所欲，施於人。）

Follow the golden rule. 要遵守金科玉律；己所欲，施於人。(= *Do as you would be done by*.) 也可説成：Be civil.（要有教養。）Be nice.（人要好。）

follow〔ˋfalo〕v. 遵循

golden〔ˋgoldn̩〕adj. 黃金的；金色的

rule〔rul〕n. 規則；規定

golden rule 黃金法則；金科玉律【即「己所欲，施於人」】

Do as you would be done by. 是一句諺語，意思是「你要別人怎麼對你，你就怎麼對別人；己所欲，施於人。」(= *Do as you would have done to you*.)

Treat others as you want to be treated. 想要別人怎麼對待你，你就怎麼對待別人；己所欲，施於人；己所不欲，勿施於人。(= *Treat others the way you want to be treated*.) treat〔trit〕v. 對待

Give all you can.（盡你所能地付出。）也可説成：Donate.（要捐獻。）Volunteer anything you can.（要自願提供任何你能提供的。）

give〔 gɪv 〕*v.* 給與；付出；贈送；捐助

all one can 力所能及；竭盡全力

Give to live well.（付出才能過得好。）也可説成：
Give to others and your life will be better.
（要對別人付出，你的生活才會更好。）

Give to receive.（付出才能獲得。）也可説成：If you
give to others, you will be rewarded with
something good.（如果你對別人付出，你就會有好的
回報。） receive〔 rɪ'siv 〕*v.* 收到；得到

Have sympathy. 要有同情心。（= *Have compassion.*
= *Be sympathetic.* = *Be compassionate.*)
sympathy〔'sɪmpəθɪ 〕*n.* 同情；同情心

Have empathy.（要有同理心。）也可説成：Be
understanding.（要體諒別人。）
empathy〔'ɛmpəθɪ 〕*n.* 共感；共鳴；同理心

Put yourself in others' shoes. 要設身處地為別人著
想。(= *Imagine yourself in the position of someone
else in order to understand that person's point of
view.*) put〔 pʊt 〕*v.* 使處於（某種狀態）

shoe〔 ʃu 〕*n.* 鞋子

in one's shoes 站在別人的立場；設身處地

PART 1

Unit 3
不要選邊站

Don't take sides.
不要選邊站。

Be on everyone's side.
要站同一國。

Be friendly to all.
對人人友善。

Everyone is unique.
人皆獨一無二。

Everyone to his taste.
【諺】人人各有所好。

To each his own.
【諺】人皆不同愛好。

Never blame others.
不要責備。

**Never point a finger
at others.**
不要指責。

**It reflects badly
on you.**
招致非議。

PART 1

Unit 3 背景說明

　　一個團體中往往有幾個小集團，不要選邊站為上策，要對每一個人友善。

Don't take sides. (不要偏袒任何一邊。) 也可說成： Don't favor one over the other. (不要偏愛兩者中的任何一個。) Don't choose a position. (不要選邊站。)　　side〔saɪd〕*n.* 一邊　　***take sides*** 偏袒

Be on everyone's side. (要站在每個人的那一邊。) 也可說成：Support everyone. (要支持每一個人。)
be on *one's* ***side*** 和某人同一邊

Be friendly to all. (要對所有人友善。) 也可說成：Always be friendly. (一定要友善。) Always be nice. (一定要親切。)　　friendly〔'frɛndlɪ〕*adj.* 友善的

Everyone is unique. (每個人都是獨一無二的。) 也可說成：We're all different. (我們全都不一樣。)
unique〔ju'nik〕*adj.* 獨特的；獨一無二的

Everyone to his taste. 人各有所好。(= *Every man to his taste.*) 是一句諺語，源自 Everyone is entitled to his own taste. (每個人都有權利擁有自己的愛好。) 也可說成：There is no accounting for tastes. (【諺】人的喜好是無法說明的；人各有所好。)
taste〔test〕*n.* 愛好

To each his own. 是一句諺語，意思是「人各有所好。」
（ = *Everyone to his taste.*) 源自 Everyone is
entitled to his own tastes. (每個人都有權利擁有自
己的喜好。) (= *Everyone is entitled to his own
preferences.*) 這句話源自莎士比亞著名的悲劇「哈姆
雷特」(Hamlet)。

Never blame others. (絕不要責備別人。) 也可說成：
Never fault others. (絕不要指責別人。) Never
accuse others. (絕不要譴責別人。)
blame〔blem〕*v.* 責備

Never point a finger at others. 絕不要指責別人。
(= *Never blame others.* = *Don't accuse others.*)
point〔pɔɪnt〕*v.* 把 (手指) 指向…
point a finger at 指責

It reflects badly on you. (這會對你有不良的影響。)
也可說成：It harms your reputation. (這會損害你
的名聲。) It makes you look bad. (這會使你看起
來很糟。)
reflect〔rɪˈflɛkt〕*v.* 反射；反映；招致非議；帶來恥辱；
帶來影響
badly〔ˈbædlɪ〕*adv.* 壞地
reflect badly on sb. 給某人帶來損害

PART 1

Unit 4
改 進

Improve!
改進！

Advance!
進步！

Onward and upward!
向上！

Dream big dreams.
要敢做大夢。

Reach for the stars.
設立大目標。

The sky is your limit.
潛力無限大。

Be a go-getter.
志在必得。

Pursue your ambitions.
追尋志向。

Leave your comfort zone.
遠離舒適。

BOOK 4・PART 1

PART 1

Unit 4 背景說明

我不願意回到過去，因為我今天比昨天好。

Improve! (要改進！) 也可說成：Get better! (要變得更好！) Get stronger! (要變得更強大！)
improve〔 ɪm'pruv 〕v. 改善；改進

Advance! (要進步！) 也可說成：Progress! (要進步！) Make progress! (要進步！)
advance〔 əd'væns 〕v. 前進；進步；進展

Onward and upward! 是慣用句，字面的意思是「要向前、向上！」源自 Move onward and upward! 也就是「要努力向上；要步步高升；要越來越成功！」也可說成：Advance to a better condition! (要進步到更好的情況！) Keep progressing! (要持續進步！)
(= *Keep advancing!*)　　　onward〔'ɑnwəd 〕adj., adv. 向前的 (地) (= *moving forward*)
upward〔'ʌpwəd 〕adj., adv. 向上的 (地) (= *going higher*)

美國人常喜歡說：***Dream big dreams.*** 鼓勵別人要有遠大的夢想。美國前總統歐巴馬 (Obama) 給一位十歲的小女孩的親筆簽名，也附加了這句鼓勵她的話。

也可説成：Be ambitious.（要有志氣。）Don't limit yourself.（不要限制自己。）

dream〔drim〕*v.* 做（夢）；夢見（…的夢） *n.* 夢；夢想

Reach for the stars. 要伸手去摘星星，引申爲「要設定不易達成的目標。」(= *Try to achieve something difficult*.) ***reach for*** 伸手去拿

star〔stɑr〕*n.* 星星

The sky is your limit. 天空是你的界限，引申爲「你的潛力無限大。」(= *Your potential is unlimited*.) 源自 The sky's the limit. (= *Anything is possible*.)

sky〔skaɪ〕*n.* 天空

limit〔'lɪmɪt〕*n.* 界線；界限；極限

Be a go-getter.（要有衝勁和進取心。）也可説成：Be a self-starter.（做事要主動。）Be a dynamo.（要做一個精力充沛的人。） go-getter〔'go'gɛtɚ〕*n.* 幹勁十足的人；有衝勁和進取心的人

Pursue your ambitions.（追求你的志向。）也可説成：Pursue what you want.（追求你想要的。）

pursue〔pɚ'su〕*v.* 追求

ambition〔æm'bɪʃən〕*n.* 志向；抱負；野心

Leave your comfort zone. 離開你的舒適圈。(= *Go beyond your comfort level*.)

comfort〔'kʌmfɚt〕*n.* 舒適   zone〔zon〕*n.* 地區

comfort zone 舒適圈【指讓人感到舒服而不費力氣的狀況】

PART 1

Unit 5
使其成真

Make it real.
使其成真。

Make it certain.
將它確認。

Make it final.
設定結局。

Carry it out.
實行。

Commit to it.
投入。

Complete the task.
完成任務。

Stick to it.

堅持下去。

Stick with it.

堅韌不拔。

Stick it out.

堅持到底。

PART 1

Unit 5 背景說明

美國人常說：Go for it! Just do it! Make it happen! 意思都是「趕快去做吧！」可接著說：*Make it real.*（使它成真。）（= *Get it done.*）*Make it certain*.（讓它確定。）（= *Confirm it.*）*Make it final*.（使它終結。）（= *Finalize it.* = *Complete it.* = *Bring it to a close.*）等來加強語氣。　　real〔'riəl〕*adj.* 真的
certain〔'sɜtn̩〕*adj.* 確定的
final〔'faɪnl̩〕*adj.* 最終的；最後的；決定性的；不可變更的
make final 使最後確定下來

Carry it out.（要實行。）也可說成：Accomplish it.（要完成。）（= *Achieve it.* = *Complete it.*）
carry out 實行；執行
Commit to it. 要投入。（= *Be committed to it.* = *Commit yourself to it.* = *Devote yourself to it.* = *Dedicate yourself to it.* = *Immerse yourself in it.* = *Throw yourself into it.*）　　commit〔kə'mɪt〕*v.* 致力於
Complete the task. 要完成任務。（= *Finish the job.*）
complete〔kəm'plit〕*v.* 完成
task〔tæsk〕*n.* 任務；工作

Stick to it. 堅持下去；堅持到底。（= *Stick with it.* = *Stick it out.* = *Stay at it.* = *Keep going.* = *Hang in there.* = *Persevere.*）也可說成：Don't quit.（不要放棄。）（= *Don't give up.*）Don't stop.（不要停止。）
stick〔stɪk〕*v.* 刺；黏住　　*stick to* 堅持
stick with 堅持做　　*stick it out* 堅持到底

PART 1

Unit 6
世無速藥

There's no magic pill.

世無速藥。

Change doesn't happen overnight.

非一朝變。

Just work hard and stay focused.

專心致志。

Show up.

出現。

Be there.

在場。

**80% of success
is showing up.**

百分之八十成功靠出現。

BOOK 4・PART 1

BOOK 4 · PART 1

There are no shortcuts.

人生無捷徑。

There are no life hacks.

生活無妙招。

You have to do the work.

要腳踏實地。

PART 1

Unit 6 背景説明

很多人想要一夜致富，急得不得了，每個人都急，
但是沒有成功；如果一直急到底，就能成功。

There's no magic pill. 沒有神奇的藥丸。(= *There is
no wonder drug.* = *There is no miracle drug.*
= *There is no cure-all.* = *There is no silver bullet.*)
magic〔ˈmædʒɪk〕*adj.* 有魔力的；神奇的
pill〔pɪl〕*n.* 藥丸

Change doesn't happen overnight. (改變不會一夜之
間就發生。) 也可説成：Change takes time. (改變需
要時間。) change〔tʃendʒ〕*n.* 改變
happen〔ˈhæpən〕*v.* 發生
overnight〔ˈovɚˈnaɪt〕*adv.* 一夜之間

Just work hard and stay focused. (只要努力並且專
心。) 也可説成：You need to put in the work and
not get distracted. (你必須付出努力，並且不能分心。)
work hard 努力 stay〔ste〕*v.* 保持
focused〔ˈfokəst〕*adj.* 專注的

Show up. 要出現。(= *Appear.* = *Put in an
appearance.*) 也可説成：Participate. (要參與。)
(= *Take part.*)

Be there. (要在那裡；要在場。) 也可説成：Appear.
(要出現。) Arrive. (要到場。) Take part. (要參
與。) Don't give up. (不要放棄。)

80% of success is showing up. (百分之八十的成功是
靠出現。) 也可説成：If you just show up, you will
have an 80% chance of succeeding. (你只要出現，
就會有百分之八十的成功機率。) If you don't try, you
can't win. (如果你不嘗試，就不可能贏。)

80% 百分之八十【唸成 eighty percent】
success〔 sək'sɛs〕 *n.* 成功

There are no shortcuts. (人生無捷徑。) 也可説成：
There is no miracle drug. (沒有特效藥。) There
is no easy solution. (沒有容易的解決辦法。)
shortcut〔'ʃɔrt,kʌt〕 *n.* 捷徑

There are no life hacks. (沒有生活小妙招。) 也可説成：
There is no wonder drug. (沒有萬靈丹。) There is
no easy solution. (沒有容易的解決辦法。)
hack〔 hæk〕 *n.* 好的方案；好的建議（= *a good solution or
piece of advice*） ***life hack*** 生活小技能；生活妙招

You have to do the work. (你必須做這個工作。) 也可
説成：The work needs to be done. (這個工作必須
要做。) There is no avoiding the work. (不可能
避開這個工作。) ***the work*** 在此指 the necessary
actions or steps to accomplish the goal（達成目
標所必須採取的行動或步驟）。

PART 1

Unit 7
立大目標

Set a big goal.
立大目標。

Break it down into steps.
拆解步驟。

Complete one step at a time.
依序完成。

Enjoy the process.
享受過程。

Enjoy every step.
享受步驟。

Process over outcome.
過程重於結果。

BOOK 4・PART 1

Intensity is overrated.
一時努力被高估。

Consistency is underrated.
持之以恆被低估。

Small steps lead to big gains.
聚沙成塔。

PART 1

Unit 7 背景説明

　　設定大的目標，一步一步完成，要學會享受過程，
先努力，不要想結果。

Set a big goal. （設定一個大的目標。）也可説成：Be
ambitious. （要有抱負。）Set your sights high. （要
設定很高的目標。）

set〔sɛt〕*v.* 設定　　　goal〔gol〕*n.* 目標

Break it down into steps. 要把它分解成幾個步驟。
（*= Divide it into steps.*）

break down 分解　　step〔stɛp〕*n.* 一步；步驟

Complete one step at a time. （一次完成一個步驟。）
也可説成：Do it one step at a time. （一步一步地
做。）（*= Do it step by step. = Do it bit by bit.*）

complete〔kəmˋplit〕*v.* 完成　　***at a time*** 一次

Enjoy the process. （要享受過程。）也可説成：Take
pleasure in the procedure. （要以過程爲樂。）

process〔ˋprɑsɛs〕*n.* 過程

Enjoy every step. （要享受每一個步驟。）也可説成：
Enjoy every step towards your goal. （要享受每
一個達成目標的步驟。）Enjoy every part of the
process. （要享受過程中的每一個部分。）

Process over outcome. 過程重於結果。(= *Value process over outcome*.) 是慣用句，類似的有：
Health over wealth. (健康重於財富。) Quality over quantity. (質勝過量。) 這些句子沒有動詞，能夠被認可，可見多常用。

over〔'ovɚ〕*prep.* 在…之上
outcome〔'aʊtˌkʌm〕*n.* 結果

Intensity is overrated. (強度被高估；一時努力被高估。) 也可說成：It's not that important to be intense. (強烈沒那麼重要。) Too much importance is placed on intensity. (強度被過度重視。)

intensity〔ɪn'tɛnsətɪ〕*n.* 強度；強烈；認真；全心投入
overrate〔ˌovɚ'ret〕*v.* 高估

Consistency is underrated. (持之以恆被低估。) 也可說成：Consistency is more important. (持之以恆比較重要。) People don't pay enough attention to consistency. (人們不夠注意持之以恆。)

consistency〔kən'sɪstənsɪ〕*n.* 連貫性；一致性；持之以恆　underrate〔ˌʌndɚ'ret〕*v.* 低估；輕視

Small steps lead to big gains. (小步驟累積大財富。) 也可說成：A little progress can lead to success. (小小的進展能使人成功。) Doing things step by step results in success. (一步一步地做事終會成功。)

lead to 導致；造成　　gains〔genz〕*n. pl.* 收益；利潤

PART 1

Unit 8
事要簡化

Keep things simple.
事要簡化。

Lighten your load.
人勿重擔。

Make your life easier.
生活輕鬆。

Enjoy nice things.
享受美好。

Be kind to yourself.
慈悲待己。

Treat yourself well.
善待己身。

BOOK 4 · PART 1

Relax and enjoy.
輕鬆享受。

Let it all hang loose.
全然放鬆。

Just let it all hang out.
就是放鬆。

PART 1

Unit 8 背景説明

事情要簡化，生活才輕鬆。

Keep things simple. (事情要簡化。) 也可說成：Don't complicate things. (不要把事情複雜化。)

simple〔'sɪmpl̩〕*adj.* 簡單的

Lighten your load. (減輕你的負擔。) 也可說成：Get rid of some of your burdens. (要除去你的一些負擔。) Let some things go. (要放下某些東西。)　lighten〔'laɪtn̩〕*v.* 減輕　load〔lod〕*n.* 負荷；重擔 (= *burden*)

Make your life easier. (要讓你的生活輕鬆一點。) 也可說成：Live a less stressful life. (要過著比較沒壓力的生活。)

Enjoy nice things. (享受美好的事物。) 也可說成：Treat yourself. (款待你自己。)　enjoy〔ɪn'dʒɔɪ〕*v.* 享受

Be kind to yourself. (要對自己好。) 也可說成：***Treat yourself well***. (要善待自己。) Be good to yourself. (要對自己好。)　kind〔kaɪnd〕*adj.* 親切的；仁慈的

treat〔trit〕*v.* 對待

我們學過 Let it all hang out. (完全放鬆。) 為了避免重複，加上一個 Just，再加上一句 Let it all hang loose. 合在一起，就不會忘記了。你可以常常對人說：***Relax and enjoy***. ***Let it all hang loose***. ***Just let it all hang out***. 意思是「要完全放鬆。」

relax〔rɪ'læks〕*v.* 放鬆　hang〔hæŋ〕*v.* 懸掛
loose〔lus〕*adj.* 鬆的　***hang loose*** 放鬆
let it all hang loose 完全放鬆 (= *let it all hang out*)

PART 1

Unit 9
重視離線

It's important to disconnect.
重視離線。

Put your phone away.
收起手機。

Unplug to unwind.
不續電得自由。

BOOK 4 • PART 1

Get offline.

離線。

Disconnect from technology.

遠離高科技。

Reconnect with each other.

聯結人脈。

BOOK 4 • PART 1

Disconnect from the world.

與世隔絕。

Reconnect with yourself.

聯結自我。

Enjoy your own company.

享受一人。

PART 1

Unit 9 背景說明

有時把手機關機，與世隔絕，再打開手機，會很快樂。

It's important to disconnect. （切斷連絡很重要。）
也可說成：Turning off all your devices is
important. （關掉你所有的裝置很重要。）
important〔ɪmˈpɔrtn̩t〕*adj.* 重要的
disconnect〔͵dɪskəˈnɛkt〕*v.* 切斷（連絡）；斷線＜*from*＞

Put your phone away. （把你的手機收起來。）也可說
成：Turn off your phone. （關掉你的手機。）Stop
checking your phone. （停止看你的手機。）
put away 收拾；把…收起來
phone〔fon〕*n.* 電話；手機（＝*cell phone*）

Unplug to unwind. （拔掉插頭才能放輕鬆。）也可說
成：Disconnect in order to relax. （切斷連絡才能
放鬆。）　　unplug〔ʌnˈplʌg〕*v.* 拔去…的電源插頭
unwind〔ʌnˈwaɪnd〕*v.* 使心情輕鬆

Get offline. （要離線。）也可說成：Disconnect. （要
切斷連絡。）Unplug. （要拔掉插頭。）Log off. （要
登出。）　　get〔gɛt〕*v.* 變得
offline〔͵ɔfˈlaɪn〕*adj.* 離線的

Disconnect from technology. (和科技斷絕關係。) 也可說成：Stop using technology. (停止使用科技。) (= *Take a break from technology*.) Stop using your devices. (停止使用你的各種裝置。)

technology〔tɛkˋnɑlədʒɪ〕*n.* 科技

Reconnect with each other. (改善彼此的關係。) 也可說成：Pay attention to other people. (要注意別人。) Spend time with one another. (要找時間和彼此相處。)   reconnect〔͵rikəˋnɛkt〕*v.* 重新接上；重新連上；改善變差的關係

Disconnect from the world. (要和世界斷絕關係。) 也可說成：Stop using your devices. (停止使用你的各種裝置。)   ***the world*** 世界；世人

Reconnect with yourself. (要改善和你自己的關係。) 也可說成：Spend time by yourself. (要找時間獨處。) Get to know yourself. (要認識你自己。)

Enjoy your own company. (要享受自我的陪伴。) 也可說成：Appreciate your own company. (要重視自我的陪伴。) Enjoy spending time alone. (要享受獨處的時間。)   enjoy〔ɪnˋdʒɔɪ〕*v.* 享受

own〔on〕*adj.* 自己的

company〔ˋkʌmpənɪ〕*n.* 公司；陪伴

PART 1 總整理

Unit 1

Appreciate blessings.
知福。
Cherish blessings. 惜福。
Create more blessings.
再造福。

Don't feel inferior.
勿感自卑。
Don't feel insecure.
勿感不安。
You're better than you think. 比想像好。

Wise men are broad-minded. 君子量大。
Foolish men are narrow-minded. 小人氣大。
Be more open-minded.
偉人寬大。

Unit 2

Follow the golden rule.
遵守金科玉律。
Do as you would be done by. 【諺】己所欲，施於人。
Treat others as you want to be treated.
己所不欲，勿施於人。

Give all you can.
盡所能付出。
Give to live well.
付出過得好。
Give to receive.
有捨才有得。

Have sympathy.
要有同情心。
Have empathy.
要有同理心。
Put yourself in others' shoes. 設身處地想。

Unit 3

Don't take sides.
不要選邊站。
Be on everyone's side.
要站同一國。
Be friendly to all.
對人人友善。

Everyone is unique.
人皆獨一無二。
Everyone to his taste.
【諺】人人各有所好。
To each his own.
【諺】人皆不同愛好。

Never blame others.
不要責備。
Never point a finger at
　　others. 不要指責。
It reflects badly on you.
招致非議。

Unit 4

Improve! 改進！
Advance! 進步！
Onward and upward!
向上！

Dream big dreams.
要敢做大夢。
Reach for the stars.
設立大目標。
The sky is your limit.
潛力無限大。

Be a go-getter. 志在必得。
Pursue your ambitions.
追尋志向。
Leave your comfort zone.
遠離舒適。

Unit 5

Make it real. 使其成真。
Make it certain. 將它確認。
Make it final. 設定結局。

Carry it out. 實行。
Commit to it. 投入。
Complete the task.
完成任務。

Stick to it. 堅持下去。
Stick with it.
堅韌不拔。
Stick it out. 堅持到底。

Unit 6

There's no magic pill.
世無速藥。
Change doesn't happen
　　overnight. 非一朝變。
Just work hard and stay
　　focused. 專心致志。

Show up. 出現。
Be there. 在場。
80% of success is
　　showing up.
百分之八十成功靠出現。

There are no shortcuts.
人生無捷徑。
There are no life hacks.
生活無妙招。
You have to do the work.
要腳踏實地

BOOK 4・PART 1

Unit 7

Set a big goal. 立大目標。
Break it down into steps.
拆解步驟。
Complete one step at a
    time. 依序完成。

Enjoy the process.
享受過程。
Enjoy every step.
享受步驟。
Process over outcome.
過程重於結果。

Intensity is overrated.
一時努力被高估。
Consistency is underrated.
持之以恆被低估。
Small steps lead to big
    gains. 聚沙成塔。

Unit 8

Keep things simple.
事要簡化。
Lighten your load.
人勿重擔。
Make your life easier.
生活輕鬆。

Enjoy nice things.
享受美好。

Be kind to yourself.
慈悲待己。
Treat yourself well.
善待己身。

Relax and enjoy.
輕鬆享受。
Let it all hang loose.
全然放鬆。
Just let it all hang out.
就是放鬆。

Unit 9

It's important to
    disconnect. 重視離線。
Put your phone away.
收起手機。
Unplug to unwind.
不纜電得自由。

Get offline. 離線。
Disconnect from
    technology. 遠離高科技。
Reconnect with each
    other. 聯結人脈。

Disconnect from the
    world. 與世隔絕。
Reconnect with yourself.
聯結自我。
Enjoy your own company
享受一人。

PART 2

Unit 1
要加入

PART 2・Unit 1~9
中英文錄音QR碼
英文唸2遍，中文唸1遍

Join in.
要加入。

Pitch in.
要參與。

Chip in.
參一腳。

Contribute!
付出！

Participate!
參與！

Play a part!
參與其中！

Get very involved.
深入其中。

Get close to it.
與之接近。

Be on it like white on rice.
形影不離。

PART 2

Unit 1 背景說明

要在團體中出類拔萃，就要深入參與（Get very involved.），領袖是自然產生的。

Join in. 要加入。(= *Participate*. = *Take part*.)
【比 Join.語氣強】　　join〔 dʒɔɪn 〕*v.* 參加

Pitch in. (要參與。) 也可說成：Help out. (要幫忙。)
Lend a hand. (要伸出援手；要幫忙。)
pitch〔 pɪtʃ 〕*v.* 投擲
pitch in 把⋯投入；參與；同心協力；做出貢獻

Chip in. (要出一份力。) 也可說成：Contribute. (要付出。) Make a contribution. (要有貢獻。)
chip〔 tʃɪp 〕*n.* 碎片；薄片；錢；籌碼
chip in 出一份力；為⋯出錢；湊錢【源自賭博時丟入籌碼（chip）】

Contribute! 要付出！(= *Give!*) 也可說成：Donate! (要捐獻！) Help! (要幫忙！)
contribute〔 kən'trɪbjut 〕*v.* 貢獻

Participate! 要參與！(= *Take part!* = *Play a part!*)
participate〔 par'tɪsə,pet 〕*v.* 參與

BOOK 4・PART 2

Play a part! 扮演某個角色！(= *Play a role!*); 要參
與！(= *Take part!* = *Participate!* = *Get involved!*)

play〔ple〕*v.* 扮演　　part〔part〕*n.* 角色 (= *role*)

Get very involved. 要深入參與。(= *Get extremely*
involved. = *Involve yourself in it.* = *Really*
participate.)

involved〔ɪn'valvd〕*adj.* 有關的；牽涉在內的

Get close to it. (要接近它。) 也可說成：Get
involved. (要參與。)

close〔klos〕*adj.* 接近的 < *to* >

Be on it like white on rice. (要緊盯著它。) 也可
說成：Be very involved in it. (要深入參與。)
Be very interested in it. (要對它非常感興趣。)
Work closely with it. (要跟它密切合作。)

on〔an〕*prep.* 接近　　white〔hwaɪt〕*n.* 白色
rice〔raɪs〕*n.* 米　　*like white on rice* 就像米上面
的白色，兩者幾乎密不可分，引申為「極其近的；
極其親密的」(= *be extremely close*)。

be on…like white on rice 緊盯著… (= *watch…*
closely)

PART 2

Unit 2
一言九鼎

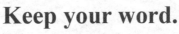

Keep your word.
一言九鼎。

Honor your word.
一諾千金。

Your word is your bond.
言出必行。

Keep your promise.
遵守承諾。

**Stay true to your
promise.**
信守承諾。

**Don't break your
promise.**
切勿食言。

Do as you promised.
言出必行。

Do as you agreed.
遵照諾言。

**Hold up your end
of the bargain.**
恪守承諾。

PART 2

Unit 2 背景説明

　　一百次遵守諾言，只要一次不遵守諾言，信用就破產了，像鏡子破了，無法復原。這一回九句話意思相同。

Keep your word. 要遵守諾言。
= Honor your word. 要遵守諾言。
= Your word is your bond. 總是信守諾言。

Keep your promise. 要遵守承諾。
= Stay true to your promise. 要信守諾言。
= Don't break your promise. 不要食言。

Do as you promised. 要言出必行。
= Do as you agreed. 你同意的事要做到。
= Hold up your end of the bargain. 要信守承諾。

one's **word** 諾言　　honor〔'ɑnɚ〕*v.* 承兌；支付；實踐
honor one's **word** 信守諾言
bond〔bɑnd〕*n.* 約定；契約

promise〔'prɑmɪs〕*n.* 承諾；諾言　　stay〔ste〕*v.* 保持
true〔tru〕*adj.* 忠實的；信守…的 < *to* >
stay true to one's **promise** 信守承諾
break〔brek〕*v.* 打破；違反；未遵守
break one's **promise** 未遵守諾言；食言

agree〔ə'gri〕*v.* 同意　　*hold up* 舉起；堅持；保持
end〔ɛnd〕*n.* 一頭；一端；部份；方面 (= *part*)
bargain〔'bɑrgɪn〕*n.* 協議；契約；交易
hold up one's **end of the bargain** 履行約定的承諾

PART 2

Unit 3
相信自己

Believe in yourself.
相信自己。

Your potential is unlimited.
潛力無限。

The world is yours to conquer.
征服世界。

BOOK 4・PART 2

You're capable.
你有能力。

You're competent.
你很能幹。

Nothing can stop you.
無法可擋。

You will succeed.
你會成功。

You're the right person.
天選之人。

I'm confident you can do it.
信你可及。

PART 2

Unit 3 背景説明

稱讚是美德，要常說稱讚的話，多鼓勵，少責備。

Believe in yourself. (要相信自己。) 也可説成：Have confidence in yourself. (要對你自己有信心。) Have confidence in your abilities. (要對你的能力有信心。) I believe you. 是「我相信你說的話。」 I believe in you. 是「我信任你；我相信你的能力。」 任何及物動詞加上介詞，就形成另一個意思，像 hear (聽到)，hear from (收到⋯的信息)。

believe in 相信；信任

Your potential is unlimited. 你的潛力無限。(= *Your potential is limitless.*) 也可説成：There is nothing you can't do. (沒有什麼你做不到的事。)

potential (pəˈtɛnʃəl) *n.* 潛力
unlimited (ʌnˈlɪmɪtɪd) *adj.* 無限的

The world is yours to conquer. 這個世界由你來征服，也就是「你一定會成功。」

conquer (ˈkɑŋkə) *v.* 征服

You're capable. 你有能力。(= *You're able.* = *You're competent.*)　　capable (ˈkepəbḷ) *adj.* 有能力的

You're competent. 你很能幹。(= *You're capable.* = *You're skilled.*)

competent 〔'kɑmpətənt 〕 *adj.* 能幹的；有能力的；能勝任的

Nothing can stop you. (沒有什麼能阻擋你。) 也可說成：You're unstoppable. (你是不可阻擋的。) You cannot be defeated. (你不可能被打敗。)

stop 〔 stɑp 〕 *v.* 阻止；妨礙

You'll succeed. 你會成功。(= *You'll triumph.* = *You'll prevail.* = *You will make it.*)

succeed 〔 sək'sid 〕 *v.* 成功

You're the right person. 你是適合的人選。(= *You're the most suitable person.* = *You're the best person for the job.* = *You're the best one to do it.*)

right 〔 raɪt 〕 *adj.* 對的；正確的；適當的

I'm confident you can do it. 我相信你做得到。(= *I believe that you can do it.*) 也可說成：I know you will succeed. (我知道你會成功。)

confident 〔'kɑnfədənt 〕 *adj.* 有信心的；確信的

PART 2

Unit 4
勿掛心

**Don't take it
to heart.**
勿掛心。

**Don't take it
too hard.**
勿傷感。

**Don't take it
seriously.**
勿當真。

Don't take offense.
切勿生氣。

Don't be offended.
勿感冒犯。

It's not an attack.
並非攻擊。

**Get rid of any
bad feeling.**
除去惡感。

**Get it out of your
system.**
擺脫煩惱。

Get it off your chest.
吐露心事。

PART 2

Unit 4 背景説明

不小心説錯話，就可以説這些話來補救。

Don't take it to heart. 別放在心上。(= *Don't be too affected by it.*)

take sth. to heart 把某事放在心上；對某事介意；對某事耿耿於懷 (= *take sth. seriously and be deeply affected by it*)

Don't take it too hard. 別太難過。(= *Don't be too sad about it.*)

take it hard 深以爲苦；耿耿於懷；悲傷不已 (= *be upset or depressed by it*)

Don't take it too seriously. 不要把它看得太認眞；不要耿耿於懷。(= *Don't give it too much thought.* = *Don't give it too much weight.* = *Don't worry about it.*)

seriously ('sɪrɪəslɪ) *adv.* 認眞地

take sth. seriously 認眞看待某事

Don't take offense. 不要生氣。(= *Don't get angry.*)

offense (ə'fɛns) *n.* 生氣；無禮

take offense 生氣 (= *become angry or upset*)

Don't be offended. (不要覺得被冒犯。) 也可說成：
Don't be insulted. (不要覺得被侮辱。) No offense
intended. (沒有惡意。)

offend〔ə'fɛnd〕*v.* 冒犯；觸怒 (*= upset = cause anger*)

It's not an attack. (這不是攻擊。) 也可說成：I'm
not attacking you. (我不是在攻擊你。) I'm not
trying to hurt you. (我沒有想要傷害你。)

attack〔ə'tæk〕*n. v.* 攻擊

Get rid of any bad feeling. 擺脫任何不好的感覺。
(*= Cast aside any bad feeling. = Eliminate any
bad feeling.*) ***get rid of*** 擺脫；除去

feeling〔'filɪŋ〕*n.* 感覺；感受

Get it out of your system. 把它擺脫掉。(*= Get rid of
the feeling. = Get over it.*)

system〔'sɪstəm〕*n.* 系統；身體

get sth. ***out of*** one's ***system*** 擺脫 (煩惱等)

Get it off your chest. (把它傾吐出來。) 也可說成：
Express it. (把它說出來。) Unburden yourself.
(吐露自己的心事。)

chest〔tʃɛst〕*n.* 胸部；內心

get sth. ***off*** one's ***chest*** 傾吐心中的心事 (煩惱等)

PART 2

Unit 5
克服恐懼

Overcome fear.
克服恐懼。

Conquer fear.
征服恐懼。

Face your fears to succeed.
勝者無懼。

BOOK 4・PART 2

Meet the challenge.
迎接挑戰。

Accept the challenge.
接受挑戰。

Rise to the occasion.
隨機應變。

Never give up too soon.
勿棄之過早。

There may still be a chance.
皆有契機。

It's never over till it's over.
不到關頭不放棄。

PART 2

Unit 5 背景說明

碰到了困難，要面對它、接受它，解決它。恐懼無用，只是傷身。勇敢地迎接挑戰是上策。

Overcome fear. 克服恐懼。(= *Defeat your fears*.)
overcome〔͵ovɚˈkʌm〕*v.* 克服
fear〔fɪr〕*n.* 恐懼

Conquer fear. 征服恐懼。(= *Beat your fears*.)
conquer〔ˈkɑŋkɚ〕*v.* 征服

Face your fears to succeed. (面對你的恐懼才能成功。) 也可說成：If you want to succeed, you must be brave and deal with what you're afraid of.
(如果你想要成功，就必須勇敢應付你所害怕的事物。)
face〔fes〕*v.* 面對　　succeed〔səkˈsid〕*v.* 成功

Meet the challenge. (迎接挑戰。) 也可說成：Take the challenge. (接受挑戰。) Face the challenge.
(面對挑戰。)　　meet〔mit〕*v.* 迎接；面對
challenge〔ˈtʃælɪndʒ〕*n.* 挑戰

Accept the challenge. (接受挑戰。) 也可說成：
Confront the challenge. (要面對挑戰。)
accept〔əkˈsɛpt〕*v.* 接受

Rise to the occasion. (勇敢應戰；隨機應變。) 也可説
成：Face the challenge. (要面對挑戰。) Face the
test. (要面對考驗。) Take the responsibility. (要負
起責任。)　rise〔 raɪz 〕*v.* 起立；能應付；經得起 *< to >*
occasion〔 ə'keʒən 〕*n.* 場合；特別的大事
rise to the occasion　隨機應變；成功面對困難；臨危
不亂 (= *rise to the challenge*)

Never give up too soon. 絕不要太早放棄。(= *Don't
quit so fast.*)
give up　放棄　　soon〔 sun 〕*adv.* 早；快

There may still be a chance. 可能仍然還有機會。
(= *It may still be possible.*)
still〔 stɪl 〕*adv.* 仍然　　chance〔 tʃæns 〕*n.* 機會

It's never over till it's over. (事情不到結束前，都沒有
結束；直到最後時刻，才能一見分曉。) 也可説成：It's
not final. (還沒有到最後。) It's not the end. (還沒
有結束。) Things will change. (情況還會有變化。)
It's not over till the fat lady sings. (不到最後，不
見眞章；事情還不到最後，可能還有變數。)【源自德國作
曲家華格納的一部歌劇，劇中女武神出來時，就
是整部戲的大結局】　over〔 'ovɚ 〕*adv.*
結束；完畢　　till〔 tɪl 〕*conj.* 直到 (= *until*)
never…till~　直到~才…

PART 2

Unit 6
驕傲地走

Walk proudly.
驕傲地走。

Move with style.
優雅地走。

Show your stuff.
展現實力。

BOOK 4・PART 2

Have more energy.
注入活力。

Look more alert.
體現機敏。

Put some pep in your step.
昂首闊步。

Be less shy.
少害羞。

Be more outgoing.
外向些。

Come out of your shell.
解放吧。

PART 2

Unit 6 背景説明

平常走路的姿勢很重要，抬頭挺胸、昂首闊步，人
人佩服；垂頭喪氣，沒有人會同情你，自己最吃虧。

Walk proudly.（要驕傲地走。）也可説成：Walk
confidently.（要有自信地走。）（= *Move
confidently*.）　　proudly〔'praʊdlɪ〕*adv.* 驕傲地

Move with style.　要優雅地走。（= *Walk with
elegance*.）　　move〔muv〕*v.* 移動；走動
style〔staɪl〕*n.* 風格；優雅；風度

Show your stuff.　要展現你的能力。（= *Show what you
have*. = *Show what you are able to do*. = *Show what
you're capable of*.）也可説成：Show your skills.
（要展現你的技能。）　　show〔ʃo〕*v.* 展現
stuff〔stʌf〕*n.* 東西；特質　　*show one's stuff* 展現
某人的能力（= *show one's ability*）

Have more energy.　要更有活力。（= *Show more
energy*. = *Be more energetic*. = *Be more lively*.）
energy〔'ɛnədʒɪ〕*n.* 精力；活力

Look more alert.（要看起來更機靈。）也可説成：
Look more energetic.（要看起來有活力。）

look〔lʊk〕v. 看起來

alert〔ə'lɝt〕adj. 警覺的;機警的;機靈的

Put some pep in your step. 在你的步伐中注入一些活
力,引申為「要更有活力。」(= *Be more energetic.*)
也可說成:Be more enthusiastic. (要更熱情。)
(= *Be more zealous.*)

pep〔pɛp〕n. 元氣;活力;精力

step〔stɛp〕n. 腳步;足跡;步調

put some pep in one's ***step*** 要更有活力

Be less shy. 不要那麼害羞。(= *Don't be so shy.*)

less〔lɛs〕adv. 較少　　shy〔ʃaɪ〕adj. 害羞的

Be more outgoing. (要外向一點。) 也可說成:Be
sociable. (要善於交際。) Be friendly. (要友善。)

outgoing〔'aʊtˌgoɪŋ〕adj. 外向的;開朗的;愛交際的

Come out of your shell. 要從你的殼裡出來,引申為
「不要再沈默害羞了。」(= *Stop being shy.*)源自烏
龜遇到危險時,總是躲進龜殼中,而小鳥
必須破殼而出,才能自由飛翔。也可說成:
Be more sociable. (要更愛交際。)
Overcome your shyness. (要克服
你的害羞。)　　shell〔ʃɛl〕n. 殼

come out of one's ***shell*** 不再害羞;不再沈默

PART 2

Unit 7
有志氣

Be ambitious.
有志氣。

Be brave.
有勇氣。

**You'll be successful
for sure.**
必成功。

Pursue your passion.
追尋所愛。

**Find what makes
you happy.**
找出悅事。

Follow your dream!
追求夢想！

Push yourself.

鞭策自己。

Never be satisfied.

永不滿足。

Stay hungry, stay foolish.

求知若渴。

PART 2

Unit 7 背景説明

　　難得活一次，做你喜歡做的事情，不會累，最好是一石多鳥。我們用「完美英語之心靈盛宴」在「快手」、「抖音」上拍短視頻，作爲「董事長完美英語班」的上課教材，又編輯成書，一石三鳥。

Be ambitious.（要有志氣；要有抱負。）也可説成：
Raise your expectations.（要有更高的期望。）
Want more.（要想得到更多。）
ambitious〔æmˈbɪʃəs〕*adj.* 有抱負的

Be brave. 要勇敢。(= *Be courageous.* = *Be daring.*
= *Be bold.* = *Be fearless.*)
brave〔brev〕*adj.* 勇敢的

You'll be successful for sure. 你一定會成功。(= *You
will certainly succeed.*)
successful〔səkˈsɛsfəl〕*adj.* 成功的　***for sure*** 一定

Pursue your passion. 追求你所喜愛的事；做你喜愛的事。(= *Do what you love.*)
pursue〔pɚˈsu〕*v.* 追求 (= *go after*)；進行；從事
passion〔ˈpæʃən〕*n.* 熱情；熱愛的事；愛好

Find what makes you happy. 要找到能使你快樂的事。(= *Discover what gives you happiness.*)

Follow your dream! 追求你的夢想！(= *Pursue your dream!*) 也可説成：Make your dream come true! (要讓你的夢想實現！) Make your dreams come true! (要讓你的夢想實現！) Go after what you want! (追求你想要的！)   follow〔ˋfalo〕*v.* 追隨； 追求；為…而奮鬥   dream〔drim〕*n.* 夢；夢想

Push yourself. (要鞭策自己。) 可加長為：Always push yourself. (一定要鞭策自己。) 也可説成：Work hard. (要努力。)
push〔puʃ〕*v.* 推；推動；驅策 (= *compel* = *force*)

Never be satisfied. 永不滿足。(= *Always want more.*) 也可説成：Don't be complacent. (不要自滿。)
satisfied〔ˋsætɪsˏfaɪd〕*adj.* 滿意的；滿足的

Stay hungry, stay foolish. (保持飢餓，保持愚笨；求知 若飢，虛心若愚。) 這是賈伯斯 (Steve Jobs) 在 2005 年美國史丹佛大學畢業典禮上，送給畢業生的話，勉勵 學生們帶著傻氣勇往直前，學習任何有趣的事物。也可 説成：Never stop learning. (要不停學習。) Always try new things. (要一直嘗試新事物。) Keep trying even if people say it cannot be done. (即使大家都 說辦不到，還是要持續努力。)   stay〔ste〕*v.* 保持 hungry〔ˋhʌŋgrɪ〕*adj.* 飢餓的；渴望的
foolish〔ˋfulɪʃ〕*adj.* 愚蠢的

PART 2

Unit 8
格外努力

Give extra effort.
格外努力。

Do more than others.
做勝他人。

Go out of your way.
特別努力。

BOOK 4 • PART 2

Bend over backwards.

全力以赴。

Do more than required.

多過要求。

Exceed what's expected.

超乎預期。

**Try every way
  possible.**
嘗試一切。

**Do everything
  you can.**
竭盡一切。

**Use every trick
  in the book.**
渾身解數。

BOOK 4 · PART 2

PART 2

Unit 8 背景説明

別人工作八小時，你也工作八小時，不可能成功。唯有全心投入，竭盡一切，使出渾身解數，才有成功的機會。

Give extra effort. 要格外努力。(= *Try harder.* = *Work harder.*)　　give〔gɪv〕*v.* 付出
extra〔'ɛkstrə〕*adj.* 額外的；特別的；格外的
effort〔'ɛfət〕*n.* 努力

Do more than others. (要做得比其他人多。) 也可説成：Do more. (要多做一點。) Surpass expectations. (要超出預期。)

Go out of your way. 要特別努力。(= *Take special pains.* = *Exert yourself.* = *Bend over backwards.*)
go out of** one's **way 特別努力 (= *do something even though it causes one some inconvenience*)

Bend over backwards. 竭盡全力；全力以赴。(= *Do all you can.*) 也可説成：Make extra effort. (要格外努力。) Go out of your way. (要特別努力。)
bend〔bɛnd〕*v.* 彎曲
backwards〔'bæk,wərdz〕*adv.* 往後
bend over backwards 後仰；拼命 (做某事)

Do more than required. 要做得比要求的多。(= *Do more than is required.* = *Do more than what is required.*) 　　require〔 rɪ'kwaɪr 〕*v.* 要求

Exceed what's expected. (要超乎預期。) 也可說成： Do more than others expect. (要做得比別人期望的多。) Do more than you are expected to do. (要做得比別人預期的多。) Exceed expectations. (要超出預期。)　　exceed〔 ɪk'sid 〕*v.* 超過 expect〔 ɪk'spɛkt 〕*v.* 期待；預期

Try every way possible. 「要嘗試每一個可能的方法。」 也就是「要嘗試各種方法。」(= *Try every possible way.*)　　try〔 traɪ 〕*v.* 嘗試　　way〔 we 〕*n.* 方法 possible〔 'pɑsəbl̩ 〕*adj.* 可能的

Do everything you can. 要盡全力。(= *Do all you can.* = *Do as much as you can.*)

Use every trick in the book. 要使出渾身解數。(= *Try every way.* = *Do everything possible.* = *Try every available method to achieve it.*) trick〔 trɪk 〕*n.* 把戲；招數 ***in the book*** 記錄在案的；為人所知的 ***every trick in the book*** 每一種招數 (或計謀)；所有可能的辦法；渾身解數 (= *every possible way*)

PART 2

Unit 9
耐心等待

Wait patiently.
耐心等待。

Bide your time.
等待良機。

Good things come to those who wait.
忍為上策。

Just be patient.
給點耐心。

Wait till the end.
等到最後。

**Save the best
for last.**
別急著吃棉花糖。

Don't rush it.
別著急。

Don't be in a hurry.
別匆忙。

**Don't get ahead
of yourself.**
別操之過急。

BOOK 4 · PART 2

PART 2

Unit 9 背景說明

　　每個人都想一夜之間成功，結果都失敗了。只要目標鎖定，方法正確，就會有成功的一天。

Wait patiently. (要耐心等待。) 也可說成：Hold your horses. (稍安勿躁。)

wait〔wet〕*v.* 等；等待

patiently〔'peʃəntlɪ〕*adv.* 有耐心地

Bide your time. (等待良機。) 也可說成：Wait. (要等待。) Be patient. (要有耐心。) Wait and see. (等等看；等著瞧。)　　bide〔baɪd〕*v.* 等待

bide one's time 等待良機

Good things come to those who wait. 源自諺語：All things come to those who wait. 意思是「懂得等待的人是最大的贏家；忍為上策。」也可說成：Patience is a virtue. (忍耐是一種美德。) Patience will be rewarded. (忍耐會有回報。)

Just be patient. (就是要有耐心。) 也可說成：Be patient. (要有耐心。) Hold your horses. (稍安勿躁。) Bide your time. (等待良機。)

just〔dʒʌst〕*adv.* 只；就

patient〔'peʃənt〕*adj.* 有耐心的

Wait till the end. 要等到最後。(= *Wait till last.*)
till〔 tɪl 〕*prep.* 直到 (= *until*)
end〔 ɛnd 〕*n.* 最後；末尾

Save the best for last. 把最好的留在最後；別急著吃
棉花糖。(= *Keep the most appealing thing for the
end.*)【《先別急著吃棉花糖》是 2006 年出版的一本勵志小
說，說明成功與失敗並非取決於一個人的才智，而是是否有
「延遲享樂」的能耐，想成功，就別急著吃掉棉花糖！】
save〔 sev 〕*v.* 保存　　last〔 læst 〕*n.* 最後；結尾

Don't rush it. 別著急。(= *Don't hurry it.* = *Don't
push it.*) 也可說成：Take your time. (慢慢來。)
rush〔 rʌʃ 〕*v.* 催促；使急速行進；使趕緊　*n.* 匆忙

Don't be in a hurry. 別匆忙。(= *Don't hurry.*
= *Don't rush.*) 也可說成：Be patient. (要有耐心。)
hurry〔 ˈhɝɪ 〕*n. v.* 匆忙 (= *rush*)
in a hurry 匆忙 (= *in a rush*)

Don't get ahead of yourself. 別操之過急。(= *Don't
be in such a hurry.* = *Don't be in such a rush.*
= *Don't be hasty.* = *Don't be rash.*) 也可說成：Do
things one step at a time. (做事情要一步一步來。)
Focus on what you are doing. (專注於你正在做的
事。)　　***get ahead of*** oneself 操之過急 (= *do or
say something sooner than it ought to be done*)

PART 2 總整理

Unit 1

Join in. 要加入。
Pitch in. 要參與。
Chip in. 參一腳。

Contribute! 付出！
Participate! 參與！
Play a part! 參與其中！

Get very involved.
深入其中。
Get close to it.
與之接近。
Be on it like white on
  rice. 形影不離。

Unit 2

Keep your word.
一言九鼎。
Honor your word.
一諾千金。
Your word is your bond.
言出必行。

Keep your promise.
遵守承諾。

Stay true to your promise.
信守承諾。
Don't break your promise.
切勿食言。

Do as you promised.
言出必行。
Do as you agreed.
遵照諾言。
Hold up your end of the
  bargain. 恪守承諾。

Unit 3

Believe in yourself.
相信自己。
Your potential is
  unlimited. 潛力無限。
The world is yours to
  conquer. 征服世界。

You're capable.
你有能力。
You're competent.
你很能幹。
Nothing can stop you.
無法可擋。

You will succeed.
你會成功。
You're the right person.
天選之人。
I'm confident you can do it. 信你可及。

Unit 4

Don't take it to heart.
勿掛心。
Don't take it too hard.
勿傷感。
Don't take it seriously.
勿當真。

Don't take offense.
切勿生氣。
Don't be offended.
勿感冒犯。
It's not an attack.
並非攻擊。

Get rid of any bad feeling.
除去惡感。
Get it out of your system.
擺脫煩惱。
Get it off your chest.
吐露心事。

Unit 5

Overcome fear. 克服恐懼。
Conquer fear. 征服恐懼。
Face your fears to succeed. 勝者無懼。

Meet the challenge.
迎接挑戰。
Accept the challenge.
接受挑戰。
Rise to the occasion.
隨機應變。

Never give up too soon.
勿棄之過早。
There may still be a chance. 皆有契機。
It's never over till it's over. 不到關頭不放棄。

Unit 6

Walk proudly. 驕傲地走。
Move with style. 優雅地走。
Show your stuff. 展現實力。

Have more energy.
注入活力。
Look more alert. 體現機敏。
Put some pep in your step. 昂首闊步。

BOOK 4 · PART 2

Be less shy. 少害羞。
Be more outgoing. 外向些。
Come out of your shell.
解放吧。

Unit 7

Be ambitious. 有志氣。
Be brave. 有勇氣。
You'll be successful for
    sure. 必成功。

Pursue your passion.
追尋所愛。
Find what makes you
    happy. 找出悅事。
Follow your dream!
追求夢想！

Push yourself. 鞭策自己。
Never be satisfied.
永不滿足。
Stay hungry, stay foolish.
求知若渴。

Unit 8

Give extra effort.
格外努力。
Do more than others.
做勝他人。
Go out of your way.
特別努力。

Bend over backwards.
全力以赴。
Do more than required.
多過要求。
Exceed what's expected.
超乎預期。

Try every way possible.
嘗試一切。
Do everything you can.
竭盡一切。
Use every trick in the
    book. 渾身解數。

Unit 9

Wait patiently. 耐心等待。
Bide your time. 等待良機。
Good things come to
    those who wait.
忍為上策。

Just be patient. 給點耐心。
Wait till the end.
等到最後。
Save the best for last.
別急著吃棉花糖。

Don't rush it. 別著急。
Don't be in a hurry.
別匆忙。
Don't get ahead of
    yourself. 別操之過急。

PART 3

Unit 1
要有所改變

PART 3・Unit 1~9
中英文錄音QR碼
英文唸2遍，中文唸1遍

Make a change.
要有所改變。

Make a real difference.
要造成影響。

Make the world a better place.
讓世界更好。

Help others.
要幫助別人。

Be of service.
要提供幫助。

**Be an asset to
the world.**
為世界資產。

**Have a positive
effect on people.**
對於人有正面影響。

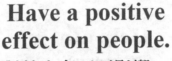

**Have a positive
effect on the earth.**
對世界有正面影響。

**Create positive change
everywhere you go.**
到處創造正面影響。

PART 3

Unit 1 背景説明

美國人常説：Make a difference. 字面的意思是「要有所不同。」引申爲「要做大事；要產生影響。」我們要把握機會，隨時隨地幫助別人。

Make a change. 要改變。(= *Change.*) 也可説成：
Do something different. (要做點不一樣的事。)
change〔 tʃendʒ 〕 *n.* 改變

Make a real difference. 要造成眞正的影響。(= *Be impactful.*) 也可説成：Do something meaningful.
(要做一些有意義的事。)　　real〔'riəl 〕 *adj.* 眞的
difference〔'dɪfərəns 〕 *n.* 不同
make a difference 造成影響

Make the world a better place. (要使世界成爲更好的地方；要使世界變得更好。) 也可説成：Do something
to improve the world. (要做點事改善這個世界。)
make〔 mek 〕 *v.* 使成爲

Help others. (要幫助別人。) 也可説成：Be helpful.
(要有幫助。) Be willing to help. (要願意幫忙。)

Be of service. 要幫忙。(= *Be helpful.* = *Be useful.*)
service〔'sɝvɪs 〕 *n.* 服務；有用；效勞；幫助
of service 有用的；有幫助的

Be an asset to the world. (要成爲世界的資產。) 也可說成：Be of use. (要有用。) Do something good for the world. (要爲世界做點好事。)

asset〔'æsɛt〕*n.* 資產 *< to >*

Have a positive effect on people. 要對人有正面的影響。(= *Influence people in a good way*.)

positive〔'pɑzətɪv〕*adj.* 正面的
effect〔ə'fɛkt , ɪ'fɛkt〕*n.* 影響 *< on >*

Have a positive effect on the earth. (要對地球有正面的影響。) 也可說成：Do something good for the world. (要爲世界做一些好事。)

earth〔ɝθ〕*n.* 地球

Create positive change everywhere you go. (無論你去到哪裡，都要創造正面的改變。) 也可說成：Make things better wherever you are. (無論你在哪裡，都要讓一切變得更好。) Improve things whenever you can. (要儘可能讓情況變得更好。)

create〔krɪ'et〕*v.* 創造
everywhere〔'ɛvrɪ͵hwɛr〕*adv.* 到處；無論何處

PART 3

Unit 2
挑戰自己

Challenge yourself.
挑戰自己。

Climb every mountain.
面對挑戰。

Change and grow.
蛻變成長。

**Work on yourself
every day.**
每天進步。

**Make strides
every year.**
每年進步。

**Plugging away
brings happiness.**
堅持生樂。

Excel!
超越巔峰！

Climb the ladder!
努力向上！

Work your hardest to succeed!
全力求勝！

PART 3

Unit 2 背景說明

　　每天進步、每年進步、堅持到底，你才會越來越快樂。一年比一年好，你會向前看，不會害怕變老。

Challenge yourself. (挑戰自己。) 也可說成：Test yourself. (考驗自己。)
challenge〔'tʃælɪndʒ〕*v. n.* 挑戰

Climb every mountain. 要爬每一座山，引申為「要接受每一個挑戰。」(= *Accept every challenge*. = *Take every challenge*.)　　climb〔klaɪm〕*v.* 爬；攀登
mountain〔'maʊntn̩〕*n.* 山

Change and grow. (要改變並且成長。) 也可說成：
Change and improve. (要改變並且進步。)
change〔tʃendʒ〕*v.* 改變　　grow〔gro〕*v.* 成長

Work on yourself every day. 每天都要致力於改善自己，引申為「每天都要讓自己更好。」(= *Better yourself every day*. = *Improve yourself every day*.)
work on 致力於；努力對付　　*work on yourself* 使自己更好 (= *better yourself* = *improve yourself*)

Make strides every year. 每年進步。(= *Advance every year*. = *Progress every year*.)

stride〔straɪd〕*n.* 大步的行走；(*pl.*) 進步
make strides 進步 (= *progress* = *advance*)

Plugging away brings happiness. (努力不懈令人
快樂。) 也可說成：Persistence will lead to
happiness. (堅忍不拔會令人快樂。)
plug〔plʌg〕*n.* 塞子；插頭　*v.* 孜孜不倦地做
plug away 堅持不懈 (= *work steadily* = *persist*
= *persevere* = *keep going*)

Excel! (要勝過別人！) 也可說成：Stand out! (要很
傑出！) Be the best! (要成爲最好的！)
excel〔ɪk'sɛl〕*v.* 突出 (= *stand out*)；勝過別人
(= *outshine everyone else*)

Climb the ladder! 爬上晉升的階梯，也就
是「要努力向上；要飛黃騰達！」也可說成：
Move up! (要向上 提升！) Go places!
(要獲得成功！) Forge ahead! (要突飛猛進！)
ladder〔'lædɚ〕*n.* 梯子；(出人頭地等的) 途徑；手段

Work your hardest to succeed! (盡全力成功！) 也
可說成：Do all you can in order to achieve your
goal! (要盡全力達成你的目標！)
work hard 努力　***work*** *one's* ***hardest*** 盡全力
succeed〔sək'sid〕*v.* 成功

PART 3

Unit 3
努力才有

Work for it.
努力才有。

Pay the price.
付出代價。

Put in the hard work.
付出努力。

**Follow your
goals forever.**

永隨目標。

Never let go.

絕不放手。

**Hold on tight to
your dreams.**

緊抓夢想。

Be sensational.
引起轟動。

**Do something
remarkable.**
引人注目。

**Set the world
on fire.**
一舉成名。

PART 3

Unit 3 背景說明

　　過去替我工作的美國人，常喜歡要求提高薪水，我就會說：*Work for it*.（努力才有。）

Pay the price.（要付出代價。）也可說成：Pay your dues.（要付出努力。）

price〔praɪs〕*n.* 價格；代價

Put in the hard work.（要付出努力。）也可說成：Be willing to work hard.（要願意努力。）Don't take shortcuts.（不要走捷徑。）Work hard to get what you want.（要努力獲得你想要的。）

put in 付出　　*hard work* 努力

Follow your goals forever. 要永遠追求你的目標。（= *Always pursue your goals*.）也可說成：Never give up on what you want.（絕不要放棄你想要的。）

follow〔'falo〕*v.* 追隨；追求（= *go after*）

goal〔gol〕*n.* 目標　　forever〔fə'ɛvə〕*adv.* 永遠

Never let go.（絕不放手。）也可說成：Never give up.（絕不放棄。）

let go 放開；鬆手；放下

Hold on tight to your dreams. (緊緊抓住你的夢想。)
也可説成：Don't give up on your dreams. (不要放
棄你的夢想。) (= *Never give up your dreams*.)
hold on to 堅持；緊抓；抓住不放
tight〔taɪt〕*adv.* 緊緊地；牢牢地

Be sensational. (要引起轟動。) 也可説成：Be
amazing. (要令人驚奇。) Be extraordinary. (要令
人驚訝。)　　sensational〔sɛn'seʃənḷ〕*adj.* 轟動的；
極好的

Do something remarkable.　要做了不起的事。(= *Do
something outstanding*. = *Do something amazing*.)
remarkable〔rɪ'mɑrkəbḷ〕*adj.* 引人注目的；出色的；
非凡的；卓越的

Set the world on fire. (要一舉成名。) 也可説成：
Make a name for yourself. (要功成名就。) Do
something sensational. (要做轟轟烈烈的事。)
(= *Do something outstanding*. = *Do something
remarkable*.)
set ~ on fire 放火燒～
set the world on fire 大爲成功；一舉成名；轟動世界

PART 3

Unit 4
不報仇

Don't take revenge.
不報仇。

Don't play dirty.
不耍陰。

Let karma do
the work.
因果自罰。

Forget tit for tat.
忘卻以牙還牙。

**Forget an eye
for an eye.**
忘卻以眼還眼。

Just let it go.
放手吧。

**Never hurt those
who hurt you.**

絕不傷傷你之人。

**Never return
bad for bad.**

絕不冤冤相報。

**Two wrongs don't
make a right.**

【諺】積非不能成是。

PART 3

Unit 4 背景説明

　　有仇不要報，浪費心思，划不來。不如把它放下（Let it go.），老天爺自然會懲罰他。(Let karma do the work.)

Don't take revenge. 不要報仇。(= *Don't seek vengeance. = Don't try to get even.*)
revenge〔rɪˋvɛndʒ〕*n.* 報仇；報復
take revenge 報仇；報復

Don't play dirty. (不要耍花招。) 也可說成：Don't cheat. (不要欺騙。) Don't hit below the belt. (不要用不正當的手段攻擊別人。)
play dirty 欺騙；耍花招

Let karma do the work. (讓因果報應來做這工作。) 也可說成：What goes around comes around. (【諺】善有善報，惡有惡報。)　　karma〔ˋkɑrmə〕*n.* 羯磨；業【宗教名詞】；命運；因果報應

Forget tit for tat. (不要想以牙還牙。) 也可說成：Don't try to get even. (不要想報復。)
forget〔fɚˋgɛt〕*v.* 忘記；不再把…放在心上
tit〔tɪt〕*n.* 山雀；呆子　　tat〔tæt〕*n.* 輕打
tit for tat 以牙還牙；針鋒相對；一報還一報

Forget an eye for an eye. 不要想以眼還眼。
(= *Forget tit for tat.*) 也可說成：Forget getting
revenge. (不要想報仇。) (= *Don't try to get even.*)

an eye for an eye 以牙還牙；以眼還眼

Just let it go. 就算了吧。(= *Just forget about it.*)

just〔dʒʌst〕*adv.* 就　　***let it go*** 放手別管；不讓某事
困擾你；就此罷休；不再追究

Never hurt those who hurt you. (絕不要傷害傷害你
的人。) 也可說成：Don't hit back. (不要反擊。)
Don't take revenge. (不要報仇。)

hurt〔hɜt〕*v.* 傷害【三態同形】

Never return bad for bad. 絕不要冤冤相報。(= *Never
do something bad in return.*)

return〔rɪ'tɜn〕*v.* 回報　　bad〔bæd〕*n.* 壞；壞的事物

return bad for bad 以怨報怨

Two wrongs don't make a right. 【諺】積非不能成
是；別人錯了，你照做也不對。(= *It is not right for
you to act in a similar way.*) 也可說成：Revenge
is wrong. (報仇是錯的。) There's no excuse for
bad behavior. (不良的行為沒有任何藉口。)

wrong〔rɔŋ〕*n.* 壞事；不良的行為

make〔mek〕*v.* 等於　　right〔raɪt〕*n.* 正當的行為

PART 3

Unit 5
寬容大量

Be forgiving.
寬容大量。

To err is human.
【諺】人皆有錯。

We all make mistakes.
人皆犯錯。

Get over it.

忘卻。

Get past it.

遺忘。

Stop thinking about it.

勿想。

Think positively.
樂觀思考。

Focus on the future.
專注未來。

Focus on this
wonderful life.
專注美好人生。

PART 3

Unit 5 背景説明

　　　人皆犯錯，原諒別人，也要原諒自己。樂觀思考，
專注未來，專注美好人生。説起來容易，做起來難，朝
這個目標前進，你會很快樂。

Be forgiving.（要寬宏大量。）也可説成：Forgive
others.（要原諒別人。）Be compassionate.（要有
同情心。）Be merciful.（要慈悲。）
forgiving〔fɚˋgɪvɪŋ〕*adj.* 寬容的；寬宏大量的

To err is human.（犯錯是人；人皆有錯。）是一句諺語，
也可説成：To err is human, to forgive, divine.
（【諺】犯錯是人，寬恕是神。）　err〔ɝ, ɛr〕*v.* 犯錯
human〔ˋhjumən〕*adj.* 人的

We all make mistakes. 我們都會犯錯。(= *Everyone
makes mistakes.*) 也可説成：Even Homer
sometimes nods.（【諺】智者千慮，必有一失。）
mistake〔məˋstek〕*n.* 錯誤
make a mistake 犯錯

Get over it. 忘了吧。(= *Forget about it.*) 也可説成：
Move on.（繼續向前進。）
get over 克服；把⋯忘掉

Get past it. 忘了吧。(= *Forget about it.*) 也可說成：
Let it go. (算了吧。) Come to terms with it. (要
逐漸接受。)　　***get past*** 克服；越過

Stop thinking about it. (不要再想它。) 也可說成：
Forget about it. (忘了吧。)
stop + V-ing 停止…
think about 考慮；想到

Think positively. 要正向思考。(= *Think positive.*)
也可說成：Be positive. (要樂觀。) Be optimistic.
(要樂觀。)
positively〔ˈpɑzətɪvlɪ〕*adv.* 正面地；積極地

Focus on the future. (專注於未來。) 也可說成：
Keep your eye on the future. (專注於未來。)
Look to the future. (展望未來。)
focus〔ˈfokəs〕*v.* 專注　　***focus on*** 專注於
future〔ˈfjutʃɚ〕*n.* 未來

Focus on this wonderful life. 專注於現在美好的人
生。(= *Concentrate on how good life is.*) 也可說
成：Remember how wonderful life is. (要記得
人生有多美好。)　　***this life*** 今生
wonderful〔ˈwʌndɚfəl〕*adj.* 極好的；很棒的

PART 3

Unit 6
人生是一場
自助餐

Life is a buffet.
人生是一場自助餐。

Fill up your plate.
裝滿你的盤子。

Really pig out.
瘋狂享用。

Life is a banquet.
人生如盛宴。

Feast like a king.
饗用如國王。

Enjoy every bite.
享受每一口。

Life is a party.

人生如派對。

Celebrate every day!

天天慶祝！

Really whoop it up!

盡情狂歡！

PART 3

Unit 6　背景説明

　　人只能活一次（You only live once.），要盡情享受人生。浪費時間，就等於浪費生命。

Life is a buffet.（人生是一場自助餐。）也可説成：There is a variety of things in life.（人生有各式各樣的事物。）There are many opportunities in life.（人生有很多機會。）　　buffet〔bʌˋfe〕*n.* 自助餐；吃到飽（= *all-you-can-eat buffet*）

Fill up your plate.（要把你的盤子裝滿。）也可説成：Take as much as you can.（要儘可能多拿一點。）
fill up 裝滿；填滿　　plate〔plet〕*n.* 盤子

Really pig out.（眞的要大吃特吃。）也可説成：Eat to your heart's content.（要盡情地吃。）
really〔ˋriəlɪ〕*adv.* 眞地　　pig〔pɪg〕*n.* 豬　*v.* 狼吞虎嚥；大吃　***pig out*** 狼吞虎嚥地大吃

Life is a banquet.（人生是一場盛宴。）也可説成：There is a variety of opportunities in life.（人生有各式各樣的機會。）There are many things in life.（人生有很多事物。）
banquet〔ˋbæŋkwɪt〕*n.* 盛宴

Feast like a king.（要吃得像國王。）也可說成：
Eat well.（要吃得好。）Take only the best.（只
拿最好的。）　　feast〔fist〕*n.* 盛宴　*v.* 參加宴會；
盡情地吃；享受　　like〔laɪk〕*prep.* 像
king〔kɪŋ〕*n.* 國王

Enjoy every bite.（每一口都要好好享用。）也可說成：
Enjoy every second.（要享受每一秒。）Enjoy
everything you do.（要好好享受你做的每一件事。）
enjoy〔ɪn'dʒɔɪ〕*v.* 享受　　bite〔baɪt〕*n.* 一口（食物）

Life is a party.（人生是一場派對。）也可說成：Life is
great.（人生很美好。）Life is fun.（人生很有趣。）
party〔'pɑrtɪ〕*n.* 派對

Celebrate every day!（要每天慶祝！）也可說成：
Enjoy every day!（要享受每一天！）Be thankful
for every day!（要對每一天心存感激！）
（= *Appreciate every day!*）
celebrate〔'sɛlə,bret〕*v.* 慶祝；歡樂

Really whoop it up!（真的要盡情狂歡！）也可說成：
Enjoy yourself!（要玩得愉快！）（= *Have fun!*
= *Have a good time!* = *Have a ball!*）
whoop〔hup, hwup, wup〕*v.* 高喊；呐喊
whoop it up 狂歡；歡鬧
美國人常說：Let's whoop it up!（我們狂歡吧！）

PART 3

Unit 7
常表感謝

Always express thanks.

常表感謝。

Always show gratitude.

常表感激。

Don't take a kindness for granted.

勿視好為應當。

**Always repay
a favor.**
要報恩。

**Do whatever
you can.**
要盡力。

**Recognize that
you owe a debt.**
要懂人情。

Be appreciative.
要心存感激。

Thank others profusely.
要一再道謝。

You can never be too grateful.
感謝不嫌多。

PART 3

Unit 7 背景説明

有人肯借你錢，非常難得，要珍惜，要表示感謝；不還錢，就是恩將仇報，這種習慣非常可怕。

Always express thanks. (一定要表達感謝。) 也可説成：Never forget to express your gratitude. (絶不要忘記表達你的感激。)　express〔ɪkˈsprɛs〕*v.* 表達　thanks〔θæŋks〕*n. pl.* 感謝；感激

Always show gratitude.　一定要表示感激。(= *Always be grateful.*)　show〔ʃo〕*v.* 展現；表示 gratitude〔ˈgrætəˌtjud〕*n.* 感激

Don't take a kindness for granted. (不要把別人的幫助視爲理所當然。) 也可説成：Appreciate other people's help. (要感激別人的幫助。) ***take…for granted*** 把…視爲理所當然 kindness〔ˈkaɪndnɪs〕*n.* 仁慈；善意；親切的行爲 (= *kind act*)

Always repay a favor. (一定要回報恩惠。) 也可説成：If someone does you a favor, do him a favor in return. (如果有人幫助你，也要幫助他作爲回報。) repay〔rɪˈpe〕*v.* 回報　favor〔ˈfevɚ〕*n.* 恩惠

Do whatever you can. (要盡你所能。) 也可說成：Do anything you can to help him. (要盡力幫助他。)

whatever〔hwɑt'ɛvɚ〕*pron.* 任何…的事物；不管什麼

Recognize that you owe a debt. (要知道你欠了一個人情。) 也可說成：Remember that you owe him. (要記得你欠他人情。)

recognize〔'rɛkəg,naɪz〕*v.* 承認；認清

owe〔o〕*v.* 欠　　debt〔dɛt〕*n.* 債務；情義

owe a debt 欠了一筆債；欠了一個人情

Be appreciative. 要心存感激。(= *Be grateful.* = *Be thankful.*)

appreciative〔ə'priʃɪ,etɪv〕*adj.* 感激的

Thank others profusely. 要一再地向別人道謝。(= *Be effusive in your thanks.*) 也可說成：Express your gratitude freely. (要儘量表達感激。)

profusely〔prə'fjuslɪ〕*adv.* 大量地；豐富地

You can never be too grateful. 你再怎麼感激也不爲過。(= *It's impossible to be too grateful.* = *It's not possible to have too much gratitude.*)

can never be too 再…也不爲過；越…越好

grateful〔'gretfəl〕*adj.* 感激的

PART 3

Unit 8
你心地很善良

Tell people: 要跟別人說：

You're too kind.
你心地很善良。

**I'm stunned by
your generosity.**
慷慨令我折服。

**You've touched
my heart.**
所為令我感動。

Always say: 一定要說：

I'm so grateful for all you've done.
我感激你所為。

How can I ever repay you?
我該如何報答？

Words are not enough.
言語無法形容。

Remember to express
your gratitude:
要記得表達你的感激：

I'm moved to tears.
感動落淚。

I'm overwhelmed.
無法承受。

A thousand thanks.
萬分感謝。

PART 3

Unit 8 背景說明

光說 "Thank you." 是不夠的，要一次說三句，還要在不同時間說三次。

kind〔kaɪnd〕*adj.* 親切的；好心的

I'm stunned by your generosity. 你的慷慨使我驚訝。（ = *I'm amazed by how generous you are.* = *Your kindness is amazing.*）

stun〔stʌn〕*v.* 使吃驚；使目瞪口呆

generosity〔ˌdʒɛnəˈrɑsətɪ〕*n.* 慷慨；大方

You've touched my heart.（你感動了我的心。）也可說成：I'm so moved by what you did.（你所做的事讓我非常感動。）　　touch〔tʌtʃ〕*v.* 感動

touch one's heart 感動某人的心

grateful〔ˈgretfəl〕*adj.* 感激的

be grateful for 對…心存感激

How can I ever repay you?（我究竟該如何報答你？）句中的 ever（究竟）用來加強語氣。也可說成：How can I ever thank you?（我要如何感謝你？）

ever〔ˈɛvɚ〕*adv.* 究竟；到底

repay〔rɪˈpe〕*v.* 回報

BOOK 4・PART 3

Words are not enough. (再多的言辭都是不夠的。) 也
可說成：I have to do more than just say thank
you. (我不能只是說謝謝你，我必須做更多。)
words〔 wɝdz 〕*n. pl.* 言辭；話
enough〔 ə'nʌf , ɪ'nʌf 〕*adj.* 足夠的

express〔 ɪk'sprɛs 〕*v.* 表達
gratitude〔'grætə,tjud 〕*n.* 感激

I'm moved to tears. 我感動得落淚。(= *I'm so touched*
I could cry.) 也可說成：I'm deeply touched. (我
深受感動。)
move〔 muv 〕*v.* 使感動　　tear〔 tɪr 〕*n.* 眼淚
be moved to tears 感動得落淚

I'm overwhelmed. (我激動得不知所措。) 也可說
成：I'm speechless. (我說不出話來。) I'm
flabbergasted. (我大吃一驚。) I'm amazed.
(我非常驚訝。)
overwhelm〔,ovɚ'hwɛlm 〕*v.* 使難以承受；使不知所措

A thousand thanks. 千謝萬謝；感激不盡；多謝。
(= *Many thanks*. = *Thank you so much*.)
thousand〔'θaʊzn̩d 〕*n.* 千
thanks〔 θæŋks 〕*n. pl.* 感謝；感激

BOOK 4・PART 3

PART 3

Unit 9
你幫了大忙

Say: 要說：

You made a big difference.

你幫了大忙。

You really helped so much.

你幫助很多。

All my thanks to you.

我很感謝你。

Tell others: 要跟別人說：

Your kindness is touching.
深感好意。

I'm full of gratitude.
滿懷感激。

Thank you from the bottom of my heart.
由衷感謝。

Express to others:
要向別人表達：

I'm indebted to you.
我感謝你。

I'm ever so grateful.
我很感激。

How can I return the favor?
如何報恩？

PART 3

Unit 9 背景説明

　　養成常説感謝的話的習慣，每一次都要用不同的句子，要累積很多高檔的句子，如：All my thanks to you.（我很感謝你。）

You made a big difference.（你產生很大的影響。）
也可説成：What you did really helped.（你所做的真的很有幫助。）What you did means a lot.（你所做的意義重大。）　　difference〔'dɪfərəns〕*n.* 不同
make a difference 產生影響

You really helped so much.（你眞的幫了很多忙。）
也可説成：You were a big help.（你幫了大忙。）

All my thanks to you. 我很感謝你。(= *I'm extremely grateful.* = *I'm so grateful to you.*)
thanks〔θæŋks〕*n. pl.* 感謝；感激

Your kindness is touching. 你的好意令人感動。
(= *Your kindness is moving.*) 也可説成：You've touched my heart.（你感動了我的心。）
kindness〔'kaɪndnɪs〕*n.* 仁慈；好意；親切的行爲
touching〔'tʌtʃɪŋ〕*adj.* 令人感動的（ = *moving* ）

I'm full of gratitude. (我充滿感激。) 也可説成：I'm extremely grateful. (我非常感激。)

full〔fʊl〕*adj.* 充滿的　　***be full of*** 充滿了

gratitude〔'grætə,tjud〕*n.* 感激

Thank you from the bottom of my heart. (我由衷地感謝你。) 也可説成：I can't thank you enough.
(我再怎麼感謝你都不夠。)

bottom〔'batəm〕*n.* 底部

from the bottom of *one's* ***heart*** 從內心深處；由衷地；真誠地

express〔ɪk'sprɛs〕*v.* 表達

I'm indebted to you. (我感激你。) 也可説成：I owe you. (我感謝你。) I owe you one. (我欠你一次人情。)　　indebted〔ɪn'dɛtɪd〕*adj.* 感激的

be indebted to 感激

I'm ever so grateful. 我非常感激。(= *I'm extremely grateful*.)　　***ever so*** 非常

grateful〔'gretfəl〕*adj.* 感激的

How can I return the favor? (我該如何報答你的恩惠？) 也可説成：How can I repay you? (我該如何報答你？)　　return〔rɪ'tɜn〕*v.* 回報；報答

favor〔'fevɚ〕*n.* 恩惠

PART 3　總整理

Unit 1

Make a change.
要有所改變。
Make a real difference.
要造成影響。
Make the world a better
　place. 讓世界更好。

Help others. 要幫助別人。
Be of service. 要提供幫助。
Be an asset to the world.
為世界資產。

Have a positive effect on
　people. 對於人有正面影響。
Have a positive effect on
　the earth.
對世界有正面影響。
Create positive change
　everywhere you go.
到處創造正面影響。

Unit 2

Challenge yourself.
挑戰自己。
Climb every mountain.
面對挑戰。
Change and grow.
蛻變成長。

Work on yourself every
　day. 每天進步。
Make strides every year.
每年進步。
Plugging away brings
　happiness. 堅持生樂。

Excel! 超越巔峰！
Climb the ladder!
努力向上！
Work your hardest to
　succeed! 全力求勝！

Unit 3

Work for it. 努力才有。
Pay the price. 付出代價。
Put in the hard work.
付出努力。

Follow your goals forever.
永隨目標。
Never let go. 絕不放手。
Hold on tight to your
　dreams. 緊抓夢想。

Be sensational. 引起轟動。
Do something remarkable.
引人注目。
Set the world on fire.
一舉成名。

Unit 4

Don't take revenge.
不報仇。
Don't play dirty.　不要陰。
Let karma do the work.
因果自罰。

Forget tit for tat.
忘卻以牙還牙。
Forget an eye for an eye.
忘卻以眼還眼。
Just let it go.　放手吧。

Never hurt those who hurt
　you.　絕不傷傷你之人。
Never return bad for bad.
絕不冤冤相報。
Two wrongs don't make a
　right.　【諺】積非不能成是。

Unit 5

Be forgiving.　寬容大量。
To err is human.
【諺】人皆有錯。
We all make mistakes.
人皆犯錯。

Get over it.　忘卻。
Get past it.　遺忘。
Stop thinking about it.
勿想。

Think positively.　樂觀思考。

Focus on the future.
專注未來。
Focus on this wonderful
　life.　專注美好人生。

Unit 6

Life is a buffet.
人生是一場自助餐。
Fill up your plate.
裝滿你的盤子。
Really pig out.　瘋狂享用。

Life is a banquet.
人生如盛宴。
Feast like a king.
饗用如國王。
Enjoy every bite.
享受每一口。

Life is a party.　人生如派對。
Celebrate every day!
天天慶祝！
Really whoop it up!
盡情狂歡！

Unit 7

Always express thanks.
常表感謝。
Always show gratitude.
常表感激。
Don't take a kindness for
　granted.　勿視好為應當。

Always repay a favor.
要報恩。
Do whatever you can.
要盡力。
Recognize that you owe
a debt.　要懂人情。

Be appreciative.
要心存感激。
Thank others profusely.
要一再道謝。
You can never be too
grateful.　感謝不嫌多。

Unit 8

Tell people:　要跟別人說：
You're too kind.
你心地很善良。
I'm stunned by your
generosity.
慷慨令我折服。
You've touched my heart.
所爲令我感動。

Always say:　一定要說：
I'm so grateful for all
you've done.
我感激你所爲。
How can I ever repay
you?　我該如何報答？
Words are not enough.
言語無法形容。

*Remember to express your
gratitude:*
要記得表達你的感激：
I'm moved to tears.　感動落淚。
I'm overwhelmed.　無法承受。
A thousand thanks.　萬分感謝。

Unit 9

Say:　要說：
You made a big difference.
你幫了大忙。
You really helped so much.
你幫助很多。
All my thanks to you.
我很感謝你。

Tell others:　要跟別人說：
Your kindness is touching.
深感好意。
I'm full of gratitude.
滿懷感激。
Thank you from the bottom
of my heart.　由衷感謝。

Express to others:
要向別人表達：
I'm indebted to you.
我感謝你。
I'm ever so grateful.
我很感激。
How can I return the favor?
如何報恩？

【劉毅老師的話】

Aim higher. 目標更高。

Aspire higher. 渴望更高。

Shoot higher. 志向更高。

人生到處是驚喜

有了「董事長完美英語班」，改變了我的人生，每天都在興奮中度過！

Life is beautiful. (生活絢爛。)
Life is amazing. (生命精彩。)
Life is full of surprises. (充滿驚喜。)

遇見二十多年前的學生，才華橫溢的王宣雯老師，協助我完成夢想，每月 50 萬元新台幣聘請她，非常值得。

魚翅大王吳昌林，讓我見識到真正的頂級美食，我把壽德大樓一樓出租給他，開雙語文創俱樂部，原價 29 萬，他出價 25 萬，但我只租 23 萬新台幣。

陳斯鴻同學的原子量能手環，幫助我更健康、睡得更好。朱芳其同學的負離子床墊，改善了我不好睡的問題。董事長班同學，人人都會「讓利」，我買到許多好的東西，都物超所值。

我請董事長班同學陳瀅瀅、卓豪盛做交誼廳的裝潢，比外面服務更好，而且優惠，和同學做生意特別安心，又有好的品質保障。

我一生的願望，是希望 14 億中國人都喜歡開口說英語。把長的句子，改編成短的三句，才記得住，說出來有力量。我背得下去，才當教材，在董事長班上過後，才放入《完美英語之心靈盛宴》，有靈魂的書必成經典。

Live happy. (活得開心。)
Die happy. (死得安樂。)
Live a life with no regrets. (生而無憾。)

用文法規則，無法造出前兩句，要當成慣用句來看。no regrets 是慣用語，一定要用複數形。這三句話，打動人心，背好以後，可以拯救悲觀的心靈，到死之前都要快樂，才無遺憾。

劉毅

PART 1

Unit 1
不要小氣

PART 1・Unit 1~9
中英文錄音QR碼
英文唸2遍，中文唸1遍

Don't be cheap.
不要小氣。

Don't be stingy.
不要吝嗇。

Try to treat others first.
搶先請客。

Give back.
要回饋。

Return favors.
要報答。

Give more, gain more.
付出多，得到多。

Enjoy giving.
樂於付出。

Enjoy sharing.
樂於分享。

You'll always win.
定會獲益。

PART 1

Unit 1 背景説明

　　「滴水之恩，當湧泉相報。」別人請你吃飯的時候，要搶著付錢，這是中國的文化。對別人的付出，不要忘記回報。

Don't be cheap. 不要小氣。(= *Don't be miserly.*
= *Don't be ungenerous.* = *Don't be parsimonious.*)
cheap〔tʃip〕*adj.* 便宜的；吝嗇的；小氣的

Don't be stingy. 不要吝嗇。(= *Don't be a
pennypincher.*)
stingy〔'stɪndʒɪ〕*adj.* 吝嗇的；小氣的

Try to treat others first. (要儘量先請別人。) 也可説成：Pay for others before they have a chance to pay for you. (在別人有機會為你付錢之前，先為他們付錢。) Offer to pay for others first. (要先主動為別人付錢。)
try to V. 試圖…；努力…
treat〔trit〕*v.* 款待；宴請　　first〔fɜst〕*adv.* 先

Give back. ①要歸還。②要回饋。(= *Return the favor.*
= *Reciprocate.*)

Return favors. 要報答恩惠。(= *Repay favors.*
= *Repay kindness.* = *Repay good deeds.*)
return 〔 rɪ'tɝn 〕 *v.* 回報；報答
favor 〔'fevɚ 〕 *n.* 恩惠

Give more, ***gain more***. 付出越多，得到越多。
(= *Give more and get more.* = *The more you
give, the more you will get.* = *If you give more,
you will get more.*)
give 〔 gɪv 〕 *v.* 給與；付出
gain 〔 gen 〕 *v.* 獲得

Enjoy giving. 樂於付出。(= *Find pleasure in
giving.* = *Take pleasure in being generous.*)
enjoy + ***V-ing*** 喜歡…

Enjoy sharing. 樂於分享。(= *Find pleasure in
sharing.* = *Take pleasure in giving some of
what you have.*)
share 〔 ʃɛr 〕 *v.* 分享

You'll always win. 你一定會贏，在此引申為「你
一定會獲益。」(= *You'll always benefit.*)
win 〔 wɪn 〕 *v.* 贏；獲勝；成功

PART 1

Unit 2
要有勇氣

Be courageous.
要有勇氣。

Grow a spine.
長點骨氣。

Get a backbone.
拿出骨氣。

BOOK 5・PART 1

Do it without fear.
做事無懼。

Don't worry or care.
無所擔憂。

Throw caution to the wind.
拋開謹慎。

Accept challenges.

接受挑戰。

Choose tough tasks.

迎難而上。

**The rest of your
life will be easy.**

餘生將安好。

PART 1

Unit 2 背景說明

只要不是生與死的問題，就沒什麼好害怕的。要拿出勇氣，接受挑戰。

Be courageous. (要有勇氣。) 也可說成：Be brave.
(要勇敢。) Be fearless. (要無所畏懼。) Be daring.
(要大膽。)

courageous〔 kə'redʒəs 〕*adj.* 有勇氣的

Grow Get Have	a	spine. backbone.	(長點骨氣；要有骨氣。)

grow〔 gro 〕*v.* 生長
spine〔 spaɪn 〕*n.* 脊柱；脊椎骨；勇氣
backbone〔'bæk,bon 〕*n.* 脊椎骨 (= *spine*)；骨氣
(= *courage and determination*)

Do it without fear. (要毫無恐懼地做。) 也可說成：
Do it confidently. (要有信心地做。)
fear〔 fɪr 〕*n.* 害怕；恐懼

Don't worry or care. (不要擔心。) 也可說成：Don't
be apprehensive. (不要憂慮。) Don't be uneasy.
(不要不安。) Be fearless. (要無所畏懼。)

worry〔'wɝɪ〕*v.* 擔心

care〔kɛr〕*v.* 在乎;憂慮;擔心

Throw caution to the wind. 字面的意思是「要把謹慎
   拋到九霄雲外。」即是「要不顧一切;要魯莽行事;要變
   得大膽;要勇於冒險。」(= *Take a risk.*) 也可說成:
   Take the bull by the horns.(要不畏艱難。)Go
   for it.(去做吧。)Just do it.(做就對了。)

throw〔θro〕*v.* 丟   caution〔'kɔʃən〕*n.* 謹慎;小心

wind〔wɪnd〕*n.* 風   ***throw ~ to the wind*** 讓風把~
   吹走;對~置之不理;不考慮 (= *fling ~ to the wind*)

Accept challenges.(要接受挑戰。)也可說成:Face
   challenges.(要面對挑戰。)

accept〔ək'sɛpt〕*v.* 接受

challenge〔'tʃælɪndʒ〕*n.* 挑戰

Choose tough tasks.(要選擇艱難的任務。)也可說
   成:Choose difficult over easy.(選擇困難,而非
   輕鬆的工作。)   choose〔tʃuz〕*v.* 選擇

tough〔tʌf〕*adj.* 困難的 (= *difficult*)

task〔tæsk〕*n.* 工作;任務

The rest of your life will be easy.(你的餘生將會很
   輕鬆。)也可說成:Your future will be smooth.
   (你的未來將是坦途。)   rest〔rɛst〕*n.* 剩餘

easy〔'izɪ〕*adj.* 容易的;輕鬆的

PART 1

Unit 3
裝作你會

Pretend you can.
裝作你會。

**Make believe
you can.**
假裝你會。

**Fake it till you
make it.**
弄假成真。

Achieve.
達成目標。

Achieve your potential.
發揮潛力。

**Great achievements
will follow.**
偉業將至。

Anything is possible.
世事皆可能。

Nothing is impossible.
無事不可達。

You can be or do anything.
萬事皆可達。

PART 1

Unit 3 背景説明

不會要裝會，裝久了，就會弄假成真。

Pretend you can. 假裝你會。(= *Act as if you can.*
= *Make believe that you can do it.*)
pretend〔prɪ'tɛnd〕*v.* 假裝

Make believe you can. 假裝你會。(= *Pretend that
you can.*)　　***make believe*** 假裝

Fake it till you make it. 一直假裝，直到你成功；成功，
從假裝開始。(= *Pretend that you can do it until you
actually can.*) 也可説成：Just pretend that you
know what you're doing and eventually you
will. (只要假裝你知道自己在做什麼，最後你就會知道
自己在做什麼。)【成功的心理技巧— modeling (模仿)：
假裝你是某人，然後直到你成為某人，學習他們怎麼做事，
並利用他們的方法，再加以改進】
fake〔fek〕*v.* 假裝；假裝⋯的樣子
till〔tɪl〕*conj.* 直到 (= *until*)　　***make it*** 成功；辦到

Achieve. 要達成目標。(= *Realize your goals.*) 也可
説成：Succeed. (要成功。) (= *Be successful.*)
achieve〔ə'tʃiv〕*v.* 達成；實現；達成目的

Achieve your potential. 要發揮你的潛力。(= *Be the best you can be.* = *Use all of your capabilities.*)

potential〔pəˈtɛnʃəl〕*n.* 潛力

achieve/fulfill/realize one's potential 發揮潛力

Great achievements will follow. 偉大的成就會隨之而來。(= *Then you will achieve great things.* = *Then you will be very successful.*)

great〔gret〕*adj.* 大的;偉大的

achievements〔əˈtʃivmənts〕*n. pl.* 成就

follow〔ˈfɑlo〕*v.* 跟隨;隨之而來

Anything is possible. 任何事都有可能。(= *Anything can happen.*)　possible〔ˈpɑsəbl̩〕*adj.* 可能的

Nothing is impossible. 沒有什麼是不可能的。
(= *Anything is possible.*)

impossible〔ɪmˈpɑsəbl̩〕*adj.* 不可能的

You can be or do anything. 你可以成為任何人或做任何事。(= *You can become anything you want or achieve anything you want.*) 也可說成:You can achieve whatever you want. (你可以達成任何你想達成的事。) You have no limits. (你沒有任何限制。)

be anything 成為任何人 (= *be whatever you want to be*)

BOOK 5・PART 1

PART 1

Unit 4
要現代化

Be modern.
要現代化。

Be up to date.
要最新的。

Keep up with the times.
要隨時代。

Get more informed.
廣納訊息。

Become more aware.
先知先覺。

Keep your mind open.
打開心胸。

Know what's going on.

知了其事。

Know what's happening.

知其發生。

Keep an ear to the ground.

保持警惕。

PART 1

Unit 4 背景說明

要注意周圍發生什麼事，要跟上時代，才不會被淘汰。

Be modern. 要現代化；要跟得上時代。(= *Keep up with the times.*) 也可説成：Be forward-looking.
(要有遠見。)

modern〔ˈmɑdən〕*adj.* 現代化的；時髦的；摩登的

Be up to date. (要知道最新的趨勢。) 也可説成：Be with it. (要消息靈通。) Be contemporary. (要跟得上時代。) Be fashionable. (要跟得上流行。)

up to date 不落後的；現代的；最新的 (= *modern* = *current*)

Keep up with the times. 要跟得上時代。(= *Move with the times.* = *Keep up to date.*) 也可説成：Stay informed. (要消息靈通。) Adapt to change.
(要適應改變。)   ***keep up with*** 跟得上

times〔taɪmz〕*n. pl.* 時代

Get more informed. 消息要更靈通一點。(= *Be better informed.*) 也可説成：Learn more. (要多知道一點。) Find out what's going on. (要知道發生了什麼事。) Find out what you need to know. (要知道你必須知道的事。)   get〔gɛt〕*v.* 變得

informed〔ɪnˈfɔrmd〕*adj.* 消息靈通的；見多識廣的

Become more aware. 要多知道一些。(= *Be better informed.*) 也可說成：Be knowledgeable. (要知識豐富。)

aware〔ə'wɛr〕*adj.* 知道的；察覺到的

Keep your mind open. 保持開明的心態。(= *Be open-minded.* = *Be broad-minded.*) 也可說成：Be willing to consider new ideas. (要願意考慮新的想法。)　　keep〔kip〕*v.* 使保持

mind〔maɪnd〕*n.* 心；精神；頭腦；想法

open〔'opən〕*adj.* 開放的；立刻接受的；不拒絕的；沒有偏見的

Know what's going on. 要知道發生了什麼事。(= ***Know what's happening.***)

go on 發生 (= *happen*)

Keep an ear to the ground. (要隨時注意事情的發展。) 把耳朵貼在地面上，可以聽到遠方的動靜，引申為「隨時提高警覺；隨時關注事情的發展。」或「隨時注意大家在說什麼。」也可說成：Stay alert. (要保持警覺。) Be observant. (觀察力要敏銳。)

ear〔ɪr〕*n.* 耳朵

ground〔graʊnd〕*n.* 地面

keep an ear to the ground 留心可能發生的事 (= *have an ear to the ground*)

PART 1

Unit 5
開 始

Start!
開始！

Get started.
發動。

Get moving.
出發。

Get going.
起動。

Take action.
行動。

Get a move on.
趕快。

First things first!
要事第一！

Do the important
stuff first!
要事先做！

Focus on the important.
專注要事。

BOOK 5・PART 1

PART 1

Unit 5 背景說明

光說沒有用，要開始做，重要的事情擺在第一位。

Start! 開始！(= ***Get started***.)
start〔start〕*v.* 開始；使開始

Get moving. 開始行動。(= ***Get going***. = ***Get started***.
= ***Get the ball rolling***. = ***Make a start***. = ***Get down to
business***.)　　move〔muv〕*v.* 動；移動　*n.* 移動；動作

Get going. ①出發。②開始；開始動手做。(= ***Get moving***.)

Take action. 採取行動。(= ***Do something***.) 也可說成：
Take the initiative. (率先開始。)
action〔'ækʃən〕*n.* 行動

Get a move on. ①趕快；趕快行動。(= ***Hurry up***.)
②開始。(= ***Begin***. = ***Start***. = ***Get going***. = ***Take action***.)

First things first! (最重要的事情先做！) 也可說成：Set
your priorities! (確定你的優先事項！) Prioritize! (列出
優先順序！)　　first〔fɝst〕*adj.* 第一的；首要的　*adv.* 先

Do the important stuff first! 先做重要的事！(= ***Tackle
the most important things first!***)
important〔ɪm'pɔrtṇt〕*adj.* 重要的
stuff〔stʌf〕*n.* 東西；說或做的事

Focus on the important. 專注於重要的事。
(= ***Concentrate on what is important***.)
focus〔'fokəs〕*v.* 聚焦；集中　　***focus on*** 專注於
the important 重要的事 (= ***important things***)

PART 1

Unit 6
無法次次勝

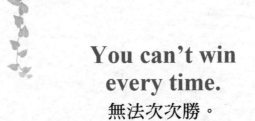

You can't win every time.
無法次次勝。

Even the best lose sometimes.
勝者時而輸。

Everyone loses now and then.
人皆可能輸。

There are no mistakes in life.

生活中無過失。

There are only lessons.

只有人生課題。

Learn from trial and error.

錯中學，誤中試。

Respect failure.
重視失敗。

Learn from mistakes.
前車之鑑。

Use failure as a stepping stone to success.
失敗為成功之母。

PART 1

Unit 6　背景說明

失敗爲成功之母，只要目標鎖定，記取教訓，不屈不撓，必能成功。

You can't win every time. （你不可能每次都贏。）也可說成：It's impossible to succeed every time.
（不可能每次都成功。）　　win〔wɪn〕*v.* 贏；獲勝
every time *每次*

Even the best lose sometimes. （即使是最屬害的人有時也會輸。）也可說成：Everyone loses sometimes.
（每個人都偶爾會輸。）No matter how good you are, you can't always win. （無論你有多好，也不可能總是贏。）　　***the best*** *最好的人*（= *the best people*）；最屬害的人（= *the most skilled/capable people*）
sometimes〔'sʌm,taɪmz〕*adv.* 有時候　　lose〔luz〕*v.* 輸

Everyone loses now and then. 每個人偶爾都會輸。
（= *We all lose sometimes.* = *We can't always win.*）
now and then *偶爾*（= *every now and then* = *sometimes*）

There are no mistakes in life. （人生中沒有錯誤。）
也可說成：You can learn from every experience.
（你可以從每個經驗中學習。）
mistake〔mə'stek〕*n.* 錯誤

There are only lessons. (只有教訓。) 也可說成：
  Mistakes are valuable learning experiences. (錯
  誤是珍貴的學習經驗。)
lesson〔'lɛsn̩〕*n.* 教訓

Learn from trial and error. (從嘗試錯誤中學習。) 也
  可說成：Learn from your mistakes. (從你的錯誤中
  學習。) Learn from experience. (從經驗中學習。)
trial〔'traɪəl〕*n.* 嘗試；試驗   error〔'ɛrɚ〕*n.* 錯誤
trial and error 嘗試錯誤；反覆試驗；不斷摸索

Respect failure. 要重視失敗。(= *Appreciate failure.*
  = *Value your failures.*)
respect〔rɪ'spɛkt〕*v.* 尊敬；尊重；重視
failure〔'feljɚ〕*n.* 失敗

Learn from mistakes. (要從錯誤中學習。) 也可說成：
  Remember your mistakes and avoid making them
  again. (要記得你的錯誤，避免再犯。)

Use failure as a stepping stone. (把失敗當作墊腳石。)
  也可說成：Use your failure to succeed. (利用你的
  失敗獲得成功。) Learn from your failure in order
  to succeed. (要從你的失敗中學習，以獲得成功。)
use A as B 把 A 用作 B   step〔stɛp〕*v.* 踩；踏
stepping stone 墊腳石；跳板
success〔sək'sɛs〕*n.* 成功

PART 1

Unit 7
不要崩潰

Don't fall apart.
不要崩潰。

Don't fall to pieces.
不要分裂。

Don't have a breakdown.
不要瓦解。

Get it together.
振作起來。

Pull yourself together.
冷靜自己。

Grin and bear it.
逆來順受。

BOOK 5 · PART 1

Stay calm.
保持冷靜。

Control yourself.
控制自己。

Compose yourself.
鎮靜下來。

PART 1

Unit 7 背景説明

碰到不順利的情況，要保持冷靜，逆來順受，不要崩潰。

Don't fall apart. 不要崩潰。(= ***Don't fall to pieces.***
= ***Don't have a breakdown.*** = *Don't break down.*)
也可説成：Don't freak out. (不要抓狂。) Don't
lose control. (不要失控。) Don't lose it. (不要失
控。)　　***fall apart*** 崩潰　　piece〔pis〕*n.* 一片
fall to pieces (在精神方面) 崩潰；垮掉；極度緊張
breakdown〔'brek,daun〕*n.* 崩潰；精神失常；神經衰弱
have a breakdown 崩潰 (= *break down*)

Get it together. (要振作起來；要打起精神。) 也可説
成：Get your act together. (要有條有理地做事。)
Pull your socks up. (加把勁；振作起來。) Shape
up. (要表現得更好。)

Pull yourself together . 控制自己；鎮靜下來；重新
振作起來。(= *Calm down.* = *Compose yourself.*
= *Regain your composure.* = *Control yourself.*
= *Regain your self-control.* = *Get a grip.* = *Get
a hold of yourself.*)

BOOK 5・PART 1

Grin and bear it. (要逆來順受。) 也可說成：Stay
and endure it. (不要放棄，要忍耐。) Keep going.
(要持續前進。) Tough it out. (要挺過去；要度過難
關。)　　grin〔grɪn〕*v.* 露齒而笑
bear〔bɛr〕*v.* 忍受

Stay calm. 要保持冷靜。(= *Keep cool.* = *Keep your*
head.)　　stay〔ste〕*v.* 保持
calm〔kɑm〕*adj.* 冷靜的

Control yourself. 要控制自己。(= *Take a hold of*
yourself.) 也可說成：Compose yourself. (鎮靜
下來。) Take it easy. (放輕鬆。)
control〔kən'trol〕*v.* 控制

Compose yourself. (鎮靜下來。) 也可
說成：Regain your composure. (要
恢復鎮定。) Calm down. (冷靜下來。)
Control yourself. (要控制自己。)
compose〔kəm'poz〕*v.* 組成；使鎮定；使平靜

PART 1

Unit 8
接受它

Take it.
接受它。

Tolerate it.
忍受它。

Withstand it.
頂住它。

Ride it out.
度過難關。

Tough it out.
逆來順受。

Weather the storm.
抵禦風暴。

BOOK 5・PART 1

Get strong.
要堅強。

Get tough.
要強硬。

Stay and endure it.
堅守它。

PART 1

Unit 8　背景説明

碰到不好的事，要接受它，忍受它，頂住它。

Take it. 接受它。(= *Accept it.*) 也可説成：Grin and bear it. (逆來順受。) Don't complain. (不要抱怨。)

take〔tek〕*v.* 承擔；接受；容忍

Tolerate it. 忍受它。(= *Endure it.* = *Put up with it.*)

tolerate〔'tɑləˌret〕*v.* 忍受；容忍

Withstand it. 挺住；要忍耐。(= *Endure it.* = *Tolerate it.* = *Put up with it.* = *Cope with it.* = *Stand fast.* = *Stand firm.* = *Tough it out.* = *Hold your ground.* = *Don't give up.* = *Survive it.*)

withstand〔wɪð'stænd〕*v.* 經受；承受；頂住；抵擋；經得起

Ride it out. (要度過難關。) 也可説成：Take it on the chin. (無怨無悔地承受。) Take things as they come. (既來之，則安之；隨遇而安。) Take it in stride. (處之泰然。)

ride out 安全度過 (暴風雨)；經受得起 (= *withstand*)

【源自船隻等待暴風雨過去】

Tough it out. 要逆來順受；挺過去。(= *Cope with*
it. = *Put up with it.* = *See it through.* = *Grin and*
bear it.)

tough〔tʌf〕*adj.* 堅韌的；剛強的；強壯的；不屈不撓的

tough out 咬緊牙關挺過（壓力、困難等）

Weather the storm. (要平安度過風暴。) 也可說成：
Cope with it. (要應付。) (= *Deal with it.*) Endure
it. (要忍受。) Survive. (要存活。) Carry on. (要
繼續進行。)

weather〔'wɛðɚ〕*n.* 天氣 *v.* 平安度過（暴風雨）；經受
得起　　storm〔stɔrm〕*n.* 暴風雨

Get strong. 要堅強。(= *Be stronger.* = *Toughen up.*)

get〔gɛt〕*v.* 變得

strong〔strɔŋ〕*adj.* 強壯的；堅強的

Get tough. 要堅強。(= *Get stronger.* = *Toughen up.*)

Stay and endure it. (留下來忍受一切；不要放棄，要忍
耐。) 也可說成：Stick it out. (要堅持到底。) Put
up with it. (要忍耐。) Grin and bear it. (要逆來
順受。) Don't give up. (不要放棄。)

stay〔ste〕*v.* 停留 (= *don't leave*)；保持
(某種狀態)；不放棄 (= *don't quit*)

endure〔ɪn'djʊr〕*v.* 忍受

PART 1

Unit 9
我今幸運

BOOK 5・PART 1

Today is my day.
我今幸運。

I am a winner.
我是勝者。

I can do anything.
無所不能。

I love living.
我熱愛生活。

I'm high on life.
精彩人生。

**I'm happy to
be alive.**
樂於活著。

BOOK 5・PART 1

I thank God.
感謝上帝。

I praise the Lord.
讚美主。

I'm a lucky person.
我是個幸運兒。

PART 1

Unit 9 背景説明

　　只要能活著，每天都是上帝給你的好日子，要享受人生，做你想做的事。

***Today is my day*.** 今天是我的日子，引申爲「我今天眞幸運。」(= *Today is my lucky day*.) 也可說成：Everything is going great today. (今天一切都很順利。) 相反的說法是：Today isn't my day. (我今天眞倒楣。)

***I'm a winner*.** (我是贏家。) 也可說成：I'm successful. (我很成功。) I'm admirable. (我值得欽佩。) I'm deserving. (我值得獎賞。) I'm a hot shot. (我是高手。) I'm a champ. (我是冠軍。)
winner 〔ˈwɪnɚ〕 *n.* 勝利者；贏家【相反的是 loser 〔ˈluzɚ〕 *n.* 失敗者；輸家；魯蛇 (網路用語)】

***I can do anything*.** (我可以做任何事。) 也可說成：Nothing is impossible for me. (對我而言，沒有什麼是不可能的。)

***I love living*.** (我熱愛生活。) 也可說成：I appreciate life. (我重視生活。) Life is great. (人生很棒。)
living 〔ˈlɪvɪŋ〕 *n.* 生活

***I'm high on life*.** 我熱愛生活；我珍惜生命。(= *I'm excited about life.* = *I'm thrilled about life.* = *I'm enthusiastic about life.*) 也可說成：I'm excited just to be alive. (能活著我就很興奮了。) Life gives me energy. (生命給我活力。)

high〔haɪ〕*adj.* 陶醉的；興奮的 (= *excited* = *thrilled* = *enthusiastic*)

be high on 對…充滿熱忱 (= *be enthusiastic about*)

***I'm happy to be alive*.** 我很高興我能活著。(= *I'm glad I'm alive.* = *I'm glad I'm still living.* = *I'm glad I'm still alive.*)

alive〔ə'laɪv〕*adj.* 活著的

***I thank God*.** (我感謝上帝。)

= ***I praise the Lord*.** (我讚美主。)

= I'm grateful to the Almighty. (我感激上帝。)

God〔gɑd〕*n.* 上帝　　praise〔prez〕*v.* 稱讚

lord〔lɔrd〕*n.* 君主　　***the Lord*** 主；上帝；耶穌基督

***I'm a lucky person*.** (我是個幸運兒。) 也可說成：I'm a lucky dog. (我是個幸運兒。) I'm a fortunate soul. (我是個幸運的人。) I'm very fortunate. (我非常幸運。)

lucky〔'lʌkɪ〕*adj.* 幸運的 (= *fortunate*)

PART 1 總整理

Unit 1

Don't be cheap.　不要小氣。
Don't be stingy.　不要吝嗇。
Try to treat others first.
要先請客。

Give back.　要回饋。
Return favors.　要報答。
Give more, gain more.
付出多，得到多。

Enjoy giving.　樂於付出。
Enjoy sharing.　樂於分享。
You'll always win.
定會獲益。

Unit 2

Be courageous.　要有勇氣。
Grow a spine.　長點骨氣。
Get a backbone.　拿出骨氣。

Do it without fear.
故事無懼。
Don't worry or care.
無所擔憂。
Throw caution to the
　wind.　拋開謹慎。

Accept challenges.
接受挑戰。
Choose tough tasks.
迎難而上。
The rest of your life will
　be easy.　餘生將安好。

Unit 3

Pretend you can.
裝作你會。
Make believe you can.
假裝你會。
Fake it till you make it.
弄假成真。

Achieve.　達成目標。
Achieve your potential.
發揮潛力。
Great achievements will
　follow.　偉業將至。

Anything is possible.
世事皆可能。
Nothing is impossible.
無事不可達。
You can be or do anything.
萬事皆可達。

BOOK 5・PART 1

Unit 4

Be modern.　要現代化。
Be up to date.　要最新的。
Keep up with the times.
要隨時代。

Get more informed.
廣納訊息。
Become more aware.
先知先覺。
Keep your mind open.
打開心胸。

Know what's going on.
知了其事。
Know what's happening.
知其發生。
Keep an ear to the ground.
保持警惕。

Unit 5

Start!　開始！
Get started.　發動。
Get moving.　出發。

Get going.　起動。
Take action.　行動。
Get a move on.　趕快。

First things first!
要事第一！
Do the important stuff
　first!　要事先做！
Focus on the important.
專注要事。

Unit 6

You can't win every time.
無法次次勝。
Even the best lose
　sometimes.　勝者時而輸。
Everyone loses now and
　then.　人皆可能輸。

There are no mistakes in
　life.　生活中無過失。
There are only lessons.
只有人生課題。
Learn from trial and error
錯中學，誤中試。

Respect failure.　重視失敗。
Learn from mistakes.
前車之鑑。
Use failure as a stepping
　stone to success.
失敗為成功之母。

Unit 7

Don't fall apart.
不要崩潰。
Don't fall to pieces.
不要分裂。
Don't have a breakdown.
不要瓦解。

Get it together.
振作起來。
Pull yourself together.
冷靜自己。
Grin and bear it.
逆來順受。

Stay calm.
保持冷靜。
Control yourself.
控制自己。
Compose yourself.
鎮靜下來。

Unit 8

Take it.　接受它。
Tolerate it.　忍受它。
Withstand it.　頂住它。

Ride it out.　度過難關。
Tough it out.　逆來順受。
Weather the storm.
抵禦風暴。

Get strong.　要堅強。
Get tough.　要強硬。
Stay and endure it.
堅守它。

Unit 9

Today is my day.
我今幸運。
I am a winner.　我是勝者。
I can do anything.
無所不能。

I love living.
我熱愛生活。
I'm high on life.
精彩人生。
I'm happy to be alive.
樂於活著。

I thank God.　感謝上帝。
I praise the Lord.　讚美主。
I'm a lucky person.
我是個幸運兒。

PART 2

Unit 1
持續學習

PART 2・Unit 1~9
中英文錄音QR碼
英文唸2遍，中文唸1遍

Always learn.
持續學習。

Learn all the time.
不斷學習。

**Learn around
the clock.**
日夜學習。

Always work hard.
努力工作。

Work like a dog.
埋頭苦幹。

**Work your fingers
to the bone.**
全力幹活。

**Always make time
for fun.**
一定要找時間玩樂。

Satisfy your soul.
要滿足自身的心靈。

**All work and no play isn't
good for the soul.**
工作不玩，無益心靈。

BOOK 5 · PART 2

PART 2

Unit 1　背景説明

　　我的座右銘是：Study hard, work hard, play hard. 我們把它分解成三組九句。

Always learn. 要一直學習。(= ***Learn all the time***.)
也可説成：***Learn around the clock***. (要日夜不停地學習。) (= *Learn nonstop*.) Never stop learning.
(絕不要停止學習。)

always〔'ɔlwez〕*adv.* 一直；總是

all the time 一直；總是　　clock〔klɑk〕*n.* 時鐘

around the clock 全天地；不分晝夜地；整天整夜；夜以繼日

Always work hard. (總是努力工作。) 也可説成：
　Always give it your all. (總是全力以赴。)

work hard 努力；努力工作

Work like a dog. 要勤奮地工作。(= *Work very hard*.)

Work your fingers to the bone. 要工作到手指磨破，看到骨頭，也就是「要拼命工作。」(= *Work like hell*. = *Work like a slave*.)

bone〔bon〕*n.* 骨頭　　finger〔'fɪŋɚ〕*n.* 手指

***Always make time for fun*.** 一定要找時間玩樂。
(= *Set aside some time to have a good time.*) 也
可說成：Set aside some time to relax. (要騰出時
間放輕鬆。)

make time 騰出時間　　fun〔 fʌn 〕*n.* 樂趣；消遣

***Satisfy your soul*.** 要滿足你的心靈。(= *Do something good for your soul.* = *Do something for your spirit.*)　satisfy〔'sætɪs,faɪ〕*v.* 滿足

soul〔 sol 〕*n.* 靈魂；心靈

***All work and no play isn't good for the soul*.** (只
工作，不遊樂，對心靈沒好處。) 也可說成：Working
all the time isn't good for your mental health.
(一直工作對你的心理健康沒好處。) Too much
work isn't good for your emotional health. (太
多的工作對你的情緒健康沒好處。)

all work and no play (只工作，不遊樂) 源自諺語：
All work and no play makes Jack a dull boy.
(只工作，不遊樂，會變成呆子。)

PART 2

Unit 2
放慢腳步

Slow down.
放慢腳步。

Take time to look around.
歷時環顧。

Don't miss something wonderful.
勿失美好。

Don't rush life.
別倉促生活。

Life isn't a race.
生活非競賽。

Enjoy every moment.
享受每一刻。

Appreciate life.
重視生活。

Cherish our beautiful world.
珍惜美景。

Stop and smell the roses.
停下享受。

PART 2

Unit 2　背景説明

　　每天生活、工作，不要太緊張，有時要放慢腳步，
停下來享受一下。

Slow down.　放慢腳步；放輕鬆。(= *Take it easy*.)

Take time to look around.　要花時間環顧四周。
　(= *Spend time looking around*.) 也可説成：
Appreciate the moment. (要珍惜當下。)
take time 花時間　　***look around*** 環顧四周

Don't miss something wonderful. (不要錯過美好
　的事物。) 也可説成：Don't lose the chance to
experience something great. (不要失去可以體驗
美好事物的機會。)
miss (mɪs) *v.* 錯過
wonderful ('wʌndəfəl) *adj.* 極好的；很棒的

Don't rush life.　不要匆忙過生活。(= *Don't rush*
　through life.) 也可説成：Don't be in such a hurry
to grow up/get married/get a job/have kids. (不
要這麼急著長大 / 結婚 / 找工作 / 生小孩。)
rush (rʌʃ) *v.* 匆忙　　life (laɪf) *n.* 生命；人生；生活
rush life 匆忙過生活

Life isn't a race. 生活不是競賽。(= *Life isn't a competition*.) 也可説成：Don't rush through life. (不要匆忙過生活。)　　race〔res〕*n.* 賽跑；比賽

Enjoy every moment. (要享受每一刻。) 也可説成：Appreciate every moment. (要重視每一刻。) Live in the present. (要活在當下。)
enjoy〔ɪn'dʒɔɪ〕*v.* 享受　　moment〔'momənt〕*n.* 時刻

Appreciate life. ①要重視生活。(= *Value life*.) ②要品味生活。(= *Savor life*.)
appreciate〔ə'priʃɪˌet〕*v.* 重視；欣賞；感激

Cherish our beautiful world. (要珍惜我們美麗的世界。) 也可説成：Treasure the beauty of the world. (要珍惜世界之美。) Treasure the Earth. (要珍惜地球。)　　cherish〔'tʃɛrɪʃ〕*v.* 珍惜

Stop and smell the roses. 要停下來聞玫瑰花香，引申爲「要停下來，享受生活。」(= *Enjoy life's pleasures*.) 源自高爾夫球選手 Walter Hagen 的自傳："Don't hurry. Don't worry. And be sure to smell the flowers along the way." (不要急。不要擔心。一定要聞聞沿途的花香。) 也可説成：Seize the day. (把握時機。) Carpe diem. (及時行樂。)
smell〔smɛl〕*v.* 聞　　rose〔roz〕*n.* 玫瑰

PART 2

Unit 3
賺到錢

Money comes.
賺到錢。

Money goes.
花掉錢。

Friendship is always there.
友誼永存。

Make quality friends.
結交優質的朋友。

**Hang out with
like-minded people.**
和志同道合的人在一起。

**Who you go with is
who you are.**
觀其友而知其人。

**Making friends
makes life beautiful.**
交朋友使人生美好。

**To improve makes life
meaningful.**
進步使人生有意義。

**That we keep
advancing makes
life wonderful.**
持續進步使人生精彩。

BOOK 5・PART 2

PART 2

Unit 3　背景説明

　　找到志同道合的朋友，很不容易，一定要珍惜他們，
不要怕花錢，友誼第一。

Money comes. (錢來。) 也可説成：You earn money.
(你賺錢。) You receive money. (你得到錢。)

Money goes. (錢去。) 也可説成：You spend money.
(你花錢。) You lose money. (你失去錢。)

Friendship is always there. (友誼永遠存在。) 也可説
成：Friendship never disappears. (友誼絕不會消
失。)　　friendship〔'frɛndʃɪp〕 n. 友誼

Make quality friends. (結交優質的朋友。) 也可説
成：Make good friends. (要交好的朋友。)
Keep good company. (要結交益友。)
quality〔'kwɑlətɪ〕 n. 品質　adj. 品質好的；優質的；
高級的

Hang out with like-minded people.　要和志同道合的
人在一起。(= *Spend time with like-minded people.*)
hang out with sb.　和某人一起玩
like-minded〔'laɪk'maɪndɪd〕 adj. 志趣相投的；看法
相同的

Who you go with is who you are. (你和什麼樣的人交往，你就是什麼樣的人。) 也可說成：You will be judged by the company you keep. (別人會以你結交的朋友來評斷你。) A man is known by the company he keeps. (【諺】觀其友，知其人；物以類聚。)　who〔hu〕*pron.* 怎樣的人

go with 和⋯交往

動名詞、不定詞、名詞子句當主詞，動詞用單數。

Making friends makes life beautiful. 交朋友使人生更美好。(= *Friends make life better.*)

make friends 交朋友

To improve makes life meaningful. 進步使人生更有意義。(= *Bettering yourself makes your life more meaningful.*)

improve〔ɪm'pruv〕*v.* 改善；進步

meaningful〔'minɪŋfəl〕*adj.* 有意義的

That we keep advancing makes life wonderful. 持續進步使人生精彩。(= *Personal progress makes life fantastic.*) that 引導名詞子句做句子的主詞。

keep + V-ing 持續⋯

advance〔əd'væns〕*v.* 進步

wonderful〔'wʌndəfəl〕*adj.* 極好的；很棒的

BOOK 5・PART 2

PART 2

Unit 4
勿皺眉

No frowns.
勿皺眉。

No angry faces.
勿生氣。

No dirty looks.
勿瞪人。

BOOK 5 • PART 2

Don't leave angry.
憤怒時不離。

Don't go away upset.
生氣時不走。

Don't storm off.
勿生氣走掉。

**Anger isn't
about others.**
憤怒無關他人。

Anger is about you.
生氣關乎自己。

**Don't punish yourself
for others' mistakes.**
勿拿他人錯懲罰自己。

PART 2

Unit 4 背景說明

生氣是用別人的錯誤懲罰自己。

No frowns. 不要皺眉頭。(= *Don't frown*.) 源自 No frowns are allowed. (不准皺眉頭。) 也可說成：I don't want to see any frowns. (我不想看見有任何人皺眉頭。) 「No + (動) 名詞」表「禁止…」。

frown〔fraʊn〕*n. v.* 皺眉頭

No angry faces. 不要有生氣的臉，也就是「不要有生氣的表情。」(= *Don't look angry*.) 源自 No angry faces are allowed. (不准有生氣的表情。) 也可說成：I don't want to see any angry faces. (我不想看見任何生氣的表情。)

angry〔'æŋgrɪ〕*adj.* 生氣的
face〔fes〕*n.* 臉；臉色；表情

No dirty looks. (不要瞪人家。) 源自 No dirty looks are allowed. (不准瞪人家。) 也可說成：I don't want to see any dirty looks. (我不想看見有人瞪人家。) dirty〔'dɝtɪ〕*adj.* (臉色) 難看的

looks〔lʊks〕*n. pl.* 表情【*give sb. a dirty look* 瞪某人】

Don't leave angry. (生氣時不要離開。) 源自 Don't leave while you are still angry. (當你還在生氣時，不要離開。) leave〔liv〕*v.* 離開

Don't go away upset. (不高興時，不要走掉。) 源自
Don't go away while you are still upset. (當你
還在不高興時，不要走掉。) ***go away*** 走開；離開
upset〔ʌp'sɛt〕*adj.* 不高興的

Don't storm off. 不要氣沖沖地走掉。(= *Don't leave
in an angry way*.) storm〔stɔrm〕*n.* 暴風雨
v. 颳暴風雨；咆哮；猛衝 ***storm off*** 氣沖沖地走掉

Anger isn't about others. 生氣和他人無關。(= *Your
anger is not related to others*.) 也可說成：Your
anger is not anyone else's responsibility. (你的
憤怒不是其他任何人的責任。)
anger〔'æŋgɚ〕*n.* 憤怒；生氣
about〔ə'baʊt〕*prep.* 關於；有關

Anger is about you. (生氣和你有關。) 也可說成：
Your anger is due to you. (你會生氣都是因為
你。) You are in control of your anger. (你能控
制你的怒氣。) Your anger is your responsibility.
(你會生氣是你的責任。)

Don't punish yourself for others' mistakes. (不要
因為別人的錯誤而懲罰自己。) 也可說成：When you
get angry with others, you are just punishing
yourself. (當你對別人生氣時，你只是在懲罰你自己。)
punish〔'pʌnɪʃ〕*v.* 處罰；懲罰
mistake〔mə'stek〕*n.* 錯誤

PART 2

Unit 5
何謂幸福？

What is happiness?
何謂幸福？

Love what you're doing.
愛你所做的事。

Love who you're with.
愛你身旁的人。

Happiness is a mindset.
樂是心態。

Choose happiness.
選擇快樂。

You'll always benefit.
定會獲益。

Live happy.
活得開心。

Die happy.
死得安樂。

**Live a life with
no regrets.**
生而無憾。

BOOK 5 • PART 2

PART 2

Unit 5 背景說明

　　幸福就是做你喜歡做的事，愛你身旁的人，活得開心，一生就沒有遺憾了。

What is happiness? 什麼是幸福？(= *What does happiness mean?*) 也可說成：How do you define happiness? (你會如何定義幸福？)

happiness〔ˈhæpɪnɪs〕*n.* 快樂；幸福

Love what you're doing. (愛你正在做的事。) 也可說成：Love what you do. (愛你所做的事。) Love your job. (愛你的工作。) Find some pleasure in everything you do. (在你做的所有的事當中尋找一些樂趣。)

Love who you're with. 愛和你在一起的人。(= *Love the person you are with.* = *Love the people you spend time with.*)　with〔wɪð, wɪθ〕*prep.* 和…一起

Happiness is a mindset. (快樂是一種心態。) 也可說成：Happiness is an attitude. (快樂是一種態度。)

mindset〔ˈmaɪndˌsɛt〕*n.* 心態

Choose happiness. 要選擇快樂。(= *Choose to be happy.* = *Decide to be happy.*)

choose〔tʃuz〕*v.* 選擇

You'll always benefit. 你一定會獲益。(= *You'll always win.*) 也可說成：You can't lose. (你不會有損失；你不可能吃虧。)

benefit〔'bɛnəfɪt〕*v.* 獲益

Live happy. 要活得快樂。(= *Live a happy life.* = *Be happy.*)

live〔lɪv〕*v.* 生活；過 (…生活)

happy〔'hæpɪ〕*adj.* 快樂的

Die happy. (要死得快樂。) 也可說成：Be happy until the day you die. (要直到死前都很快樂。) Be happy all your life. (要一輩子都很快樂。)

die〔daɪ〕*v.* 死

Live a life with no regrets. (要過著沒有遺憾的生活。) 也可說成：Don't have any regrets. (不要有任何的遺憾。) Don't feel remorse for the things you do. (對你所做的事不要覺得懊惱。)

live a ~ life 過著~生活

regret〔rɪ'grɛt〕*n.* 後悔；遺憾

with no regrets 沒有後悔；毫無遺憾

PART 2

Unit 6
正面想法

Positive mind.
正面想法。

Positive vibes.
正面能量。

Positive life.
正面人生。

Good vibes only.
唯好能量。

No bad vibes.
無壞能量。

Spread positive
energy everywhere.
處處傳播正能量。

Spread happiness.

散播歡樂。

Radiate love and joy.

散發愛悅。

Let your light shine.

閃耀自己。

PART 2

Unit 6 背景說明

外國人常說：Good vibes only. 句中的 vibe 源自 vibration（震動），表示要傳播正能量，不要傳播負能量。

Positive mind. 正面的想法。(= *Positive thoughts.* = *Good thoughts.*) 源自 You should have a positive mind. (你應該要有正面的想法。) 也可說成：Positive attitude. (正面的態度。) (= *Good attitude.*)

positive〔ˈpɑzətɪv〕*adj.* 正面的；積極的；樂觀的
mind〔maɪnd〕*n.* 心；精神；頭腦；想法

Positive vibes. 正面的能量；正面的感受。(= *Positive feelings.* = *Good feelings.*) 源自 You should have positive vibes. (你應該要有正能量；你應該要有正面的感受。)

vibes〔vaɪbz〕*n. pl.* (給人的) 印象；情緒上的激動；(某地、某種局面或某支曲子的) 氣氛；氛圍 (= *vibrations*)

Positive life. (積極的人生。) 源自 You should have a positive life. (你應該要有積極的人生。) 也可說成：Good life. (美好的人生。) Optimistic life. (樂觀的人生。)

Good vibes only. 只能有正能量；只能有好的想法。
(= *Only good thoughts*.)

No bad vibes. 不能有負能量；不能有壞的想法。
(= *No bad thoughts*.)

Spread positive energy everywhere. 要到處散播正能
量。(= *Spread good energy everywhere*.) 也可説
成：Show positivity wherever you go. (無論你
去那裡，都要展現正能量。) Influence others with
your positivity. (用你的正能量影響別人。)
spread〔 sprɛd 〕*v.* 散播；傳播
energy〔ˈɛnɚdʒɪ〕*n.* 能量
everywhere〔ˈɛvrɪˌhwɛr〕*adv.* 到處

Spread happiness. (散播快樂。) 也可説成：Make
others feel happy. (要使別人覺得快樂。)
happiness〔ˈhæpɪnɪs〕*n.* 快樂；幸福

Radiate love and joy. 要散發愛和快樂。(= *Spread
love and joy*.)　　radiate〔ˈredɪˌet〕*v.* 散發；輻射
joy〔 dʒɔɪ 〕*n.* 快樂；高興

Let your light shine. (要讓你的光芒閃耀。) 也可説
成：Let others see how good you are. (要讓別人
知道你有多好。)【源自「聖經」】
light〔 laɪt 〕*n.* 光；光芒　　shine〔 ʃaɪn 〕*v.* 閃耀

PART 2

Unit 7
身體痛無可避

Pain is inevitable.
身體痛無可避。

Suffering is optional.
精神苦有選擇。

It's all in your mind.
全憑你如何想。

Pain makes you stronger.
痛苦令人堅強。

Tears make you wiser.
眼淚讓你聰慧。

**Learn from yesterday,
hope for tomorrow.**
吸取教訓，希望明天。

Be physically fit.
身體要健康。

Be mentally strong.
心理要堅強。

Be morally upright.
品德要正直。

PART 2

Unit 7　背景説明

　　痛苦有兩種，身體的痛苦和精神上的痛苦。精神上的痛苦是可以改變的，換個想法，海闊天空。

Pain is inevitable.（身體上的痛苦是無可避免的。）也可説成：You can't avoid some pain.（你無法避免某些疼痛。）

pain〔pen〕*n.*（身體上的）痛苦；疼痛
inevitable〔ɪnˈɛvətəbḷ〕*adj.* 無法避免的

Suffering is optional.（精神上的痛苦是可選擇的。）也可説成：You don't have to suffer.（你不必受苦。）

suffering〔ˈsʌfərɪŋ〕*n.* 苦難；折磨
optional〔ˈɑpʃənḷ〕*adj.* 可選擇的

Pain is inevitable, suffering is optional. 這個句子出自日本知名作家村上春樹的書，關於馬拉松賽跑，他説了這句話，pain 是「身體的疼痛」，無法避免，而 suffering 是「苦難；折磨」，你可以選擇不要去做。

It's all in your mind.（這全看你心裡怎麼想。）也可説成：What you feel depends on your attitude.（你的感受取決於你的態度。）

mind〔maɪnd〕*n.* 心；精神；頭腦；想法

Pain makes you stronger. (痛苦會使你更堅強。)
也可説成：Heartache will make you a more
resilient person. (心痛會使你成為更有韌性的人。)
strong〔strɔŋ〕*adj.* 堅強的

Tears make you wiser. (眼淚會讓你更有智慧。) 也
可説成：Experiencing sadness will make you
wiser. (經歷悲傷會使你更有智慧。)
tear〔tɪr〕*n.* 眼淚　　wise〔waɪz〕*adj.* 有智慧的

Learn from yesterday, ***hope for tomorrow.*** 向昨天
學習，為明天懷抱希望。(= *Learn from yesterday
and hope for tomorrow.*) 源自愛因斯坦的名言：
Learn from yesterday, live for today, and hope
for tomorrow. 　***hope for*** 希望

Be physically fit. 身體要健康。(= *Be in good shape.*
= *Be in good condition.* = *Be in good health.*)
physically〔ˈfɪzɪk!ɪ〕*adv.* 身體上
fit〔fɪt〕*adj.* 健康的 (= *healthy*)

Be mentally strong. 心理要堅強。(= *Have a strong
mind.*) 也可説成：Be mentally healthy. (心理要健
康。) 　　mentally〔ˈmɛnt!ɪ〕*adv.* 精神上；心理上

Be morally upright. 品德要正直。(= *Be moral.* = *Be
honorable.*) 　　morally〔ˈmɔrəlɪ〕*adv.* 道德上
upright〔ˈʌpˌraɪt〕*adj.* 端正的；正直的

PART 2

Unit 8
把別人放在
第一位

Put others first.
把別人放在第一位。

Think of others first.
先想到別人。

You will end up first.
你最後會變成第一。

Care about others.
關懷他人。

Help those
around you.
幫助周圍。

Be a shoulder to
lean on.
可被依靠。

Try hard to be helpful.
盡力去助人。

**Make a special
effort to do good.**
努力做好事。

**Go out of your way
for people.**
竭力去助人。

PART 2

Unit 8　背景說明

　　把別人放在第一位，先想到別人，關懷別人，自己最受益。

Put others first. (把別人放在第一位。) 也可說成：Be selfless. (要無私。)　　***put…first*** 把…放在首位
others〔ˈʌðɚz〕*pron.* 別人

Think of others first.　要先想到別人。(= *Consider other people first*.)　　***think of*** 想到
first〔fɜst〕*adv.* 先

You will end up first.　你最後會變成第一。(= *In the end, you'll be on top*.) 也可說成：You'll win. (你會獲勝。)　　***end up*** 以…結束；最後變成…
first〔fɜst〕*adv.* 首要地；最先地　　*adj.* 第一的，居首位的

Care about others.　要關心別人。(= *Be concerned about others*.)　　***care about*** 關心

Help those around you. (要幫助你周圍的人。) 也可說成：Help your friends and family. (要幫助你的朋友和家人。) Help people who are close to you. (要幫助和你親近的人。)
around〔əˈraʊnd〕*prep.* 在…周圍

Be a shoulder to lean on. 要當一個可以依靠的肩膀，
引申爲「要當一個可以依靠的人。」而 a shoulder to
cry on 則是指「可以傾吐心事的人」。也可說成：Be
helpful.（要幫助別人。）Be supportive.（要支持別
人。）Support those who need help.（要支持需要
幫助的人。）　　　shoulder〔ˈʃoldə〕*n.* 肩膀
lean〔lin〕*v.* 倚靠；依賴＜*on*＞

Try hard to be helpful. 要努力成爲有用的人。(＝*Do*
your best to be useful.) 也可說成：Do your best
to help others.（要盡力幫助別人。）　　***try hard*** 努力
helpful〔ˈhɛlpfəl〕*adj.* 有幫助的；有用的

Make a special effort to do good. 要特別努力做好
事。(＝*Try hard to do a good deed.* ＝ *Go out of*
your way to do good deeds.)
special〔ˈspɛʃəl〕*adj.* 特別的　　effort〔ˈɛfət〕*n.* 努力
make a special effort 特別努力　　***do good*** 做好事

Go out of your way for people. 要非常努力幫助別
人。(＝*Help others even if it inconveniences you.*
＝ *Make a special effort to help others.*)
go out of your way （特別是爲其他人）非常努力地做；
　　費盡心思地做【字面的意思是「離開你要走的路」，也就是
　　「特地去幫助別人」】

BOOK 5・PART 2

PART 2

Unit 9
同意眾人意見

Agree with everybody.
同意眾人意見。

You'll fit right in.
你會完全融入。

Go along to get along.
認同才能相處。

Give great service.
提供一流服務。

Be eager to help.
要熱心去助人。

**Always aim to
please others.**
致力取悅他人。

More love, less hate.

多一點愛，少一點恨。

More smiling, less worrying.

多一點微笑，少一點擔心。

More compassion, less judgment.

多一點同情，少一點批評。

PART 2

Unit 9 背景説明

要融入一個團體，要先認同他們的核心價值。

Agree with everybody. (要同意每個人。) 也可説成：
Be agreeable. (要欣然同意；要討人喜歡。) Never
contradict anyone. (絕不要反駁任何人。)
agree〔ə'gri〕*v.* 同意　　***agree with*** 同意；和…意見一致

You'll fit right in. (你就能完全融入。) 也可説成：
You'll be accepted. (你就會被接受。) You'll be
part of the group. (你會成爲團體的一部份。)
fit in 融入；相處融洽
right〔raɪt〕*adv.* 完全地；徹底地

Go along to get along. 同意別人以期與人相處融洽；
隨波逐流；委曲求全。(= *Conform in order to have
acceptance and security*.) 也可説成：Do what is
expected in order to have a good relationship
with others. (做符合期待的事，以和別人有良好的關
係。) ***go along*** 同意；贊成
get along 進展；和睦相處

Give great service. (要提供很棒的服務。) 也可説成：
Be helpful. (要幫助別人。) Do the best you can
to help. (要盡力幫助別人。)

give〔gɪv〕*v.* 給予；提供
great〔gret〕*adj.* 很棒的；極好的
service〔'sɝvɪs〕*n.* 服務

Be eager to help. 要熱心助人。(= *Be enthusiastic about helping.*) 也可說成：Always be ready to help. (要總是願意幫助別人。)
eager〔'igɚ〕*adj.* 渴望的；熱切的
be eager to V. 渴望…

Always aim to please others. 始終致力於取悅他人。
(= *Always try to make others happy.*)
aim〔em〕*v.* 瞄準；指望；企圖
aim to V. 指望 (做某事)　　please〔pliz〕*v.* 取悅

More love, less hate. 多一點愛，少一點恨。(= *Love more and hate less.* = *Love people more and hate people less.*)　　hate〔het〕*n. v.* 憎恨

More smiling, less worrying. 多一點微笑，少一點擔心。(= *Smile more and worry less.*)
smile〔smaɪl〕*v.* 微笑　　worry〔'wɝɪ〕*v.* 擔心

More compassion, less judgment. 多一點同情，少一點批評。(= *Be more compassionate and less judgmental.*)
compassion〔kəm'pæʃən〕*n.* 同情
judgment〔'dʒʌdʒmənt〕*n.* 判斷；批評

PART 2 總整理

Unit 1

Always learn. 持續學習。
Learn all the time.
不斷學習。
Learn around the clock.
日夜學習。

Always work hard.
努力工作。
Work like a dog. 埋頭苦幹。
Work your fingers to the
bone. 全力幹活。

Always make time for
fun. 一定要找時間玩樂。
Satisfy your soul.
要滿足自身的心靈。
All work and no play isn't
good for the soul.
工作不玩,無益心靈。

Unit 2

Slow down. 放慢腳步。
Take time to look around.
歷時環顧。
Don't miss something
wonderful. 勿失美好。

Don't rush life.
別倉促生活。
Life isn't a race.
生活非競賽。
Enjoy every moment.
享受每一刻。

Appreciate life.
重視生活。
Cherish our beautiful
world. 珍惜美景。
Stop and smell the roses.
停下享受。

Unit 3

Money comes. 賺到錢。
Money goes. 花掉錢。
Friendship is always
there. 友誼永存。

Make quality friends.
結交優質的朋友。
Hang out with like-
minded people.
和志同道合的人在一起。
Who you go with is who
you are.
觀其友而知其人。

Making friends makes
    life beautiful.
交朋友使人生美好。
To improve makes life
    meaningful.
進步使人生有意義。
That we keep advancing
    makes life wonderful.
持續進步使人生精彩。

Unit 4

No frowns. 勿皺眉。
No angry faces. 勿生氣。
No dirty looks. 勿瞪人。

Don't leave angry.
憤怒時不離。
Don't go away upset.
生氣時不走。
Don't storm off. 勿生氣走掉。

Anger isn't about others.
憤怒無關他人。
Anger is about you.
生氣關乎自己。
Don't punish yourself for
    others' mistakes.
勿拿他人錯懲罰自己。

Unit 5

What is happiness?
何謂幸福？

Love what you're doing.
愛你所做的事。
Love who you're with.
愛你身旁的人。

Happiness is a mindset.
樂是心態。
Choose happiness.
選擇快樂。
You'll always benefit.
定會獲益。

Live happy. 活得開心。
Die happy. 死得安樂。
Live a life with no regrets.
生而無憾。

Unit 6

Positive mind. 正面想法。
Positive vibes. 正面能量。
Positive life. 正面人生。

Good vibes only. 唯好能量。
No bad vibes. 無壞能量。
Spread positive energy
    everywhere.
處處傳播正能量。

Spread happiness. 散播歡樂。
Radiate love and joy.
散發愛悅。
Let your light shine.
閃耀自己。

Unit 7

Pain is inevitable.
身體痛無可避。
Suffering is optional.
精神苦有選擇。
It's all in your mind.
全憑你如何想。

Pain makes you stronger.
痛苦令人堅強。
Tears make you wiser.
眼淚讓你聰慧。
Learn from yesterday,
  hope for tomorrow.
吸取教訓，希望明天。

Be physically fit.
身體要健康。
Be mentally strong.
心理要堅強。
Be morally upright.
品德要正直。

Unit 8

Put others first.
把別人放在第一位。
Think of others first.
先想到別人。
You will end up first.
你最後會變成第一。

Care about others. 關懷他人。
Help those around you.
幫助周圍。

Be a shoulder to lean on.
可被依靠。

Try hard to be helpful.
盡力去助人。
Make a special effort to
  do good.
努力做好事。
Go out of your way for
  people. 竭力去助人。

Unit 9

Agree with everybody.
同意眾人意見。
You'll fit right in.
你會完全融入。
Go along to get along.
認同才能相處。

Give great service.
提供一流服務。
Be eager to help.
要熱心去助人。
Always aim to please
  others. 致力取悅他人。

More love, less hate.
多一點愛，少一點恨。
More smiling, less
  worrying.
多一點微笑，少一點擔心。
More compassion, less
  judgment.
多一點同情，少一點批評。

PART 3

Unit 1
進 步

PART 3・Unit 1~9
中英文錄音QR碼
英文唸2遍，中文唸1遍

Progress.
進步。

Develop.
發展。

Get better.
改善。

**Life doesn't
improve by chance.**
生活不會無故改善。

**Life improves
by change.**
改變才會改善生活。

Just keep changing.
只要持之以恆改變。

Keep improving.
持續改善。

Keep progressing.
持續進步。

**Keep working
on yourself.**
不斷改進。

PART 3

Unit 1　背景說明

　　小孩因為長大而快樂，我們因為進步而快樂。只要今天比昨天好，今年比去年好，你就不會害怕變老。

Progress. 　要進步。(= *Advance.* = *Move forward.* = *Improve.* = *Make progress.*) 也可說成：***Develop.*** (要發展。) Grow. (要成長。) ***Get better.*** (要改善。)
progress〔prə'grɛs〕*v.* 進步　　〔'prɑgrɛs〕*n.*
develop〔dɪ'vɛləp〕*v.* 發展　　get〔gɛt〕*v.* 變得

Life doesn't improve by chance. (生活不會無故改善。) 也可說成：Don't count on luck to improve your life. (不要想依賴運氣來改善生活。)
improve〔ɪm'pruv〕*v.* 改善；進步 (= *get better*)
chance〔tʃæns〕*n.* 機會；偶然；運氣
by chance 偶然地；意外地

Life improves by change. 　要改變，生活才會改善。(= *Your life will improve only if you change.*)
change〔tʃendʒ〕*v. n.* 改變

Just keep changing. 　只要持續改變。(= *Continue to change.*) 　***keep + V-ing*** 持續…

Keep improving. 　要持續進步。(= ***Keep progressing.*** = ***Keep working on yourself.***)
work on 致力於　　***work on yourself*** 改善自己；讓自己更好 (= *better yourself* = *improve yourself*)

PART 3

Unit 2
投資自己

Invest in yourself.
投資自己。

It pays off.
非常值得。

You will benefit.
你會獲益。

Eat healthy food.
吃健康食物。

Drink enough water.
喝足夠的水。

Move your body.
動一動身體。

Take a class.
上課。

Attend a party.
聚會。

Try something new.
嘗鮮。

PART 3

Unit 2 背景説明

　　每天吃健康的食物、上課、參加聚會、嘗試新的事物，都算是投資自己。

Invest in yourself. (要投資自己。) 也可説成：Put money/time into your own improvement. (投入金錢/時間，使自己更好。)　　invest〔ɪnˋvɛst〕v. 投資 <*in*>

It pays off. 這非常值得。(= *It's worth it.*)
pay off 得到回報；有收穫

You will benefit. (你會獲益。) 也可説成：You'll be better off. (你的情況會變得更好。)
benefit〔ˋbɛnəfɪt〕v. 獲益

Eat healthy food. 要吃健康的食物。(= *Eat good food.*)
healthy〔ˋhɛlθɪ〕adj. 健康的

Drink enough water. (要喝足夠的水。) 也可説成：Be sure to drink enough water. (一定要喝足夠的水。)

Move your body. (要動一動你的身體。) 也可説成：Stay active. (要經常運動。)　　move〔muv〕v. 移動

Take a class. 要上課。(= *Enroll in a class.* = *Sign up for a class.*)

Attend a party. 要參加聚會。(= *Go to a party.*)
attend〔əˋtɛnd〕v. 參加　　party〔ˋpɑrtɪ〕n. 派對；聚會

Try something new. 要嘗試新事物。(= *Try new things.* = *Do something you've never done before.*)
try〔traɪ〕v. 嘗試

PART 3

Unit 3
有尊嚴

Have dignity.
有尊嚴。

Have morals.
有操守。

Have character.
有品格。

Beauty is temporary.
美貌是暫時的。

**Personality is
permanent.**
個性是長期的。

**Good character
prevails.**
好的性格佔優勢。

Beauty catches attention.

美貌可獲注目。

Character catches the heart.

品格可獲人心。

Character comes first.

性格在第一位。

PART 3

Unit 3　背景説明

　　美麗是暫時的，可獲得注目；好的個性是長期的，人人喜歡和你在一起。

Have dignity. 要有尊嚴。(= *Have honor*.) 也可説成：
　Be respectable. (要值得尊敬。)
dignity〔ˈdɪgnətɪ〕*n.* 尊嚴

Have morals. (要有道德。) 也可説成：Have integrity.
　(要正直。) Be moral. (要合乎道德。)(= *Be ethical*.)
morals〔ˈmɔrəlz〕*n. pl.* 行為原則；道德；品行

Have character. (要有品格。) 也可説成：Have
　good character. (要有好的品格。) Be a good
　person. (要做個好人。) Be an upright person.
　(要做個正直的人。)
character〔ˈkærɪktɚ〕*n.* 性格；人格；品性；品格

Beauty is temporary. (美麗是暫時的。) 也可説成：
　Beauty fades. (美麗會消失。) (= *Good looks
　fade*.) Beauty doesn't last. (美麗不持久。)
beauty〔ˈbjutɪ〕*n.* 美；美麗
temporary〔ˈtɛmpəˌrɛrɪ〕*adj.* 暫時的

Personality is permanent. (個性是永久的。) 也可説
　成：Personality lasts a lifetime. (個性會持續一生。)

One's personality never changes. (一個人的個性永遠不會變。)

personality〔ˌpɝsn̩ˈælətɪ〕*n.* 個性

permanent〔ˈpɝmənənt〕*adj.* 永久的

Good character prevails. 好的性格佔優勢。(= *Good character wins.*) 也可説成 : A person of good character will succeed. (性格好的人會成功。)

prevail〔prɪˈvel〕*v.* 盛行;勝過;戰勝;優勝;佔優勢

Beauty catches attention. (美麗會引人注目。) 也可説成 : Being beautiful will make others notice you. (漂亮會使人注意到你。)

catch〔kætʃ〕*v.* 抓住;引起 (注意)

attention〔əˈtɛnʃən〕*n.* 注意 (力)

Character catches the heart. (品格能擄獲人心。) 也可説成 : Having a good character will make others love you. (有好的品格會使人愛你。)

heart〔hɑrt〕*n.* 心　　***catch one's heart*** 抓住某人的心;把某人迷住 (= *capture one's heart*)

Character comes first. 性格最重要。(= *Character is most important.*) 也可説成 : Your character is more important. (你的品格更重要。)

come first 首先要考慮到的;是最重要的人 (或事物)

PART 3

Unit 4
消除嫉妒

Eliminate envy.
消除嫉妒。

Discard doubt.
拋開疑慮。

**Leave no space
for stress.**
不留壓力。

Forget fear.
不要恐懼。

Abolish anger.
不要憤怒。

Get rid of greed.
不要貪心。

Laugh when you can.
能笑盡可能笑。

Apologize when you should.
該賠罪則賠罪。

Let go of what you can't change.
無力改則放下。

PART 3

Unit 4 背景説明

恐懼、憤怒、貪心、嫉妒，都要消除，你才會快樂。

> 背誦密碼：**E**liminate **e**nvy.
> **Di**scard **d**oubt.
> Leave no **s**pace for **s**tress.

Eliminate envy. 消除嫉妒。(= *Don't be envious.*)
eliminate〔ɪ'lɪmə,net〕*v.* 除去
envy〔'ɛnvɪ〕*n.* 嫉妒

Discard doubt. (抛棄懷疑。) 也可説成：Don't
doubt yourself. (不要懷疑自己。) 或 Don't be
suspicious. (不要心存懷疑。)
discard〔dɪs'kɑrd〕*v.* 抛棄
doubt〔daʊt〕*n.* 懷疑

Leave no space for stress. 不要留空間給壓力，也就
是「不要有壓力。」(= *Don't allow stress into your
life.*) 也可説成：Don't succumb to stress. (不要
向壓力屈服。)
leave〔liv〕*v.* 留下 space〔spes〕*n.* 空間
stress〔strɛs〕*n.* 壓力 (= *pressure*)

> 背誦密碼：**F**orget **f**ear.
> **A**bolish **a**nger.
> **G**et rid of **g**reed.

Forget fear. 忘了恐懼；不要恐懼。(= *Don't be afraid*.)

forget〔fɚ'gɛt〕*v.* 忘記　　fear〔fɪr〕*n.* 害怕；恐懼

Abolish anger. 廢除憤怒；不要憤怒。(= *Don't get angry*.)　　abolish〔ə'balɪʃ〕*v.* 廢除

anger〔'æŋgɚ〕*n.* 憤怒；生氣

Get rid of greed. 擺脫貪心；不要貪心。(= *Don't be greedy*.)　　***get rid of*** 擺脫；除去

greed〔grid〕*n.* 貪心；貪婪

Laugh when you can. 能笑的時候就笑。(= *Laugh whenever possible*.)　　laugh〔læf〕*v.* 笑

Apologize when you should. (該道歉時就道歉。) 也可說成：Apologize when you are at fault. (當你有錯時就道歉。)　　apologize〔ə'palə,dʒaɪz〕*v.* 道歉

Let go of what you can't change. 你無法改變的，就放下。(= *Don't worry about the things that you cannot change*.) 也可說成：Don't hold on to regrets. (不要一直後悔。)

let go of 放開；鬆手；放下

change〔tʃendʒ〕*v.* 改變

PART 3

Unit 5
情或理先？

Be kind or be right?
情或理先？

Just be kind.
情在前面。

It's always the right choice.
正確選擇。

Choose love.
選擇愛。

Choose light.
擇光明。

**Choose
compassion.**
要同情。

Be kind to the poor.
善良待貧。

Be kind to the rich.
良善待富。

Be kind to the unkind.
善待不善。

PART 3

Unit 5 背景説明

當你有「情」或「理」要選擇的時候，要選擇「情」，符合中國人的「情理法」。

Be kind or be right? 該仁慈還是該正直？(= *Should you be kind or should you be right?*) 也可説成：Should you be nice or should you insist on being correct? (你應該要對人好，還是要堅持正確的事？)

kind〔kaɪnd〕*adj.* 親切的；仁慈的

right〔raɪt〕*adj.* 正確的；正直的

Just be kind. 就是要仁慈。(= *Simply be nice.*)

It's always the right choice. (這永遠是正確的選擇。) 也可説成：Being nice is always the best thing to do. (對人好永遠是最應該做的事。)

choice〔tʃɔɪs〕*n.* 選擇

Choose love. (選擇愛。) 也可説成：Choose to love others. (要選擇愛人。) Accept love from others. (要接受別人的愛。)

choose〔tʃuz〕*v.* 選擇

Choose light. (選擇光明。) 也可說成：Be optimistic.
(要樂觀。) Be good. (要做好人。) Don't be evil.
(不要做壞人。)　　light〔 laɪt 〕*n.* 光；光亮；光輝

Choose compassion. (選擇同情。) 也可說成：
　Be compassionate. (要有同情心。)
compassion〔 kəmˊpæʃən 〕*n.* 同情

Be kind to the poor. (要對窮人好。) 也可說成：
　Have compassion for poor people. (要同情窮
　人。)　　poor〔 pʊr 〕*adj.* 貧窮的
the poor 窮人 (= *poor people*)

Be kind to the rich.　要對有錢人好。(= *Be nice to*
　wealthy people.) 也可說成：Have compassion for
　rich people. (要同情有錢人。)
rich〔 rɪtʃ 〕*adj.* 有錢的
the rich　有錢人 (= *rich people*)

Be kind to the unkind. 要對不善良的人好。(= *Be nice*
　to people who are not nice.) 也可說成：Have
　compassion for people who are not nice. (要同
　情壞人。)
unkind〔 ʌnˊkaɪnd 〕*adj.* 不親切的；冷酷的；無情的
the unkind　不善良的人 (= *unkind people*)

PART 3

Unit 6
充滿愛意

Love deeply.
充滿愛意。

Forgive quickly.
輕易饒恕。

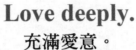

Life's too short
to be unhappy.
生命苦短。

There's no rewind.
人生無倒帶。

There's no replay.
人生無重播。

**Enjoy every moment
as it comes.**
享受每一刻。

Don't look back.
勿回頭看。

**Concentrate on
the future.**
專注未來。

**There's so much
to look forward to.**
展望將來。

PART 3

Unit 6 背景説明

儘量愛周圍的人，生命短暫，人生不能重來，要享受每一刻。

Love deeply. 要深刻地愛。(= *Love completely.*) 也可説成：Love unconditionally. (要無條件地愛。)
deeply〔ˈdiplɪ〕*adv.* 深深地

Forgive quickly. 要很快地原諒。(= *Excuse others without delay.*) forgive〔fɚˈgɪv〕*v.* 原諒
quickly〔ˈkwɪklɪ〕*adv.* 快地

Life's too short to be unhappy. (人生太短暫，不能不快樂。) 也可説成：Don't waste your time being unhappy. (不要浪費時間不快樂。)
too…to 太…以致於不
unhappy〔ʌnˈhæpɪ〕*adj.* 不快樂的

There's no rewind. (人生無倒帶。) 也可説成：You can't go back in time. (你無法回到過去。)(= *You can't go back to the past.*)
rewind〔riˈwaɪnd〕*n.* (錄音帶的) 倒轉；回轉；倒帶

There's no replay. (人生無重播。) 也可説成：You can't change the past. (你無法改變過去。)

There are no second chances. (沒有第二次機會。)
There are no do-overs. (無法重來。)
replay〔ri'ple〕*n.* 重播

Enjoy every moment as it comes. 當每一刻來臨時，
都要好好享受，引申爲「要享受每一刻。」也可説成：
Live in the present. (要活在當下。)
enjoy〔ɪn'dʒɔɪ〕*v.* 享受
moment〔'momənt〕*n.* 時刻

Don't look back. (不要回頭看。) 也可説成：Forget
about the past. (要忘了過去。) Don't think about
the past. (不要想過去。) Have no regrets. (不要有
遺憾。) ***look back*** 回頭看；回顧

Concentrate on the future. 要專注於未來。(= *Focus
on the future.*)
concentrate〔'kɑnsṇ,tret〕*v.* 專心
concentrate on 專心於　　future〔'fjutʃɚ〕*n.* 未來

There's so much to look forward to. (有很多事物
可以期待。) 也可説成：Many good things will
happen in the future. (未來會有很多好事發生。)
look forward to 期待

PART 3

Unit 7
重新開始
是一大幸福

**Starting over
is a blessing.**

重新開始是一大幸福。

**Starting over is a
chance to do better.**

重新來過會做得更好。

**Don't be afraid
to restart.**

勿怕重頭來過。

Want a new start?
想重新開始嗎？

You don't need
a new day.
不需要等到明天。

You just need
a new mindset.
只需要換個心態。

Hit the reset button.
重新開始。

**Get a new
perspective.**
新的視野。

Have a fresh start.
重獲新生。

PART 3

Unit 7　背景説明

失敗了，重新開始，反而是一大幸福，因為你會做得更好。

Starting over is a blessing. （能重新開始很幸福。）
也可説成：Making a fresh start can be a good thing. （重新開始可能是好事。）

start〔stɑrt〕*v. n.* 開始　　***start over*** 重新開始
blessing〔'blɛsɪŋ〕*n.* 幸福；幸運的事

Starting over is a chance to do better. （重新開始就有機會做得更好。）也可説成：When you start again, you can do it better than the first time.
（當你重新開始，你可以比第一次做得更好。）

chance〔tʃæns〕*n.* 機會

do better 做得更好；表現得更好

Don't be afraid to restart. 不要害怕重新開始。
（ = *Don't fear starting over*. = *Don't fear having to start again*. ）

afraid〔ə'fred〕*adj.* 害怕的
restart〔ri'stɑrt〕*v.* 重新開始

Want a new start? 想要新的開始嗎？(= *Do you want a new start?*)

You don't need a new day. 你不需要新的一天，也就是「你不需要等到明天。」(= *You don't have to wait until tomorrow.*)

You just need a new mindset. (你只需要一個新的心態。) 也可說成：You just need to change your attitude. (你只需要改變你的態度。)

just〔dʒʌst〕*adv.* 只　　mindset〔'maɪnd,sɛt〕*n.* 心態

Hit the reset button. 按下重置按鈕，引申為「重新開始。」(= *Start over.* = *Start again.*)

hit〔hɪt〕*v.* 打；打擊

reset〔'risɛt〕*n.* 重置；清零重新設定

button〔'bʌtn̩〕*n.* 按鈕　　***hit a button*** 按下按鈕

Get a new perspective. 要有新的看法。(= *Get a fresh outlook.*) 也可說成：Look at it in a different way. (要用不同的方式來看它。)

perspective〔pɚ'spɛktɪv〕*n.* 正確的眼光；透徹的看法；觀點

Have a fresh start. 要有新的開始。(= *Start over.* = *Begin again.*)　　fresh〔frɛʃ〕*adj.* 新鮮的；新的

BOOK 5・PART 3

PART 3

Unit 8
木已成舟

**What's done
is done.**
木已成舟。

You can't do it over.
無法重來。

**You can't take
it back.**
覆水難收。

Accept the situation.
接受現況。

Make it better.
讓它更好。

**Do the best you
can with it.**
善加利用。

You'll have more chances.
你還有很多機會。

There are many fish in the sea.
天涯何處無芳草。

There are plenty of pebbles on the beach.
一片森林等著你。

PART 3

Unit 8　背景説明

　　失敗了，沒關係，要接受現狀，天涯何處無芳草，
人生機會多得很。

What's done is done. (做了就是做了。) 也可說成：
　　What's done cannot be undone. (【諺】已經做了，
　　無法恢復；木已成舟；已成定局。) The past is past.
　　(過去的已經過去。)
what〔hwɑt〕*pron.* 任何⋯的事
done〔dʌn〕*adj.* 完成的

You can't do it over. (你無法重做；你無法重來。)
　　也可說成：You can't change it. (你無法改變。)
　　You can't change the past. (你無法改變過去。)
over〔ˈovɚ〕*adv.* 重覆地　　***do over*** 重做

You can't take it back. (你無法收回。) 也可說成：
　　You can't undo what you did. (你無法恢復你做過
　　的事。)　　***take back*** 撤回；收回

Accept the situation. (要接受這個情況。) 也可說成：
　　Understand your situation. (要了解你的情況。)
accept〔əkˈsɛpt〕*v.* 接受
situation〔ˌsɪtʃuˈeʃən〕*n.* 情況

Make it better. (要使它更好。) 也可說成：Improve your situation. (要改善你的情況。)

Do the best you can with it. 要善加利用它。(= *Make the most of it*. = *Make the best of it*. = *Take full advantage of it*.) 也可說成：Make the best of the situation. (要善加利用這個情況。)

do the best *one can* 盡力 (= *do one's best*)

You'll have more chances. (你會有更多的機會。) 也可說成：You'll have more opportunities in the future. (未來你會有更多的機會。)

chance〔tʃæns〕*n.* 機會

There are many fish in the sea. (海裡有很多魚。)
There are plenty of pebbles on the beach. (沙灘上有很多小圓石。) 都引申為「還有很多合適的人或機會；天涯何處無芳草。」也可說成：There are many other opportunities. (有很多其他的機會。)

fish〔fɪʃ〕*n.* 魚【單複數同形】   sea〔si〕*n.* 海

plenty〔'plɛntɪ〕*n.* 豐富；多量   *plenty of* 很多的

pebble〔'pɛbḷ〕*n.* 小圓石

beach〔bitʃ〕*n.* 海灘

PART 3

Unit 9
思慮少點

Think less.
思慮少點。

Feel more.
感受多點。

Don't overthink.
別想太多。

Do something nice.
做些好事。

Make someone's day.
讓人開心。

**Be the reason
someone smiles.**
使人開懷。

Life is beautiful.
生活絢爛。

Life is amazing.
生命精彩。

Life is full of surprises.
充滿驚喜。

PART 3

Unit 9　背景説明

　　不要想太多，人生非常美、非常精彩，處處是機會，處處是驚喜。

Think less. 想少一點，也就是「不要想太多。」
（= *Don't think too much.* ）

Feel more. （要多感受。）也可説成：Trust your
feelings.（要相信你的感覺。）　　feel〔 fil 〕*v.* 感覺

Don't overthink. 不要想太多。（= *Don't think too much.* ）
overthink〔͵ovɚˋθɪŋk〕*v.* 過度思考；想得太多

Do something nice. （做點好事。）也可説成：Do someone
a favor.（幫某人一個忙。）　　nice〔 naɪs 〕*adj.* 好的

Make someone's day. 讓某人高興。（= *Make someone
happy.* ）　　***make one's day*** 使某人高興

Be the reason someone smiles. （成爲某人微笑的原因。）
reason 後的 that 被省略了。也可説成：Make someone
smile.（讓某人微笑。）Make someone happy.（使某人快
樂。）　　reason〔ˋrizn̩〕*n.* 原因　　smile〔 smaɪl 〕*v.* 微笑

Life is beautiful.（人生很美。）也可説成：Life is fantastic.
（人生很棒。）　　***Life is amazing.*** 人生很棒。（= *Life is
wonderful.* ）　　amazing〔 əˋmezɪŋ 〕*adj.* 很棒的

Life is full of surprises. （人生充滿令人驚訝的事。）也可
説成：You never know what might happen.（你永遠
都不知道會發生什麼事。）　　***be full of*** 充滿了
surprise〔 səˋpraɪz 〕*n.* 驚訝；令人驚訝的事

PART 3 總整理

Unit 1

Progress. 進步。
Develop. 發展。
Get better. 改善。

Life doesn't improve by chance.
生活不會無故改善。
Life improves by change.
改變才會改善生活。
Just keep changing.
只要持之以恆改變。

Keep improving. 持續改善。
Keep progressing.
持續進步。
Keep working on yourself. 不斷改進。

Unit 2

Invest in yourself.
投資自己。
It pays off. 非常值得。
You will benefit. 你會獲益。

Eat healthy food.
吃健康食物。

Drink enough water.
喝足夠的水。
Move your body.
動一動身體。

Take a class. 上課。
Attend a party. 聚會。
Try something new. 嘗鮮。

Unit 3

Have dignity. 有尊嚴。
Have morals. 有操守。
Have character. 有品格。

Beauty is temporary.
美貌是暫時的。
Personality is permanent.
個性是長期的。
Good character prevails.
好的性格佔優勢。

Beauty catches attention.
美貌可獲注目。
Character catches the heart. 品格可獲人心。
Character comes first.
性格在第一位。

Unit 4

Eliminate envy. 消除嫉妒。
Discard doubt. 拋開疑慮。
Leave no space for stress.
不留壓力。

Forget fear. 不要恐懼。
Abolish anger. 不要憤怒。
Get rid of greed. 不要貪心。

Laugh when you can.
能笑盡可能笑。
Apologize when you
    should. 該賠罪則賠罪。
Let go of what you can't
    change. 無力改則放下。

Unit 5

Be kind or be right?
情或理先？
Just be kind. 情在前面。
It's always the right
    choice. 正確選擇。

Choose love. 選擇愛。
Choose light. 擇光明。
Choose compassion.
要同情。

Be kind to the poor.
善良待貧。
Be kind to the rich.
良善待富。
Be kind to the unkind.
善待不善。

Unit 6

Love deeply.
充滿愛意。
Forgive quickly.
輕易饒恕。
Life's too short to be
    unhappy. 生命苦短。

There's no rewind.
人生無倒帶。
There's no replay.
人生無重播。
Enjoy every moment as
    it comes. 享受每一刻。

Don't look back.
勿回頭看。
Concentrate on the future.
專注未來。
There's so much to look
    forward to. 展望將來。

Unit 7

Starting over is a blessing.
重新開始是一大幸福。
Starting over is a chance
to do better.
重新來過會做得更好。
Don't be afraid to restart.
勿怕重頭來過。

Want a new start?
想重新開始嗎？
You don't need a new day.
不需要等到明天。
You just need a new
mindset. 只需要換個心態。

Hit the reset button.
重新開始。
Get a new perspective.
新的視野。
Have a fresh start.
重獲新生。

Unit 8

What's done is done.
木已成舟。
You can't do it over.
無法重來。
You can't take it back.
覆水難收。

Accept the situation.
接受現況。
Make it better. 讓它更好。
Do the best you can with
it. 善加利用。

You'll have more chances.
你還有很多機會。
There are many fish in the
sea. 天涯何處無芳草。
There are plenty of
pebbles on the beach.
一片森林等著你。

Unit 9

Think less. 思慮少點。
Feel more. 感受多點。
Don't overthink. 別想太多

Do something nice.
做些好事。
Make someone's day.
讓人開心。
Be the reason someone
smiles. 使人開懷。

Life is beautiful.
生活絢爛。
Life is amazing.
生命精彩。
Life is full of surprises.
充滿驚喜。

句子索引

C

句
子
索
引

句子索引

句子索引

句子索引

句子索引

句子索引

R

句子索引

句
子
索
引

關鍵字索引

關鍵字索引

關鍵字索引

📖「句子索引」、「關鍵字索引」使用方法

1 翻開「句子索引」p.843 找到Life，
你會看到所有Life開頭的句子。

「完美英語之心靈盛宴」，它是案頭金句句典，你想到什麼，都可以從「句子索引」和「關鍵字索引」中，找到「完美英語」，也可自行造出「心靈盛宴」。例如：有關 life，可以在「句子索引」中查到：

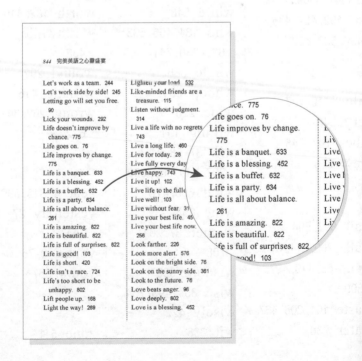

② 再用「關鍵字索引」p.863找所有
有life的句子在哪一頁。

在「關鍵字索引」p.863 中，你可查到所有包
含life的句子，把它們組合起來，便是一篇精
彩的演講稿，你說出來，出口成章，句句金
句！

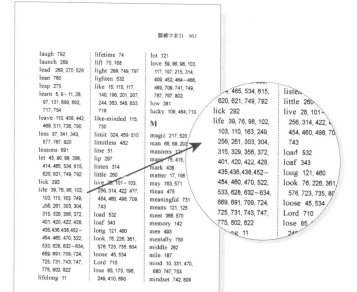

3 可以在p.39找到 Make life amazing.

📄 利用「索引」編寫出的演講稿

範例 ▶ 劉毅「董事長英語研習班」的「董事長萬用演講稿」。

Make the Most of Life 精彩活一生 英文錄音QR碼

1. Life is beautiful.
人生很美。

Life is sweet.
人生很甜。

Life is amazing.
人生真棒。

Live gracefully.
優雅生活。

Live gratefully.
感激生活。

Live generously.
大方生活。

Embrace life.
擁抱生活。

Cherish life.
珍惜生命。

Celebrate life.
慶祝生命。

2. Life is a blessing.
活著真幸福。

Health is a blessing.
健康是幸福。

Love is a blessing.
愛即是幸福。

Enjoy yourself.
享受人生。

Savor life.
品味人生。

Relish life.
欣賞人生。

Live your best life.
精彩人生。

You only get one.
生不重來。

Get all you can out of it. 盡情揮灑。

📄 利用「索引」編寫出的演講稿

3. **Life is a buffet.**
人生是一場自助餐。

Fill up your plate.
裝滿你的盤子。

Really pig out.
瘋狂享用。

Life is a banquet.
人生如盛宴。

Feast like a king.
饗用如國王。

Enjoy every bite.
享受每一口。

Life is a party.
人生如派對。

Celebrate every day! 要天天慶祝!

Really whoop it up!
要盡情狂歡!

4. **Appreciate life.**
重視生活。

Cherish our beautiful world.
珍惜美景。

Stop and smell the roses. 停下享受。

Don't rush life.
別倉促生活。

Life isn't a race.
生活非競賽。

Enjoy every moment.
享受每一刻。

Slow down. 放慢腳步。

Take time to look around.
歷時環顧。

Don't miss something wonderful.
勿失美好。

5. **Life is good!**
生活很美好!

Love life!
愛你的生活!

Live well!
好好過日子!

Enjoy life!
享受人生!

Live it up!
盡情享受人生!

Use your time well!
善用你的時間!

📖 利用「索引」編寫出的演講稿

You only live once!
人只能活一次。

**Don't waste any
　time.**
不要浪費時間。

**Make every day
　count.**
每一天都要活得有意義。

6. **Life is short.**
人生苦短。

Make the most of it.
善加利用。

**Work hard, study
　hard, play hard.**
工作、讀書、玩樂，盡情揮灑。

Treasure time.
珍愛光陰。

Time is a treasure.
時間即寶藏。

**Time beats
　diamonds or gold.**
時間勝過鑽或金。

Use time wisely.
善用時間。

**Use every hour
　and minute.**
時刻善用。

**Live life to the
　fullest.**
充實人生。

7. **Don't do too much.**
勿做太多。

Don't do too little.
勿做太少。

**Everything in
　moderation.**
一切中庸。

Create balance.
創造平衡。

Balance your life.
平衡生活。

**Life is all about
　balance.**
生活全在於平衡。

Too far east is west.
【諺】物極必反。

**Extreme right is
　extreme wrong.**
【諺】過猶不及。

📄 利用「索引」編寫出的演講稿

Find the middle ground.
尋求中庸之道。

8. **Love deeply.**
充滿愛意。

Forgive quickly.
輕易饒恕。

Life is too short to be unhappy.
生命苦短。

Don't look back.
勿回頭看。

Concentrate on the future.
專注未來。

There's so much to look forward to.
展望未來。

There's no rewind.
人生無倒帶。

There's no replay.
人生無重播。

Enjoy every moment as it comes.
享受每一刻。

9. **Having a bad day?**
今天倒楣嗎?

Take a deep breath.
做個深呼吸。

It's just a day, not a lifetime.
只是倒楣一天,不是倒楣一輩子。

You're still young!
你還年輕!

You have many opportunities.
你有很多機會。

The world is open to you.
整個世界都對你開放。

Life goes on.
生活還是得繼續。

Look to the future.
要展望未來。

Look on the bright side.
要看事物的光明面。

📖 本書製作過程

「完美英語之心靈盛宴」原來是「劉毅董事長英語研習班」的上課講義，感動了很多人。

先由美籍老師 Edward McGuire 編寫草稿，再經 Bailey Aiken 老師和 Laura E. Stewart 教授校閱，我們特別挑選出中國人能夠背得下、記得住、說得出的句子，我都先背過、使用過。

我 77 歲能背下來，相信你們也能背下來，背完之後的感覺非常好，使用後，更是讓我興奮無比。

感謝謝靜芳老師翻譯、編輯，王宣雯老師把中文修飾得更美，以前我們只要求英文句子短，容易背，儘量不超過五個字，現在連中文翻譯也要求簡短優美，學英文的時候，同時也學了中文。如 Don't put it off. (勿拖延。) 我們會在「背景說明」中，用白話文註解為「不要拖延。」

感謝美術主任白雪嬌，每一頁都要求完美，讓你看了舒服，看了還想再看。感謝蔡琇瑩老師和伍家瑤老師協助編輯。感謝工作了 40 多年的排版專家黃淑貞和蘇淑玲，她們的功力，無人能比。

這本書我隨身攜帶，心裡不舒服的時候，做個深呼吸，打開書背一背，立刻感到輕鬆，身心健康，像充了電一樣，又有了精神。

劉毅

完美英語之心靈盛宴
Perfect English for the Soul

附錄音 QR 碼　售價：990 元

主　　編 / 劉　毅

發 行 所 / 學習出版有限公司

　　　　　　TEL (02) 2704-5525

郵 撥 帳 號 / 05127272 學習出版社帳戶

登 記 證 / 局版台業 2179 號

印 刷 所 / 裕強彩色印刷有限公司

台 北 門 市 / 台北市許昌街 17 號 6F

　　　　　　TEL (02) 2331-4060

台灣總經銷 / 紅螞蟻圖書有限公司

　　　　　　TEL (02) 2795-3656

本公司網址 / www.learnbook.com.tw

電 子 郵 件 / learnbook0928@gmail.com

2023 年 9 月 21 日初版

本書改編自「完美英語心靈饗宴①～⑤」

ISBN 978-986-231-489-0

Keep advancing.
持續進步。
Keep progressing.
不斷進步。
Keep growing.
持續成長。

Find joy.
尋找喜悅。
Find light.
尋找光明。
Pursue cheer.
追求快樂。

Be kind.
友善待人。
Be gentle.
溫和待人。
Be considerate.
體貼他人。

Always learn.
不斷學習。
Always improve.
不斷改進。
Always innovate.
不斷創新。